Paint a Murder

A Bella Sarver Mystery

By

Barbara Lipkin

To my friends in the Friday figure drawing group – thanks for the companionship and the inspiration.

The Bella Sarver Mysteries

Paint a Murder
Brush With Death

This is a work of fiction. Names, characters, places and incidents are products of the author's imagination or are used fictitiously and are not to be construed as real. Any resemblance to actual events, locales, organizations or persons, living or dead, is entirely coincidental.

Text and cover ©2017 by Barbara Lipkin. All rights reserved.

ISBN-13: 978-1546357292

ISBN-10: 154635297

Prologue

Saturday night. Ken and Debbie Wilson swayed together to the music, hardly moving at all. Other couples swirled around them, but the Wilsons were wrapped in their own thoughts. The reality of gray hair and arthritic joints disappeared into the darkness as they held each other, and once again they were boy and girl, lithe and slim, hair glossy and full, dancing in the high school gym with their first love.

Suddenly, Debbie stiffened in her husband's arms. "What's wrong?" he asked.

She shook her head and snuggled closer. Stooped over these days, Ken was still a good six inches taller than his wife. Even with heels, her head barely reached his shoulder, but she was used to keeping her nose clear so she could breathe. He bent his head to touch the top of hers. They'd been married a long time.

"Nothing," she said. But a host of remembered images flooded her mind.

Karaoke night at Martingale Manor. The dance committee had done an amazing job of transforming the clubhouse into a ballroom. Crepe-paper streamers sailed above the dancers. The lights were low, and the committee had unearthed disco balls from somebody's basement. The words of an old Brenda Lee hit were projected on a screen set up at the back of the room and the woman standing on the stage belted them out, following the prompting of the bouncing ball. She was heavier than she used to be, face lined and a bit jowly. But, just for tonight, just for a little while, the old familiar music and the lights glittering in the darkness worked magic. The words wailed out over the loudspeaker, the voice a little wobbly at the edges, but clear enough.

Ken tightened his hand at Debbie's waist, moved her away from him and twirled her under his arm. The circle skirt she'd found at a local resale shop swung out wide, as if even the skirt remembered what it had been like to dance at Homecoming. She giggled, but he wasn't looking at her. He was staring at the woman on the stage, startled at first, but then a different expression shadowed his face. Debbie recognized it. She'd seen it once before.

Lily Turner wasn't on the dance floor. She'd lost her husband, Harold, a few months back. She couldn't say she was really sorry he was gone. The last few years had been a misery. Not that the many years prior had been a lot of fun, either. Harold had never quite lived up to his early promise. But they'd been together more than fifty years. At least, he'd been a decent enough dancer.

Lily felt something on her cheek and reached up to wipe it away. A tear? Really?

Lily sniffled impatiently and rose to go get a drink. "Stop it," she told herself. "You're being an idiot." The woman warbling away up there was old, at least as old as Lily. Her hair was still blond, but that meant nothing, of course. She stood straight enough, but there was no denying the sagging jaw and the bags under the eyes. Lily shook her head sadly at the silliness of it all.

The Dance Club had hired a professional bartender for the evening, a young man who dressed up for the occasion, white shirt, black vest, and all.

"What can I get you?" he asked.

Lily didn't return his cheerful smile. "White wine," she said abruptly. She took the glass he proffered without a word and turned away.

Back at her table, she turned her attention to the stage once again. Brenda Lee's song was finished, and the singer had moved on to an old Johnny Mathis standard. Lily stared. There was something familiar about the performer. She couldn't quite ... but then, it came to her. "Oh, my God," she exclaimed softly, under her breath.

Chapter One

Shirley Rogers might have reached the 'active adult' age but she could still swim like a fish. When she was a child, her parents took her and her brother to North Avenue Beach almost every summer week-end. She'd run across the burning hot sand into the freezing cold Lake Michigan waters and swim and splash and jump over the waves until her lips turned blue and still she didn't want to leave. Her father had to wade in and carry her out of the water over his shoulder, long blonde hair streaming into her eyes, laughing in protest. It was a good memory. She didn't have a lot of those.

Deer Creek was a good forty miles from the beach and these days, Shirley didn't relish the long drive east down the Eisenhower. When she found out that Martingale Manor offered both an indoor and an outdoor swimming pool at its clubhouse, she was sold. She lost no time moving into one of the compact, ranch-style townhouses. How delightful to walk out of her house to the clubhouse only a block away and be able to dive right into the pool, any time she felt like it. What a luxury.

She liked to get there early, before the water aerobics class started. Usually she was the only one there, and she could pretend it was her own private pool. She wasn't alone this morning, though. Another woman had arrived even earlier. Shirley recognized her but she didn't greet her. Early morning didn't feel like a good time for chit-chat.

Shirley stood at the edge of the pool for a few minutes, watching the other woman's strong and even strokes cleave through the water. Shirley hated it when another swimmer chopped through the water, churning it up. It made it hard for her to concentrate on her own rhythm. But today, this wasn't going to be a problem. Satisfied, she slipped into the pool, stretched her body out on the water, and began her swim. It was her favorite thing to do. Nothing else left her feeling so relaxed, so free.

Rita Cutler would be expecting her at the shop, but she could wait. Mondays were always slow, anyway. Rita could handle anything that was likely to crop up at *Ruffles and Flourishes*. She was good with the customers and she seemed to enjoy dealing with them. She was sharp, too. Sharper than Shirley had expected her to be. That might turn into an issue, but she didn't want to think about that now. She just wanted to swim.

Stop worrying. Everything will be fine. Haven't you always come out ahead of the game? But this time, she needed help. She hated asking for help. It made her feel out of control. She hated opening up her private business to strangers. *Still, sometimes you just have to trust people. And Leo is a professional, after all.*

Had it been a mistake to ask Leo to go over the books for her? She'd tried to straighten out the accounts so they'd make sense to the IRS, but the thing was – she just didn't know enough. She knew she had to pay a reasonable amount of taxes, but.... Leo was another smart one. A CPA. If only he'd stop asking so many questions. He never said anything about the answers she gave him, but she could tell he wasn't totally satisfied.

Shirley was nothing if not resourceful. She'd had to be, a woman on her own. That's what Peter never seemed to understand. It had all been up to her to make things work.

She didn't have anybody to help her. And if now she finally had it pretty good, wasn't she entitled? She'd done the best she could. It was up to him to do the same. It's a tough world out there.

Their last phone call hadn't ended on a good note. She'd call him back. Soon. Not today. Today she had other problems to think about.

Lots of times, all she needed was some free-floating time in the pool to come up with a solution. Reaching her arm out, feeling the pull of the water as she swept back against it, up the length of the pool and back again, enjoying the strength of her arms and legs. There was no better way to start the day than by swimming long laps, feeling the stretch in her shoulders, letting her thoughts drift randomly. So refreshing. When the other swimmer left the pool, it barely registered with Shirley.

Her reverie was interrupted by the noisy chatter of people arriving for the class. *Already? It feels like I only just started. How could an hour have gone by so fast?*

She wasn't the least bit tired. She flipped onto her back and began to swim cross-wise the width of the deep end while the class assembled itself at the shallow end. The warm water felt so delightful, she'd have been happy to float all day. But when one of the newcomers headed in her direction in order to get in a little pre-class warm-up, she hauled herself out of the water and headed for the ladies' locker room.

A few minutes later, Shirley stood under the steaming shower and let the hot water flow over her, loving how it made her whole body feel loose and warm. "Maybe I was actually born a mermaid," she speculated, and laughed.

She heard the last couple of stragglers slam the door as they left the locker room for the pool and Shirley knew she was finally alone. She hummed to herself as she lathered up her still-blond hair. Still blond, with a little help. Dreamily, she found herself remembering. Remembering an old Johnny Mathis number, remembering when she and her friends had slow-danced to it, back in the day. Remembering.

Her voice was deeper than it used to be, a little rusty on the high notes, but she'd always been able to carry a tune. The steam freed up her vocal chords. She tilted her head back into it and let her voice soar, really belting it out.

A door crashed open. Not the one leading out to the pool. The other one, the one from the lobby. Shirley could tell the noise came from further away. Footsteps, soft but she could hear them slap against the tiled floor.

The shower still sprayed hot, but Shirley suddenly shivered. Her voice died in her throat. Another voice rose, taking up the song where she'd left off.

"Who's there?" she called, but it came out as a whisper.

No answer, but the footsteps came closer. Shirley reached for the faucet, to turn off the water, but there wasn't any more time. The shower curtain was ripped aside.

"What...?" Shirley gasped. She never finished her question.

Chapter Two

Bella Sarver unloaded the bags containing paints, brushes and various accessory items from the hatch of her SUV and stuffed them all into the large folding shopping cart she'd placed ready behind the car. She liked to get to her painting class early so she could lay out her materials and catch her breath before her students started trooping in.

Class wasn't scheduled to begin until 9:30, but more than an hour earlier, the Martingale Manor clubhouse was already hopping. The Pilates class was working out in the great room, two people were concentrating on the jigsaw puzzle in the library, a bunch of quilters were getting a head start at their sewing machines, and a group of residents in work-out attire were already sweating in the gym.

As Bella hauled her cart across the clubhouse, a tall woman rushing in the opposite direction while staring at the phone in her hand, wet hair slicked back behind her ears, nearly ran into her, only coming to an abrupt stop at the last second.

"Bella! I didn't expect to see you here. Are you teaching this morning?"

"I am," Bella said. "I didn't expect to see you here, either, Kasia. I know you don't live here. You're definitely not over 55."

Kasia laughed and pushed a dangling strand back in place. "Shh, don't tell anybody. No, my mom lives here, and I like to pop in a few times a week to make sure she's okay. She lets me use her pool pass, too, so sometimes I come in really early to swim, if Alex takes over getting the kids off to school. I'd forgotten, but you did mention you were doing classes for this place. How do you like it?"

"Well, I love painting, as you know, and my students are really receptive, so it's fun. It's different from the Deer Creek Art League, because most of these women aren't trained artists, but some of them show promise. It doesn't matter, anyway, as long as they learn something new and enjoy themselves, right?"

"Exactly," Kasia agreed.

She and Bella were both on the Board of the DCAL. Kasia Novik was the VP in charge of Education and Bella had recently been elected President. More like, persuaded into it by some of her confederates. There hadn't been any competition for the job.

Kasia was a fairly recent addition to the membership rolls. She felt warmed by the old-timers enthusiastic welcome when she attended her first meeting, not long after moving to Deer Creek from out of state. As soon as they realized that she was not only a talented collage artist, but also meant to take an active role in running the organization, they practically turned themselves inside out to make sure she knew how thrilled they were to have her join the organization. There were way too many old timers. If the place was going to keep thriving, young blood was needed, with fresh ideas and plenty of energy.

Kasia still had a faint, barely noticeable, Eastern European accent, left over from her earliest years in Poland. Her parents had managed to leave for America shortly after the fall of Communism and never looked back into those nightmare years, with the constant struggle just to live and the omnipresent specter of a visit from the secret police if an unwise word was spoken to the wrong person. Their daughter had been too young to be aware of the situation at the time, but she'd grown up on her parents' stories, whispered when they thought she was safely asleep. She filed them deep in her memory, but they took a back seat to the adventures of adjusting to America. She'd been young enough to learn English seemingly without effort, in no time at all, but the rhythm and cadences of her first language remained.

The new Director of Education was settling well into her position. She actually seemed to be relishing the challenges of rounding up teachers, scheduling the classes, coordinating with the Park District, and keeping everybody more or less happy in the process. Dealing with the egos of a slew of artist-teachers, each of whom had their own ideas of how the job should be done, was not a task for the faint-hearted. Bella admired her attitude.

"Do you have time for a cup of coffee?" Bella invited.

Kasia checked her watch. "I should get back; I have a million things on my to-do list. Oh, well, they can wait a few minutes."

"I should get to my class, too. I need to get these things set up, but there's still time, and I wanted to ask you about the class schedule for next spring. Are we all set with teachers?"

One thing led to another. After another quarter hour or so, Kasia checked her watch again and jumped up from the table. "Damn! I'm really late now, Bella. Look, I'll see you later, okay?"

"Oops, me too." They started off in opposite directions, but then Bella turned around. "Wait a sec, Kasia. Aren't you forgetting something?"

Kasia frowned, puzzled.

"Didn't you bring a bathing suit?"

"Oh, for ….." She ran back into the locker room to grab her duffel bag.

The Martingale Manor Painting Group had already been painting together for several years before Bella came along, but since they didn't have a knowledgeable leader, they ended up just trying to copy various photos. All their paintings looked almost exactly the same. A good exercise, probably, but not very creative. Bella helped them understand that the whole point was to let your own feelings and ideas flow out on the canvas, not to try to replicate what someone else had already accomplished. Paint and brushes were just the vehicles for the process.

"It's all about the composition, ladies," Bella had announced at the first session several weeks before. "It doesn't matter how well you might paint an object, if the whole composition doesn't draw the viewer in and make him or her want to spend time with your painting, your efforts have been wasted. So we don't put our center of interest right smack in the middle of the canvas. That's a no-no. Today, we're going to really work on composition. We're going to learn how to place shapes on the canvas and how to use color and contrast to design an interesting painting. Let's get started. Use this set-up here for inspiration, and I'll come around to see how you're doing."

The small table next to her held an arrangement of bowls and flowers on top of a colorful cloth. Bella designed her still-life set-ups to be seen in the round. Her students could choose to paint the arrangement from any angle. They could use the whole thing, or select parts of the arrangement. She meant the set-up to be an inspiration that each student could make her own, rather than have seven identical paintings. As she waved her hand at the table, the light from the large, north-facing windows caught the stone on the third finger of her left hand.

"Ooh, how pretty," Joanie Passarelli cooed, grabbing Bella's hand so she could examine the ring more closely. "Looks like an engagement ring. Is it?"

The emerald was an intense green, surrounded by small diamonds set on a wide gold band. It still felt a little odd on her finger. Sometimes she looked at it and wondered what it was doing there. Art had surprised her with it on her birthday, in October, only a couple of weeks after she'd agreed to marry him.

"How did you know I love emeralds?" she asked. Maybe it wasn't the best response, but it was the first thing she could think to say.

"I knew it would go with your hair," Art said, ruffling the red mess gently. "Diamonds don't seem to suit you. Too cold."

Connie Marks, a tall, thin woman whose swingy blonde hair could fool people into thinking she was ten years younger than her actual age, joined Joanie in admiring the ring, and before she knew what happened, everybody wanted to know all about Bella's engagement.

"Aren't you the brave one," Debbie commented from across the room, glancing at the other women clustered around Bella. She'd remained standing at her easel, gripping her brush so tightly that her hand shook a little as she bent to the canvas, trying to get the foliage just right.

"Brave? I don't think getting married is an act of bravery, do you?"

Debbie smiled. "I didn't back when I was a kid. I jumped into marriage with both feet then, but I doubt if I'd do it now."

"Oh, Debbie, you know Ken is a doll," Joanie protested.

"Oh, sure, he is," Debbie agreed. "I love him to bits. It's just that I don't know if I'd get married again, if I had to do it over. It ends up being really complicated, doesn't it?"

"Life is complicated. Things that seemed simple when we were young don't seem so simple any more," Bella said. "But if you love someone, you should get married, right?"

Debbie raised an eyebrow, and the other women laughed.

Art Halperin had been one of her students in the painting holiday she'd led to Tuscany about two years earlier. Since then, they'd had several adventures together, and they'd come to depend on each other in a way neither thought they'd ever do again. Bella would have been content if Art had moved in to the townhouse with her, but he wanted a proper marriage or nothing. And a proper marriage required a suitable engagement ring. Maybe a little old-fashioned, but Art was the kind of guy who liked to do things right, and he had definite ideas of what that entailed. It was one of the things Bella loved about him. She knew he wasn't going to let her down the way her first husband had.

Art hadn't been totally in favor of her taking on the painting class at Martingale Manor. "Don't you think you're doing enough already?" he asked. "You're teaching at the Deer Creek Art League, not to mention 'presidenting' it. Now you're immersed in creating this co-op gallery besides. When will you find time to do your own work?"

"I know, Art. But actually, the more I have to do, the better my brain seems to work. If I'm not busy with something, it's hard for me to just go into my studio and paint. But when I have a million things going, I have a million ideas for paintings, too. Anyway, this won't be hard. I'll just teach this class the way I do my other beginning classes. It'll be fun."

"Okay," he said. "But don't forget to breathe!"

Debbie Wilson was already in the classroom when Bella finally made it in, after her detour for conversation with Kasia. She stood at the easel with her feet planted firmly apart, wielding her brush with abandon, her lips pressed together in concentration, putting finishing touches on the painting she'd begun the week before.

"You're here bright and early, Deb," Bella said, unpacking her supplies and setting things on the counters. "Did you bring Ken to his water aerobics class this morning?"

"Absolutely; he never misses it. I really think it does him a lot of good. He always seems to move a lot easier the rest of the day. I sort of like coming in early, too. It gives me some extra time to get myself together."

"I'll let you get to it, then, while I run to the bathroom."

Bella remembered what Art told her as she inspected her face in the locker room mirror a few minutes before class was due to begin. Breathing was fine, but who would get the work done if people didn't step up? She'd never been one to sit back and let others do what she felt she should be taking on. "Not too terrible for an old bat," she told herself. She dried her hands on a paper towel, and then ran her fingers through her short red hair, making it stand up in spikes, the way she liked it.

Bella Sarver was a small bundle of energy. Her body, usually clad in jeans and shod in brightly colored sneakers, leaned forward most of the time, ready to run on to the next project. Only the crinkles around her eyes and the puckers above her lips, brought on by the intense concentration she brought to her work, whatever it was at the moment, indicated that she was 'of a certain age.' She rubbed lotion into her hands as she stood before the mirror over the sink. She thought about applying some lipstick, but decided not to bother.

As she turned to go, she observed once again, as she had every time she'd been there before, that the locker room was an absolute mess. There was a bank of lockers arrayed along one side of the room, but nobody seemed to use them. Sample-size bottles of shampoos and conditioners festooned the counter by the sinks. Bags lay open on the benches, surrounded by damp towels and various items of clothing. Mismatched shoes were scattered randomly across the tiled floor. She might have expected to see such chaos at a school, but not where grown women hung out.

An expression her mother had used sprang to mind. *Were these people raised in a barn?* Then she laughed at herself. *Not my problem, is it?*

She had a hand on the door handle when it dawned on her that she'd been hearing the persistent rush of running water ever since she'd entered. No one else was there, was there? She knew the water aerobics class was still in session, would be for another half hour, at least. There was no other sound, just the steadily pounding water.

Was anyone in the shower? Could someone just be standing under the spray? Or had someone left the water on when they got out?

She had to get to class, but still, she hesitated. Her gut was telling her something wasn't right.

"Hello?" she called out. "Are you ok in there?"

No reply. She walked towards the back, into the alcove that housed four shower stalls, two on each side. Still no sound except the water drumming, but now she could see that it was running out over the lip of the further stall on her left. There was a drain in the center of the alcove, but it must have been blocked with something because the water was puddling all over the floor. She stared at it, not comprehending at first.

Bella was a painter. She loved the color red. Cadmium, alizarin crimson, quinacridone. Even as the names of the paint colors danced in her mind, she knew that was crazy. She wasn't looking at paint though the water was tinged with red. She was looking at blood.

Almost against her will, she stretched her hand to the shower curtain drawn across the stall and moved it aside. She could see the woman was dead. Her body under the pounding, icy spray didn't move. More to the point, her throat gaped open from a savage gash. Bella let the curtain drop, and slowly backed away.

Chapter Three

The Fourth Thursday event of the Deer Creek Art League was always well-attended. The members looked forward to getting the first look at the latest exhibit and second-guessing the judge's choice of prize winners. Not to mention the wine and snacks.

Mollie Schaeffer, as Director of Exhibits, designated a theme for each month's show, open to all members. It was usually something that could be very freely interpreted, such as "Oceans," or "Mountains," but the artists didn't have to follow even that guideline, and Bella Sarver seldom did. She generally entered whatever painting had just come off her easel.

Bella preferred to paint in series, that is, she painted a number of variations on a particular idea, until she'd said everything she wanted to say about it. Currently, she was experimenting with abstract designs, using non-representational shapes and colors. It was a departure from her previous brightly-colored landscapes and still life paintings, and she was enjoying it very much. She didn't feel like interrupting her flow to do a painting to order, one that didn't fit into the series. Coincidentally, though, the current month's theme was "Red," which happened to be the dominant color in Bella's entry.

Fabio Gompers spotted Ben Goldberg, Membership Vice-President, maneuvering his way through the guests, trying not to spill any of the wine from the glasses on his tray. Fabio grabbed a glass and raised it in a toast.

"Show's not bad, is it? I think the members may be improving."

"Most of them probably aren't at your level, Fabio, but they do their best. Anyway, they have a good time trying. Did you enter something this month?"

"It's over there," Fabio said, gesturing with his head to a spot at the far end of the room. "Didn't get first place, though."

"Well, you can't win them all, can you? Better luck next time. Anyway, it's nice to see you here. You haven't been to one of these dos in a while, have you?"

"Not my thing, really, but I figure I should show up every now and then, see what's going on. "

A jazz trio had set themselves up in a corner of the space, and their music added energy to the occasion, but also raised the noise level considerably. "Lively crowd, tonight," Art noted, raising his voice. Even so, Bella had to strain to hear him.

She looked around the gallery with a satisfied expression. "It's great to have such a fantastic turn-out. Ben's idea of having a monthly party was inspired. We never had crowds like this when we used to have our openings on Saturday mornings."

"I remember," Art said. "Most of the time, the only people who came to those were some of the board members."

They walked slowly around the room, examining the current month's show. Most of the pieces were paintings but there were a few drawings as well as a scattering of other types of works, such as sculptures, jewelry, and fiber art.

"How does a judge figure out the prizes?" Art asked. "I mean, how do you say a painting is better than a necklace or something?"

"Good question, Art. And the answer is, I don't know. It's a problem that comes up all the time. To be really fair, we should probably award prizes in different categories."

Art nodded. "I guess it really doesn't matter that much, at least in this setting."

"The lesser prizes don't, although first, second and third place carry small cash awards. But the first place winners each month get to be in the Regional Art Show every summer, and that can be something of a big deal. Still, artists just want to hang their pieces somewhere they can be seen. Prizes aren't usually that important to most of them."

"Besides," Art added, "from what I can see so far, the same few people win them every month."

Bella laughed. "You're right. And that's another problem we haven't figured out how to solve. We try to get a different judge every month, so that isn't it. Maybe it's just that those same few people are actually the best artists."

"Congratulations, Bella," Mollie said, bustling up to join them.

"What? What for?"

"Best of Show, of course."

"Who? Me?"

Mollie grabbed Bella by the arm and steered her across the room. There, between the two long windows, was Bella's latest experiment, a long canvas with an arrangement of arches and lines interspersed with little star-like shapes, painted in various shades of reds, magentas, and purples. Dark gray shapes provided contrast, a relief from all the red. It was an arresting design. It almost forced a viewer's eyes to move around the composition, focusing on the primary focal point of the intersection of complicated shapes but then being led to other sections by lines and colors. Next to the canvas, stuck onto the wall, was a large blue ribbon, with the legend "Best of Show" inscribed on the medallion.

"Well done, honey," Art said, giving her a big hug. "Good for you."

Bella grinned. "I just wanted to show the piece. I never expected to win."

She really hadn't expected any prizes. She hardly ever won at the Art League. She told herself it was because her work was usually pretty abstract, and the judges tended to prefer more representational work. Which might even be true.

"It's nice to be appreciated, though," she added.

Her attention was caught by a small painting on the next section of wall. She might not have noticed it but for the Third Place ribbon draped over its frame. It was a landscape, a river scene. Mostly dark colors, but a spot of light drew the viewer's eye, highlighting a little rowboat with some figures. It was Impressionistic in style, with rough, thick brush strokes, but it was lovely. She leaned closer to read the label. "Boating. Oil on canvas, eight by ten inches. Fabio Gompers."

"I wouldn't have recognized this as Fabio's work," she told Mollie. "It's lovely, but his work is usually a lot more polished, isn't it?"

"True," Mollie agreed. "Also, it's kind of small for him. Most of the pieces I've seen are a lot bigger."

"I thought I'd try something a little different," Fabio said, coming up to join them. "Easier on the back to work on a small piece. I can sit down while I paint."

"Yes, easier on the back and on the fingers, too," Bella said, observing that Fabio held his wine glass stiffly in his right hand, the knuckles swollen. "How's your arthritis, Fabio?"

He flexed his fingers experimentally. "I'm managing. By the way, I hope the cops didn't give you a hard time on Monday."

"Monday? Were you there? I didn't see you."

"I saw you, Bella. I'd given my name to the cops and I was on my way out. I had to go to that meeting at the Art League, remember? You were over by the fireplace, talking to some guy."

"Detective Carlson," Bella affirmed. "But what were you doing there?"

"I go to the water aerobics class three mornings a week. The exercises seem to be helping, I think."

"Don't you have to be a resident to use the pool?"

"I *am* a resident. I moved to Morningstar Manor a couple of years ago. But you're not one of my neighbors, are you?"

"No, no, I just teach a class there. I certainly didn't expect to be finding a murder victim."

"Yeah, I heard about that. Couldn't have been much fun for you, huh? Although ...."

Bella grimaced. She took a sip of wine.

"I think Bella doesn't want to think about that right now, Fabio. Why don't you go get yourself some hors d'ouevres?"

"Well, that was subtle, Mollie," Bella said, watching Fabio disappear towards the food.

"I didn't think subtlety was called for just then. And you didn't need to be reminded of what happened."

"As if I could forget."

"Anyhow - time for the announcements."

Mollie patted Bella's arm. She moved into the middle of the room and tapped her glass to attract attention. "Welcome, ladies and gentlemen. I don't want to interrupt your socializing, but I'd just like to tell you the winners of this month's show. And don't forget, most of these pieces are available for purchase."

Bella had been thinking of little else since Monday. Despite the fact that her friends teased her about finding bodies, she didn't seem to be getting used to it. And the scene in the locker room had been particularly gruesome.

She tried to put it out of her mind and concentrate on enjoying the evening. She almost succeeded.

Chapter Four

"What is it with you, Ms. Sarver?" Detective Len Carlson asked.

"I'm sorry, Detective, but it's not my fault, is it? I didn't ask for this, did I?"

"Doesn't this strike you as really strange, that you keep running across dead bodies?"

"Well, sure it does, but there it is. What was I supposed to do? Ignore it, pretend I never saw anything?"

Carlson took a deep breath and let it out slowly. He reminded himself that Bella Sarver wasn't responsible for the fact that his twelve year old Jeep Cherokee had just needed over a thousand dollars' worth of 'routine service.' Nor for the fact that the local orthodontist had told his wife last week that their oldest daughter was going to need sixty-eight hundred dollars' worth of braces on her teeth if she wanted to be able to chew properly in the future. "Calm down," he told himself. "Just do your job."

He cleared his throat. "Sorry. No, of course not. You did the right thing to call us. But you do realize this looks a little odd?"

Bella knew Detective Carlson of the Deer Creek Police Department from the previous summer, when she'd discovered a corpse at the local art fair. He and his team had done most of the leg work in that case, but it was Bella who'd put the clues together to solve the multiple mysteries set in motion by the culprit. Now here they were again. Bella was surprised at how calm she felt. Maybe it would hit her later.

Investigative Officer Melanie Jennings was first on the scene, with her team following right behind. She recognized Bella pacing impatiently in front of the women's locker room door, and asked her a few preliminary questions.

"Shall I show you the body?" Bella asked.

"No, Ms. Sarver, you just go sit down. Somebody will be with you soon."

Jennings donned her protective scene-of-crime clothing and entered the room. Her first impression was one of chaos. Had the killer made a shambles of the room in the course of committing the crime? But when she saw the body sprawled half in and half out of the shower stall, she realized that wouldn't have been necessary. Clearly, there hadn't been a fight, just a straight-forward slaying. It wouldn't have taken long.

Jennings became aware of a clamor outside the door leading to the swimming pool. She'd sent another officer around there to prevent anyone from leaving the pool area and entering the locker rooms. She opened the door to find a huddle of wet, shivering people clamoring to know what was going on. She noted that they were all female, the men in the water aerobics class having already been allowed to enter the men's locker room to shower and dress.

"I'm afraid there's been an incident. We're going to have to ask you to stay in the pool area for a while, until we clear out the locker room. The officers here will get you some towels in the meantime."

A chorus of loud protests arose from the group but Jennings retreated back into the locker room. She had no idea where the other officers were going to get towels, but that really wasn't her problem. When a couple of scene of crime officers came in, she left them to do their jobs and went to do hers.

Marlene Benson, the Activities Director of Martingale Manor, had quickly assessed the situation. She called around to some residents who were able to bring over towels and blankets from their closets, and distributed them to the water aerobics people, who were finally allowed to leave the pool area through the adjacent gym. Wrapped in their make-shift cover-ups but still in their wet swimsuits, they milled around near the fireplace for warmth. None of them were happy to have been kept waiting while the police did their thing, but at least no one was in imminent danger of pneumonia. Still.... Carlson couldn't very well interview anybody properly in that state, and all their belongings were in the locker rooms.

"How're they coming along in there?" he asked Officer Jennings, lifting his chin towards the general direction of the locker rooms.

"I'll go check, Detective. I think they're about finished."

The Medical Examiner finished her preliminary exam and allowed the body to be removed from the locker room. The SOCO team had measured and dusted for prints and taken photos. The entire room had been thoroughly searched:

shower alcoves, toilet stalls, waste baskets. The team had found all sorts of interesting and not-so-interesting objects. A lot of half-empty plastic bottles of shampoos and bath gels. Numerous towels, combs, brushes, hair dryers. Duffel bags containing dry clothes. The one thing they hadn't come across was any sort of a murder weapon.

The ME had determined that the deceased had been stabbed in the throat with a sharp object, possibly a pair of scissors. She hadn't died immediately. She'd probably been conscious for quite some time as she lay under the streaming shower, bleeding to death. Who knows how long she might have lain there, if her body blocking the drain hadn't caused the blood-tinged water to overflow the stall.

Carlson assembled his team in the clubhouse's social hall. Jennings, Detective Ron Pepper, and several other officers listened to his instructions. He knew they weren't really necessary. He was aware that everyone already knew their job. Just the same, he wanted to make sure nothing was going to be forgotten. Deer Creek was a peaceful town. The police force was used to handling drunks and giving out parking tickets. The number of murder cases they had could be counted on the fingers of one hand.

"Remember, get everybody's statement before you let them leave the building. I want them all accounted for."

"Right, sir, it's all in hand," Jennings said. "I've got people posted at both doors of both locker rooms and all the outside doors. No one is going to get past us."

"Let's just hope whoever did this hasn't already left. Could anyone have been in that locker room before we got here?"

"You mean aside from Ms. Sarver? She said she didn't see anyone."

"Yeah, but who knows who was there before Sarver came in?"

"So we're ruling her out?"

Carlson raised an eyebrow.

"I just mean, you don't think she did it, do you?"

Carlson sighed. "I wish it was that easy, but let's be realistic. If she killed the victim, all she'd have had to do was leave. No, I don't think she did it, Officer. We're going to have to do some work on this one."

In fact, not many people seemed in any hurry to leave. Painting class was obviously canceled for the day, though the Pilates class and Quilters Club were still assembled. Not that a lot of work was going on in either room. But most of the painting group still milled around the social hall, along with various others who'd remained in the building. Marlene Benson had decided that a large pot of coffee was in order, and now Bella and Carlson each had a steaming cup as they sat facing each other in the pleasant conversation grouping around the fireplace. It wasn't the ideal interview situation, with so many people hovering nearby, but that couldn't be helped.

"All right, let's start at the beginning," Carlson said.

"Well, I already told you, Detective. I heard the water running in the shower. Something about it nagged at me. Now that I think about it, it's probably that the water was the only sound. I couldn't hear anyone moving around or anything. Anyway, I was going to leave, but I didn't feel right about it. So I called out. When no one answered, I walked back there. That's when I saw the bloody water overflowing the sill. So then, I pulled the curtain aside, and saw the body. I know enough not to touch anything else, but I did reach over to turn off the water. I just used two fingers on the faucet. It was so cold. It didn't seem right to ...."

Bella took a sip of her coffee and swallowed hard.

"Okay, I get it. So then ...?"

"So then – then I went out of the locker room and called you. And that's it. That's all I know."

"You said no one else was in the locker room at the time. Did you see anyone leaving as you came in?"

"Well, no. Not from the locker room itself. There were plenty of people around. As you know, there were some exercise classes going on, and a couple of the craft rooms were in use. A few of my students had come in early, too. I already told your Officer Jennings about that. But no one else was in the locker room when I got there. I didn't notice anyone walking away from it, either. I think if there'd been somebody there, they would have said 'hi.' This is an incredibly friendly neighborhood, you know. Everybody always says 'hi.'"

"Friendly, yeah. Except for a little murder here and there."

"Murder? Are you sure?"

"Unless the victim stabbed herself in the throat, yeah, murder. You said you recognized her?"

Bella nodded. "Shirley Rogers. She owns *Ruffles and Flourishes*, the gift shop over on Main Street. I've been in there a couple of times. In fact ..., no never mind, that doesn't matter."

Carlson sighed. "Everything matters," he said. "You should know that, right? You've been through something like this before."

"No, well …. It's nothing. It's only that we were talking about her just the other day."

"We?"

"Mollie & I. And Leo. You know, he's doing some work for her right now."

"For who? Shirley Rogers?"

Bella nodded. "Right. She asked him to do something about her taxes, and he was complaining about what a mess her records are."

Carlson eyed Bella skeptically. "So Ms. Rogers owned a store right next door to your new co-op gallery. And your friend, Leo Schaeffer, is her accountant. More coincidences?"

Art Halperin had to argue his way in to the Martingale Manor clubhouse. He was neither a resident nor a guest, but he finally managed to convince the gate guard that he was needed inside. There was a police officer at the door, but Art pushed right past when he saw Bella on the sofa with the detective.

"Are you all right?" he asked anxiously, as Bella rose to meet him. He put his arms around her and held her tight, and she briefly considered whether it was okay to break down now. But breaking down was not something Bella did, so she just rested her head against his chest for a minute, and then stood back.

"I'm fine," she said.

"Bella, you're beginning to make a habit of this sort of thing," Art told her.

"Exactly what I said," Carlson chimed in. "Maybe you can do something about it, Mr. Halperin.

"I would if I could. How do you think I should go about it?" Art asked rhetorically.

Carlson shrugged.

"Can I take her home now?"

"Yeah, fine. Take her home. I know where to find her. But I'm going to want to talk to her again."

Art helped Bella gather up her equipment and they toted it all out to her car.

"What are you doing here?" Bella asked. "Did somebody call you?"

"No. I was driving by and I saw all the police cars out in front. I knew you were teaching here today, so I pulled over and tried to call you. When you didn't answer, I got worried, so I came in to look for you. That's when I heard somebody had been killed here. I figured you must be involved somehow."

"Thanks."

"I meant that in a good way, you know," Art said, grinning. He slammed the hatch shut on Bella's SUV. "I'll follow you home, ok?"

"You really don't have to do that, Art. You must have been on your way someplace, weren't you?"

"Yeah, just to one of my alumni meetings. We're trying to establish another scholarship fund for a promising new high school grad who plans to go into physics."

"So you should go. I'm perfectly fine, Art. Really."

"I know you are, Bella. But humor me. It's not every day my best girl finds a dead body. Anyway, the meeting is probably mostly over by now," he said, glancing at his watch. "Let's go put your things away and go get something to eat."

Bella knew when she'd lost an argument. "Okay, but I'm warning you, I'm going to want to argue that your group should make a point of funding a female with your scholarship."

"Some affirmative action? You're on."

It wasn't until more than an hour later, as Bella and Art were sipping their coffee after a soup and salad lunch that Bella remembered.

"What's wrong?" Art asked, seeing her face change.

"I can't believe this, Art. I completely forgot. I'm supposed to be at a meeting right now. Mollie is going to kill me."

Chapter Five

Bella Sarver did know the victim, Shirley Rogers, but not very well. She'd been in her store a few times. As Detective Carlson noted, it was just down the block from the Deer Creek Art League, on Main Street. Shirley Rogers was the reason Bella was now teaching at Martingale Manor in the first place. Hard to believe it had all started only a couple of months ago, just as summer had begun to turn into autumn. How does time go so fast?

Ruffles and Flourishes occupied 226 Main Street. The place had something of an identity issue, as it didn't seem to be sure whether it was a gift shop or an art gallery or maybe a home goods store. Shirley carried all kinds of odd things; paintings, sure, but also notecards, miscellaneous serving pieces, silk scarves, fancy dolls – anything that caught her eye when she shopped the many catalogs that arrived at her store or on-line just about daily. She looked forward to the gift shop convention at Chicago's McCormick Place every year and always came home laden with boxes and bags of stuff. If someone needed a present, or just the right objet d'art to set off a table, or the perfect accessory for a new outfit, Shirley's store was where to find it. It had only needed the right sort of ground to plant itself in in order to thrive, and Deer Creek was a very fertile climate.

The little bell fixed over the front door of *Ruffles and Flourishes* tinkled when Bella Sarver pushed it open that September day. She always enjoyed poking around the little stores in town to see what was new whenever she had some free time. Today, in honor of autumn, *Ruffles and Flourishes'* predominant color scheme was oranges and browns, with a liberal sprinkling of turkeys, pumpkins, ghosts and witches denoting the fall holidays soon to come. Shirley Rogers relished every holiday in its turn, and was never going to be accused of skipping over Halloween or Thanksgiving in the rush to get to Christmas.

"Be right with you," Shirley called out.

"No problem, Shirley," Bella told her. "I'm not in any hurry."

Ruffles and Flourishes hadn't been in its current location long. Bella wasn't certain exactly when Shirley had moved to Deer Creek, but she remembered meeting her at least a year or so earlier, when Shirley Rogers had turned up at a meeting of the Deer Creek Art League. Her store had recently opened and she said she wanted to get acquainted with the local arts community. It was part of her program to cultivate contacts among the local business owners. Networking, networking, networking. Shirley had a pretty good business sense.

Bella had first visited *Ruffles and Flourishes* shortly after that first meeting. She'd been impressed by how attractive the store was then, but now it was absolutely crammed with colorful goods, inviting customers to pick up and examine them. Bella felt like a kid in a candy shop as she moved around the displays.

She reached for a box of notecards from a pile on a table, thinking she recognized the work as that of Kasia Novik, who specialized in charming paintings of small European villages. She turned the box over to look at the label, but the name didn't ring any bells. Pretty cards, though. They'd make nice stocking stuffers for Christmas.

A small painting hanging in the little gallery alcove caught her eye. A nicely rendered landscape of a Tuscan hill town. It reminded Bella of the painting holiday she'd led there not too long before. The trip had its high points, but there'd been some unexpected complications. She leaned forward for a closer look. The signature was hard to decipher.

"You like that one?" Shirley asked, coming forward. "I do, too. It's one of our local artists, you know. Fabio Gompers. He's one of your members at the Art League, isn't he?"

"Fabio? Yes. I'm always surprised to realize that, because he's such a well-known artist. I wouldn't have expected him to bother with us. I'm kind of surprised to see his work here, as well."

Shirley shrugged. "Why not? If he can place some of his work here, so much the better. No shipping costs and the fact that he's local doesn't hurt sales any, either. I have some of Cynthia Oh's paintings, too."

"Cynthia? She's our Program Director this year. Nice work. I didn't realize you carried her pieces."

"Yes. I like to help out our local people when I can. So," Shirley said, changing directions, "I hear you're going into competition with me."

"Competition? What do you mean?"

"Your new gallery. The co-op."

"The co-op? How on earth did you hear about that? We only just decided to go ahead with it last week."

"News travels fast," Shirley replied laconically.

Bella eyed her skeptically, but Shirley was giving nothing away.

34

Not that the co-op was a big secret, but still – it wasn't at the announcement stage yet. Bella thought back to the previous week's meeting, wondering who might have spilled the beans. Maybe Kasia? Probably not Ben. Could have been Fabio. Well, it probably didn't really matter much. Word was bound to get out.

Bella remembered that a few people had voiced doubts about the project.

"Do you think we could really do it?" Kasia had asked, wavering uncertainly between wanting to do it and being nervous about taking on the commitment.

"Sure, we can. Why not?" Bella retorted. "What's to stop us?"

"I say we go for it," Mollie Schaeffer urged. "In fact, I make a motion. I move that the Deer Creek Art League rents the vacant store at 224 Main Street for the purpose of establishing a co-op art gallery."

"Thank you, Mollie," Bella said. "Do we have a second?"

"Yes, I second."

"Thank you, Kasia. All in favor?"

Eight hands went up.

"All opposed?"

One hand rose. It belonged to Becky Lemon, Board Secretary. The rest of the Board members glanced at her sourly.

Becky looked around the table. She knew she was at odds with the others, as usual, but her hand stayed defiantly raised.

"Eight, nine," Bella counted. "Leo? You're abstaining?"

Leo Schaeffer nodded. "I'm not sure about this. It'll still cost a lot, you know, even with the Pearson money. The store needs renovating; we'd have to buy new shelving, a hanging system, another PC. Where's all that going to come from?"

Anybody could have identified Mollie and Leo Schaeffer as a couple from a distance. If any two people were made for each other, it was them. They even looked alike. Both short and round, though Mollie's head was topped with a mop of curly black hair and Leo's head was shiny and bald. Their personalities complimented, rather than matched, each other. Mollie was an eternal optimist, but Leo always looked for the dark side of a situation. Maybe that came from being an accountant.

"Oh, Leo," Mollie chided. "Have a little faith. It'll work out fine. We have some surplus from our classes and sales, don't we? And our members will cough up something, especially if they want to be able to show and sell their work at the co-op. And ... you can keep the books, okay?"

It was Mollie Schaeffer who first had the idea of turning the new venue into a co-op art gallery. The Deer Creek Art League owned the nice building right on Main Street outright, but it was bursting at the seams. The League offered exhibition space to its members, along with classes, social events, and special exhibits of outside artists. When long-time member Penny Pearsons died and left a legacy to the League, the first thing the Board thought of was expansion. And when a store just one block east of the building became vacant, the solution was staring them in the face.

Undeniably, it wasn't going to happen without a lot of organizing. And Mollie was nothing if not a whiz at organizing things.

"So – Bella – what's the vote?" Mollie called out.

"Eight for, one against, one abstention. As President, I don't get a vote, except to break a tie. Ok, then. Motion carried," Bella announced. "I guess the first thing we need is a committee to get this off the ground. Rahj, will you chair that?"

"Sure, it'll be fun. I'll start organizing it right away. Mollie, we'll need you, naturally."

As the Director of Development, Rahj Patel seemed the most obvious choice to head up the effort, but he was certainly going to need lots of help.

"And Leo, what about you? We definitely need your financial expertise," Rahj told him.

"Well, if we're going to do this, I better make sure we do it right," Leo conceded. Leo, a retired CPA, was Treasurer of the DCAL.

"Terrific. So tomorrow morning, I'll call the realtor and get everything started. In fact," Rahj corrected himself, "there's no time like the present." He pulled a cell phone out of his pocket as he left the building, to walk over to the store to take a look at the "For Sale" sign and get the realtor's name and number.

A few days later, Bella held her pen poised above the signature line on the lease. As President, she had both the authority and the responsibility of signing it. She was excited about the possibilities the co-op gallery might offer to the local artists, but enough of a realist to recognize that it was big risk, too. Were they moving too fast? Maybe Leo had been right to caution them. Bella reviewed the situation in her mind.

The current Art League building served simultaneously as gallery, classroom, and meeting space. It was so full, it was getting hard to turn around without bumping into things. It was also hard to concentrate on sales with so much else going on. Undeniably, the member artists needed a space specially dedicated to showing and selling their work. Ideally, they could place their pieces with independent galleries, but that was easier said than done. The art business was tough, and on-line competition had both widened buyer's options and reduced the number of actual physical stores that could promote the artists' work. These days, the art world was pretty much a do-it-yourself enterprise, and artists needed all the help they could get.

'Let's go for it, then,' Bella told herself. She grasped the pen firmly and signed her name.

So the project was set in motion, but all the details remained to be worked out. The general membership, which included Shirley Rogers, hadn't even been notified yet. Somebody on the board must have leaked the news. Not Mollie or Leo. Rahj? Bella doubted it. That left Ben Goldberg, Fabio Gompers, or Kasia Novik. Probably not really important, but still ….

"Nothing much is really set yet, Shirley," Bella said now. "But you're right; the Art League is planning to open a co-op. But it's not really competition. It's just a co-op gallery for those of our members who want to have another venue for selling their work. It's going to be run entirely by the co-op members, and mostly financed by them, also. But it's not like your store; it's not a gift shop. No, it will be strictly an art gallery."

"Just the same, you have to admit there's some overlap there. And it'll be right next door."

"Well, maybe a little. But competition is good for business, isn't it? That's what I hear, anyway. Our co-op and your store can be the nucleus of a new arts district here in Deer Creek. That's bound to be good for all of us."

"Hmmph," Shirley mumbled. "Maybe. We'll have to see." She clearly wasn't happy about it, but she made an effort and changed the subject.

"You teach classes over at the Art League, don't you, Bella?"

"Yes, I do. Painting and drawing. Why?"

"Nothing, but I was just wondering. You know I've moved into Martingale Manor recently?"

"No, I didn't know. You mean that new active adult community south of town? And by the way, what's an 'active adult'?"

Shirley laughed. "It's a polite way of saying old people who aren't quite ready to pack it in yet. I guess it's better than calling us 'senior citizens'."

She clearly wasn't young, but no one would take Shirley Rogers for a senior citizen. Her hair was still blonde and full, thanks to a little assist from her hairdresser. Her body was a bit more comfortably padded than it used to be, and her jawline sagged just a little, but the softer lines suited her.

Bella smiled, too. "I guess. So, are the adults there active?"

"Actually, they are. I've never seen so many clubs and other activities in one place before. It's sort of like living in a permanent resort. There's tennis and bocce ball and swimming and history club and book club and … and…."

Bella waved her hand back and forth. "Stop, stop! I get the idea. Sounds great!"

"Yeah. I think I'm going to love it there. You should look into it."

Bella smiled non-commitally.

"So, anyway, there's a painting group, too, but these people really don't have a clue. They just get a photo of somebody else's painting, a Monet or somebody, and try to copy it. So then they all end up with a small, bad copy of someone else's work. That's no way to learn anything. I was wondering if you might like to teach a class there. You know, just the basics of how to get started doing a painting."

"Oh!" said Bella. "Well, yes, I might like that. Let me think about it."

Bella did think about it, with the result that, in no time at all, she'd found herself teaching a class at Martingale Manor, where the residents were indeed pretty active. Except for Shirley Rogers, of course. She was dead and Bella was involved in another murder. Strange how life works out sometimes.

Chapter Six

Rahj Patel, Co-Op Committee Chair, called the meeting to order on time. That alone was a rarity for any meeting of the Deer Creek Art League.

"I got us a two year lease on the store, and Bella's already signed it, so it looks like we're in business," he announced. "By the way, where is Bella? She should have been here by now."

"I saw her this morning at Martindale Manor. She said she'd be here right after class," Kasia said. "I'm sure she'll be here any minute."

"OK, but we'll move on without her. So -," Rahj continued, "poor Penny's legacy will pay for the rent, but this co-op has to become self-supporting if it's going to last for more than two years. Also, it would be nice if we can save a lot of the legacy for improvements, repairs and such, and not have to spend it all on rent. So – we need to establish a system."

"I agree," said Ben Goldberg. "But don't you think we should get over to the place and take a look at it first? I think seeing what sort of space we're talking about will help us understand how we should structure the operation."

Ben was one of the most organized Membership Vice-Presidents DCAL had ever had, partly because he was a very visual person. He thought in images as well as in words. And if he could visualize an event or a project, he could make it happen.

You could always find him with a pencil in hand, doodling out a design. It helped him think. Whenever he was faced with an especially difficult problem, his designs became intricate figures of overlapping circles and dots. Often enough, he colored them in with markers and then translated the sketches to very large canvases. An extremely creative young man. No wonder his work was carried in some of the high end galleries on the North Shore.

Mollie looked at her watch for the umpteenth time. It was so unusual for Bella to be late. Mollie checked her phone, but there was still no reply to her earlier text. She wondered if she should call. She sent another text, and told herself not to be silly. No doubt Bella had got sidetracked by one of her students, or held up in traffic, or something. She'd get here.

Mollie turned her attention back to the meeting, which was in the process of adjourning in order to troop down the block to the new gallery.

Number 224 Main Street was a store at the south end of downtown, bounded by Pine on the north and Brookline on the south, just across from the park. There was a Starbucks right on the corner, and then came Ruffles and Flourishes, the new co-op, which had been a children's clothing store until a month or so ago, and a small independent bookshop. You couldn't ask for a better location. Rahj turned the key in the lock and held the front door open for the others to enter.

"Oh," said Kasia. Her anticipatory smile faded as she stood at the threshold and surveyed the empty space. Empty, that is, but for some torn sheets of brown paper and wadded-up plastic bags. Dust motes danced in the sunlight coming in through the large window. Dust covered the floor and a lonely counter across one end of the room.

"Cheer up, Kasia," Mollie said. "Yes, it's a pretty depressing site at the moment, but look at the possibilities. It's a very good size. It just needs to be cleaned up and painted, and maybe a moveable wall for additional hanging space." She looked around optimistically, seeing, not the empty, dirty place in front of her but the bright, cheerful gallery it was going to become. "It only needs some elbow grease to get it in shape."

"Absolutely!" Rahj agreed. "Just what I said to myself when I took the lease. It'll be perfect. And there's tons of storage space, too, in the basement."

He led them towards the back of the store, where a door opened into a stairwell, and they all headed down the stairs. The basement was indeed a cavernous room under the entire store. It was unfinished, all concrete floors and stud walls, but there was electricity, at least. A couple of bare light bulbs hung from the ceiling and lit satisfactorily when Rahj flipped the switch by the stairs. "We don't need to finish it," he said, "unless we want to. We can just clean it up and build some shelving and such."

"I wish Bella was here. She would have liked to see this," Kasia noted.

"I know," Mollie agreed. She checked her phone again. Still nothing. "This isn't like her. I wonder if I should call Art."

"Why worry him? Let's wait a little longer. I'm sure she'll be in touch," Kasia said, trying to be reassuring, but not entirely able to hide her own anxiety.

Back at the Art League building, the committee relaxed into their chairs. "We have a ton of work to do to get ready to open by Christmas," Kasia observed. "We're going to need a lot more help."

"I didn't know we'd settled on Christmas as a goal," Rahj said.

"Well, we didn't, but we've talked about it, and why not? I think we can do it," Mollie said. "We have two months. We're just going to have to get the membership involved. Ben, that's your area, okay? You know what? We should have a contest."

"A contest?" Ben asked warily. "What sort of contest?"

"A naming contest."

Four blank faces turned to her. Mollie sighed. "Right," she began. "As you know, the co-op members are going to have to agree to a monthly fee as well as to taking regular turns working at the gallery. What if we offer a year's free membership to the person who comes up with the best name? A naming contest!"

"Brilliant! I love it," Rahj said.

That's when Mollie's phone rang. She looked at the screen. She usually hated it when the phone rang. It was almost always somebody she didn't want to talk to, like a sales person or a politician. If it even *was* an actual person rather than a robocall. But Bella's picture popped up. Finally!

"Bella!" she exclaimed. "Where are you? We were getting worried."

The other committee members stopped talking and looked anxiously at Mollie. "Tell her ...." Rahj started to say, but Mollie waved him off.

"What?" she exclaimed again, more softly. "You're not serious! I don't believe this, Bella. Not again."

"What is it?" Rahj persisted, but Mollie waved him off again.

"No, I know it's not a joke. I'm sorry. Of course, this has to be horrible for you. No, no – I get it. Do you need me to come over? Okay. I'm glad Art is with you. Call me later, all right?"

She pressed 'end.' Her fellow committee members stared at her impatiently.

"Shirley Rogers has been killed. Bella found the body."

For a moment, no one said anything, and then everybody spoke at once. Mollie raised her hand for silence. "I don't know anything else," she said. "Bella's going to call me later."

"I just saw her this morning," Fabio said. "She was fine."

"Who? Shirley? You saw Shirley? I didn't know you even knew her, Fabio," Mollie said.

"Yes," he said, frowning. Stunned? Or maybe puzzled would be a better word. "I saw Bella, too. She was talking to some guy. I bet he was one of the cops. There were a bunch of police there. I had to give them my name before they'd let me leave the building. But they didn't tell me why."

When people heard the name 'Fabio Gompers,' they usually expected to see a lean, handsome, dark-haired young Italian. Either that or a cigar-smoking, squat, bald labor boss. Fabio was neither of those things. He was the product of a union between a lovely Italian girl and a Jewish GI who helped liberate Italy at the end of the Second World War. True, he'd once had dark curly hair, but that was mostly gone now, and his physique had gone to ... had just gone. However, there must have been something in his Italian heritage that came through and endowed him with the ability to create paintings that evoked the Renaissance with their luminous portrayal of human flesh. The Deer Creek Art League considered itself blessed to count an artist of that quality among its members. However, his people skills left something to be desired.

"Where? You saw both of them? Why didn't you say something?" Mollie demanded.

"Shirley was swimming. I was just leaving the pool when she came in. I see her there some mornings. She likes to swim early, before the water aerobics class starts. She kept swimming her laps for a couple of minutes, while people came into the pool, but then she left. She was perfectly fine then. I saw you, too, Kasia."

Kasia nodded agreement. "That's right. Shirley came in a little after I did, and I left before she was done with her laps. Like you said, she was perfectly fine."

"This was at Martingale Manor? You live there, too?" Mollie asked. "Both of you?"

Fabio nodded while Kasia shook her head. "I moved in to one of the condos about a year ago," he said.

"Do you like it, Fabio?" Kasia asked. She continued before he could answer. "My mother loves it there. She moved to one of the townhouses a couple of years ago, and it's great. I like it, too. In fact, that's how I get to use the pool."

"I didn't know you could get in," Mollie said.

"Oh, yes, if you're a guest of a resident. I like to swim there when I can. It's usually not crowded early, before the classes start." Then she remembered, and her smile dimmed. "I wonder what'll happen to Shirley's store now. Does she have any kids? Does anybody know?" she asked, looking around the table.

Mollie shook her head. "I don't really know her very well. I met her when she joined the Art League, but I can't say we ever talked about much except League business. My Leo is doing some work for her, though. He might know more."

"She took some of my small still-life paintings for her gallery," Fabio announced, apropos of nothing.

"Really? But *Ruffles and Flourishes* is just a little gift shop, isn't it? I'm surprised a fancy artist like you would bother with it," Rahj commented.

Fabio shrugged. "You place your work wherever you can, don't you? And she only has some small pieces, nothing major."

"I think she has some of Cynthia's pieces, too," Kasia said.

"Does she?" Mollie asked. "It's nice of Shirley to help out our local artists. Was nice," she corrected.

Cynthia Oh was the Program Director for the Art League. She was known for her charming paintings of country cottages.

Fabio snorted. "Nice, nothing. Shirley doesn't do anything to be nice. She carries Cynthia's little paintings because they sell. Not what you'd call great art, but they're colorful, don't cost too much, and fit well in small spaces. Believe me, if they didn't move, they'd be gone."

"Come on, Fabio," Kasia protested. "The poor woman has just been killed."

"I wonder what's going to happen to her store, then. I'd better get my stuff out of there right away."

"Maybe whoever inherits will take it over," Rahj speculated.

He looked around the table, but nobody had an answer for him. "Well," he said, "there's nothing we can do about this. And our new project is going to involve a lot of work, so let's get back to business."

"Right, we have a lot to do. But it's going to be a lot of fun, as well, don't you think?" Mollie said. "It will be great to give our artists a better chance of selling their work than they have with just a piece or two in our monthly shows here at the Art League. It can be so hard to get into other galleries, as we all know. Except you, of course," she added, with a nod to Fabio.

"I've been lucky," he agreed," but I work plenty hard at it, too, you know. Gallery owners don't come looking for artists, do they? You have to get out there and push."

He shoved his chair back from the table. "I better get over to Shirley's place and see what's going on."

Chapter Seven

Leo Schaeffer was working for Shirley Rogers, but he didn't know much about her, either. He had his wife, Mollie, to thank for the introduction. If 'thank' was the right word.

He rubbed his eyes, sighed heavily, and pulled his adding machine closer. Shirley Rogers' accounting system was somewhat unusual, to say the least. She'd eschewed anything as useful as Quickbooks in favor of an old-fashioned 12 column ledger. That would have worked well enough had she arranged it as any bookkeeper had been taught – debits vs. credits, assets vs. liabilities, accounts receivable vs. accounts payable. But no, she apparently just entered her items willy-nilly, as bills came in or as she thought to send out invoices and commission checks. It was an amazing mess. The only way to straighten it out would be to go over every item, line by line, and enter it into a newly created system using accepted accounting methods. It was going to be a massive amount of work. Leo was beginning to be sorry he had ever allowed his wife to talk him into helping out.

Mollie had been talking with Shirley at a general meeting of the Deer Creek Art League and Shirley complained about having to pay her taxes. "It's so unfair," she said. "I do all the work and the government gets all the money."

"Well, really," Mollie laughed, "we all have to pay our taxes, don't we? I mean, we all use the streets and the fire protection, and we expect the entire structure of society to be there for us so we can be free to live and work here without having to think about every detail, don't we?"

"Oh, I know," Shirley waved her away. "I get it. But it's so complicated. I mean, how do I figure out how much to pay? It's easy when you get a salary, but I'm running a business. What's business income and what's personal income? What can I deduct for expenses? So many questions."

"How have you been managing so far?" Mollie asked reasonably. "After all, you've been doing this for a while, haven't you? And you seem like a pretty competent person to me."

"Thanks, but I just sort of make things up as I go along. But now I got this letter from the IRS that they want to audit my books. I don't know what to do."

"I do," Mollie told her. "My Leo is a CPA. He'll straighten it all out for you."

Which is how Leo found himself in the back office of *Ruffles and Flourishes* on a beautiful, crisp early November day when he'd much rather be out in the park, painting a nice picture of the late autumn leaves fallen on the grass, still showing bright golds and reds.

"I thought I was supposed to be retired," Leo complained to Mollie. "I have more work now than when I was working, between the Art League and your friend's businesses and such."

"Oh, don't be such a grump," Mollie teased. "You know you love it."

Leo did love it, but this …. He waved his hand at the pile of ledgers and envelopes full of … who knew what? This was too much.

He sighed again, picked a random envelope from the pile, and opened it. An invoice from a place called Fine Art USA, $100 for five small giclee prints. Great. He put it in a new pile. Accounts payable. But what about the prints? Where were they? Still in inventory? Sold? He scanned in the bill, printed the copy, and put that in another new pile. Inventory. He pushed his chair back and looked at the desk scattered with all kinds of paper. This was too big a job for one person. *Let's start again.*

""Rita," he called out.

Rita Cutler, Shirley's part-time assistant, came to the door of the office. Rita lived just a couple of blocks away, in a small condo across from the park. A retired office manager, she was thrilled when Shirley hired her to help out in the store. It was just what she wanted. A way to earn a little extra income doing something that brought her into contact with the public. She'd only been working a few months, but she was hoping she could stay on forever. She especially loved it when Shirley took some time off, like she did today. Then Rita could pretend that *Ruffles and Flourishes* belonged to her. She had all kinds of ideas of how to run the business, if only she could get Shirley to listen.

"What can I do for you, Leo? Do you want a cup of coffee?"

"No. No, thanks. I need a lot more than that. For starters, is there some sort of inventory list around here?"

Oh! I have no idea," she said, looking around at the cluttered desk, the overflowing file cabinets, and messy shelves. "I just come in and help out at the counter. I told Shirley, I could help out a lot more, with the books and things, but she likes to handle all that herself, so I just wait on customers when they come in."

"Well," Leo tried again, "when a customer asks for something, how do you know how to find it?"

"Well, actually, it's not like that," Rita said. "I mean, usually people just come in and look around, and when they find what they want, they bring it over to the counter. Or I might look around myself, if they know the sort of thing they have in mind."

Leo appeared mystified.

Rita tried again. "I mean, it's not like the supermarket, where you know you need some tomatoes so you go over to the produce counter. This is the sort of place where you just browse until something catches your eye."

"Right. Okay, let's look at it another way. When somebody wants to buy something, what do you do?"

"Well, I ring it up. I look at the tag to see how much it is, and then I punch it in on the register, and the register figures out the tax and everything, and then the customer slides in their card and pays for it."

Leo thought for a moment. "When you punch in a sale, what exactly do you do?"

"Well, let's see. The tag has the price. And the ID number, too, of course. I punch in the number first, then the price, and then the register says how much to charge."

"Where do these numbers come from?"

"I don't actually know, Leo. I assume they're some sort of inventory … oh!"

"Exactly. Oh! So there has to be an inventory record someplace, right?"

"I guess so," Rita agreed. "I never really gave it much thought. Shirley writes the numbers on the tags, and I enter them into the register when I ring up the sale. She never asked me to do anything else."

"Okay, so the register must have some way of keeping track of sales," Leo ventured.

Rita frowned. "Maybe. You know, I'm not really sure about that, Leo. You're probably right. But if it does, I have no idea how to get any reports out of it."

"Do you ever see her working on any kind of a computer print-out?"

She shook her head doubtfully. "But then, I wouldn't, would I? I never see Shirley doing any sort of record keeping. She probably does it after hours."

"I can't find any proper records on her laptop. I found a ledger where she writes things down, but it's so haphazard, I can't believe it. Do you think there's another ledger someplace that's more organized?"

"I'm sorry, Leo, but I just don't know. I mean, if it were up to me, I would have organized things differently, but Shirley just wanted me to take care of the customers, so I really didn't bother thinking about her record keeping. I did think about how to arrange the store or advertise, things like that, but she never wanted to hear any of my ideas. So I stuck to my job and kept quiet."

"Okay, I get it." Leo thought for a moment. "I can't believe anyone would try to run a business this way. If she didn't use a computer to keep business records, she must have used another paper ledger. So – let's see if we can find that ledger. And then, we better take an inventory of everything in the store and compare it with the ledger, if we can find that. Then we'll at least have some idea of what was bought and what was sold. But this is way too big a job for me. I'm going to wait until Shirley comes back. We'll have to re-negotiate, and we'll have to bring in some help. For now, I'm going home."

Fabio Gompers pushed open the front door of Ruffles and Flourishes before Leo could see himself out. Leo tried to stop him entering, telling him the place was closed, but Rita Cutler recognized Fabio and waved him in. "What can I do for you?" she asked. "Like Leo said, we're closed now."

"That's okay, Rita. I just wanted to see about my paintings. How are they moving?"

"I don't think we've sold one for a while, Fabio. People like them, but they're kind of pricey, you know."

"Yeah, I guess. I think I'll take them out, if that's okay with you."

"Well, if you want to …, but wouldn't you rather talk to Shirley about that? I'm sure she'll be in pretty soon."

"You don't need me here, do you?" Leo interjected. "I'll see you later, Rita. Thanks for your help."

"You'll never guess what happened," Mollie greeted Leo at home not long after he'd left Ruffles and Flourishes.

"You're right. I have no idea," Leo answered, moving past her. "Whatever it is will have to wait. I have a headache from trying to make sense of Shirley's so-called bookkeeping. I've never seen a mess like that in my life."

"I guess you haven't heard, then," Mollie said, following her husband into the living room.

"Heard what?" Leo flopped into a comfy chair, sprawled with his legs out, eyes closed, and one arm draped across his forehead.

"You could have saved yourself the headache, Leo. Shirley's bookkeeping methods don't make much difference now."

"What do you mean?" Only Leo's lips moved. The rest of him stayed immobile.

"You know I was at a meeting of the co-op committee this afternoon, right?" She frowned. "I must have been there while you were just down the street at *Ruffles and Flourishes*."

Mollie looked down at Leo in the chair, going over the events in her mind while she waited for him to feel her presence. Finally, he opened one eye. "And…?"

"Well, Bella called me while I was there. You'll never guess what happened."

"If it's Bella, it must be that she found another body. That seems to be her new hobby."

Mollie's face fell. "How did you know?"

Leo's eyebrows shot up into his receding hairline. "Don't tell me," he pleaded.

Mollie ignored him. "Shirley Rogers."

"What about her?"

"She's dead. Bella found her in the shower stall at Martingale Manor."

Leo sat up, then put his head in his hands, and began rocking back and forth. "Dear God," he muttered, "it's really too bad I'm not a drinking man. If I ever needed a drink, now would be the time."

Mollie took the hint. She poured a glass of wine for Leo and one for herself. "I think it's about time we started drinking, don't you?"

"And if not now, when?" he laughed, clinking his glass against hers. "L'chaim."

"L'chaim." She took a sip, then sat down in the matching chair on the other side of the end table, staring at the faux fireplace. For a while, they just sat there together, watching the electric fire go through its color changes. Leo scooped a handful of cashew nuts from the bowl on the table.

"So, how did your meeting go?"

"Well, up until Bella called me about Shirley, it was going fine. It broke up after I shared the news. I guess none of us felt like making any more decisions right then."

Leo grunted. They each took another sip of wine. The colors did their thing.

"Wait a minute. What time did you say Bella called you?"

"I guess it was around two or so. Why?"

"Was Fabio Gompers at your meeting?"

"Well, sure. You know he's on the co-op committee. What's going on, Leo?"

"So he knew about Shirley Rogers being killed?"

Mollie nodded.

"So why didn't he say anything about it to me?"

"When?"

"When he came into the store and took away his paintings."

"Really? Why would he do that? And why just then?"

"Good questions, hon. I wish I could answer them."

They sipped at their wine again.

"So what do you mean, her bookkeeping is a mess?" Mollie asked, suddenly remembering what Leo had started to tell her. "That doesn't sound like Shirley at all. She's so well-organized. That's one of the things she and I have in common. Had."

"If you'd been there, you'd have seen for yourself. There are hardly any records and no rhyme or reason to the so-called records that do exist. I don't understand how anyone could run a business that way."

Mollie bit her lip thoughtfully.

"What's the matter?"

"I don't think you *could* run a business like that. Not for very long, anyway. And Shirley's had that store for … how long? It's been a fixture on Main Street for a while now."

"I didn't realize you knew Shirley that well."

"I don't, really. We weren't friends," Mollie said. "More like acquaintances. We worked together on some committees for the Art League. Especially if there was a community thing going on downtown. She has …had…a relationship with a number of our artists, too. But you can tell what people are like, if they're detail-minded or flaky or whatever."

Leo nodded slowly. "I believe you, hon. Which means - something strange is going on there. But why would she ask me to help straighten out her accounts? She must have known I couldn't work with what she gave me."

Mollie shook her head.

"Anyway, it's out of my hands now. The police will be getting into everything and it'll be their problem."

"Yes," Mollie said slowly, "but you know, it's kind of our problem too, isn't it?"

"Is it? How?"

"Well, I mean – you looking into her books, and the co-op moving in next door, and Bella finding her like that."

"No, no, no," Leo argued, shaking his head energetically. "All coincidence. Not our concern."

Mollie raised an eyebrow, then poured a little more wine into their glasses. She was content to let the matter rest for the moment.

Chapter Eight

Martingale Manor consisted of several hundred small detached houses and several hundred more one-story townhouses, each on a pretty landscaped lot. There were a couple of ponds populated in summer by geese, ducks, egrets and herons, in park-like settings well-supplied with walking and bike paths, and benches for sitting and admiring the view. No one walking the peaceful, quiet grounds would have imagined that only ten years prior, the land was part of a large farm, one that had belonged to the Martingale family since the mid-1800's.

Like so many family farms, the remaining Martingale, a great-great-grandson of the Will Martingale who'd pushed west from the wilds of Ohio to the even wilder lands of Illinois, searching for better land on which to make a living for his growing family, hadn't been able to cope with the competition from the large factory farms that had pretty much taken over the agricultural business by then. He sold the land to a developer who had seen the opportunity to be had by catering to the growing segment of retired baby boomers with money, who wanted to downsize and be done with the chores of mowing lawns and shoveling snow, but who also demanded luxurious surroundings. The 'over-55' community he'd built had a lot in common with Disneyland, but the residents loved it.

The Clubhouse, a sprawling building of no particular style, stood just beyond the gated entrance to the community. The Clubhouse had at least four entrances at widely separated points in the building. Each entrance required a keycard to get in, but anybody could leave just by pushing open a door. There were no CCTV cameras, so that option was a bust as far as the police were concerned. People popped in and out at will, and there was absolutely no way to know who was in the building at any given time. As Detective Len Carlson stood in the middle of the building's sprawling, high-ceilinged great room and watched Bella Sarver and Art Halperin leave through the main entrance, he thought about this. The killer could have entered, done the murder and left without any of the twenty or thirty people then engaged in various activities being the wiser. Nobody could have planned that. It was just a matter of luck.

Carlson knew the scene of crime team was already hard at work around the building. He'd get their preliminary report in due course. The officers had sealed off the crime scene and taken the particulars of everyone in the building when they arrived, but who knew if the murderer was still there? Odds are, the killer would have left immediately, even before the body was discovered. Why would he or she hang around? As for finger prints, dozens of people had access to the locker room. SOCO was certainly dusting the place for prints, but that was just a matter of form. Doubtless there'd be plenty of prints, but so what?

It sure was taking a chance. Anybody could have walked into that locker room while the stabbing was taking place. For that matter, if Bella Sarver had only entered sooner, she would have been bound to see the killer. Although, Carlson ruminated, even the locker room had two entrances, one to the lobby and the other to the indoor pool. Still, nobody in his right mind would have planned a murder under such circumstances. So it had to have been impulsive. But why?

"First things first," Carlson told himself, and crossed the lobby to the ladies' locker room. He found the medical examiner just rising to her feet after examining the body, which still lay in a pool of water, half in and half out of the shower stall. The ugly wounds in the victim's throat were still seeping blood. The ME recognized Carlson and turned to him, still wearing her latex gloves.

"Be careful where you step," she warned. "It's slippery with all this water."

Carlson stopped where he was, a few feet from the body. The scene was clear enough. "What have you got, Beth?"

Beth Franklin crouched over the corpse once more. "As you can see, Len, cause of death was a stab wound to the throat."

"Time?"

"Sometime between 8 and 9 this morning. We can pin it down because the water aerobics class was going on then, and some of the people in the class saw the victim swimming across the deep end of the pool for a little while after class started. She apparently went for an early morning swim and was just finishing up when they arrived. She got out of the pool and was last seen alive entering the locker room, just a little after 8. The lady who found her called it in just before 9. So …."

"So that's pretty clear, then," Carlson finished. "How about the murder weapon? A knife of some kind?"

"Maybe," Franklin said, "but I doubt it. The wound is pretty jagged and rough. No, I'm thinking this could have done with a scissors. I'll know more for sure when I get her on the table. The poor woman didn't die right away, I can tell you that. Whoever did it just left the victim to lie there, drowning in her own blood."

Carlson could picture it. She might have been conscious for a while, lying helpless while the water, running cold, pounded her body. The autopsy remained to be done, but Carlson doubted it would get them much further ahead. No, he'd have to approach this case in a different way. Physical evidence wasn't going to get him very far. He had to look for motive.

Who was Shirley Rogers? Who hated her enough to kill her? Who was walking around with a grudge so insistent and all-pervasive that it led to murder? Carlson sighed. *Time to see what her neighbors can tell me.*

Bella Sarver usually liked to give a 'homework' assignment before she dismissed her classes for the day. . It was generally something basic, such as:

> *'This week, be sure to notice how the sky gets a more intense blue as you look straight up at it and more watery as you look out toward the horizon,' or 'this week, I want you to sketch some trees. It's easy enough to draw a generic tree, but this week, pick one and really study it to see how the branches grow out from the trunk, how the bark looks, how the leaves overlap each other. Remember, a lot of drawing is just about paying attention.'*

This week's assignment was a little more advanced, as her students had been progressing nicely for some weeks. She'd asked them to create a design from their imaginations. It could be realistic or not. Their choice.

The art room at the end of the long corridor was perfectly designed for its purpose. Large and airy, it spanned the width of the wing that jutted out from the core of the building. Long windows across the entire width of the room let in plenty of light. There was a sink and counter at one end and several long tables. Artists had only to bring their own easels and other supplies, and get to work.

Bella's students chatted about their latest assignment as they prepared for class, comparing and admiring each other's sketches while they waited for their teacher, oblivious to the drama taking place just down the hallway. But after a while, they began to wonder why Bella was so late. It wasn't like her, not at all.

Joanie Passarelli offered to go see if she could find her. She started off briskly towards the great room, but as she got further down the hallway, she saw the uniformed police officers all over the place and her steps slowed. She noticed Bella sitting on one of the couches flanking the fireplace, talking to a man who was leaning forward, listening intently, occasionally writing in the notebook he held in one hand.

While Joanie hesitated, not knowing if she should move forward or what, a female police officer approached and asked her to have a seat, indicating the group of tables at one end of the great room. Joanie saw that quite a few of her fellow residents were already siting around the tables, but she turned back to the officer.

"What's going on?" she asked, more curious than concerned.

"A woman's been killed," was the terse reply.

"A woman? Here? What do you mean killed? As in ... murdered? Who is it?"

The policewoman shrugged.

Marlene Benson overheard Joanie's questions as she passed the front door on the way back to her office, on the opposite side of the building from the classrooms. "I think it's

Shirley Rogers," she told her. "At least, that's what I heard. And yes, looks like murder."

"Shirley Rogers? I don't think I know who she is, do you, Marlene?"

"I met her once or twice, but I didn't really know her. She hasn't lived here very long."

"I better go tell the others to pack up their things. Looks like we're not having class today," Joanie said.

Officer Melanie Jennings moved from group to group, getting names and addresses, asking basic questions as to their whereabouts during what was assumed to be the relevant time frame. She was a little surprised by how calmly the 'active adults' were taking the news of the murder. She'd been a police officer for more than five years, but she was still young enough to think of anybody over sixty as pretty old, and anybody over seventy as on their last legs. She'd been prepared to treat them *very* gently but as a matter of fact, the reaction she was seeing most often was simply curiosity, with a bit of poorly concealed excitement thrown in.

"Don't worry, honey," Connie Marks, one of Bella's students, said, patting Jennings' arm. "We're not as fragile as some of us look. If we were, we wouldn't have lasted this long." She chuckled happily as she made her way over to the coffee urn and helped herself to a cup before sitting down with the others.

Debbie Wilson was relieved to spot her husband sitting at a round table with some of his water aerobics buddies. "Are you okay, Ken?" she asked anxiously, hurrying over to him.

"I'm fine," he said calmly. "Why? How are you?"

The men of the water aerobics class had fared better than the women, as they'd been allowed to shower and dress before being ushered into the lobby with the others. Ken Wilson seemed perfectly comfortable, sipping his coffee and sharing stories about sports. As a former south-sider, Ken was naturally a White Sox fan and didn't have much patience with anybody who could bring themselves to root for the Cubs. He shoved his chair over so Debbie could squeeze in at the table.

"You heard about it?" she asked.

"Sure. Somebody got herself murdered in the ladies' shower."

"I mean, you know who it is?"

He nodded. "Funny thing is, I saw her just before. She was swimming laps this morning, before water aerobics. She stayed in the pool a little while after our class started. We were probably the last people who saw her."

"Saw her alive, you mean," Debbie said.

Ken nodded again.

From across the room, Lily Turner observed the Wilsons, her expression giving nothing away. Then she turned her attention back to her work. She'd been in the sewing room, piecing squares of material together for her latest quilt when the police asked everyone to go into the lobby. There was no quilting class this morning, but she preferred being in the clubhouse, even if she didn't talk much with the other residents. There was a nice long table for her to spread out her materials, and good light in the room.

"I'd rather stay here," she told Office Jennings frostily.

"I'm sorry, ma'am, but we need to gather everyone in the building into the great room."

"Why? I'm not going anywhere."

Jennings smiled patiently. "Let me help you," she offered, as she began to gather the materials into a neat stack.

"I don't need your help," Lily said, grabbing her bag and stuffing all the fabrics into it. She left the room and Jennings had to hurry to keep up with her.

Now she sat alone at one of the tables in the great room, sorting through her colored squares, trying out different combinations. She loved quilting and she was good at it, creative. She followed the well-worn patterns women had been working for centuries but she added her own touches, just enough to make each one special. Her quilts decorated the homes of all her children and grandchildren, as well as countless cousins and in-laws. It wasn't that she was especially generous. It was just that she'd run out of places to store all her creations.

Talk about old memories! Lily remembered Shirley. Remembered the Wilsons, too. Ken and Debbie. Debbie Kowalski, as she was then. Lily remembered a lot of things. Lily's mother had told her that time would pass and she'd forget old hurts and slights, but Lily's mother was wrong. There are some things you just don't forget.

Our Lady of Cherubim was one of the several Catholic elementary schools in Bridgeport, where Shirley Rogers, nee Shirley McCarthy, had been born. Bridgeport, the south side Chicago neighborhood famously home to a lot of Chicago mayors, had also been home to Lily Dunbar. She remembered everything about Cherubim School, the black-habited nuns who presided over the classes, rulers at the ready, to rap the knuckles of any child who dared to 'act smart.' Lily remembered the other kids, too, including little Shirley McCarthy. She never got her knuckles rapped. She always knew the answers. She was the first one to jump up to clean the blackboard. Little Miss Perfect.

They all dressed alike, in uniforms passed down from older sisters and brothers, or cousins. Uniforms cost money. They were used until no one could possibly get another day out of them. The girls wore little blue plaid jumpers over crisp white blouses back then, hair tightly braided and tied with ribbons. The boys wore neat blue shirts and black pants, hair parted on the side and slicked down with water. Little ladies and gentlemen. At least when the nuns were looking.

Bridgeport was largely an Irish neighborhood in those days, but it was also home to Czechs, Lithuanians and Poles. The Irish had been there since the early days of Chicago, in the mid-nineteenth century. The others drifted in a bit later, but all remembered their immigrant roots vividly, and all had the languages and traditions they'd brought with them from the old country. All the prejudices and rivalries, too. But they were nearly all Catholic.

The local public high school was Wolfe, named after Thomas A. Wolfe, a nineteenth century Chicago politician. There was a Catholic high school for the boys and one for the girls, but it was expensive, so a lot of the kids who'd gone to parochial elementary schools went to the public high school. Lily Dunbar's and Shirley McCarthy's parents reluctantly sent their daughters to Wolfe. Debbie Kowalski went there, too.

The principal of Wolfe School was Rena C. Flannery. Miss Flannery was a stern-faced woman who owned only two suits, one blue and one grey, but they were very good suits, severely tailored to fit her spare body. If she had any vanity at all, it was about her steel gray hair, which tended to glow blue from the rinse her hairdresser applied once a month without fail. She demanded excellent performance from both teachers and students, and it was a brave child who dared to give less than her best. The good students thrived in this strictly disciplined atmosphere. The less good students were usually smart enough to look as if they were trying.

Lily Dunbar was an okay student. She liked to watch and think. She saw that the kids who pushed themselves forward sometimes got caught short when their confidence outstripped their talents. So Lily let others preen and posture. She just kept her head down and did what was expected of her. She had a few friends. Neither Shirley McCarthy nor Debbie Kowalski was among them. But Lily had known them. Both of them. Neither had changed very much. Debbie had always been a push-over. Shirley had always been a show-off. And now she was dead.

Chapter Nine

The high point of Ken Wilson's week was the Martingale Manor water aerobics class, every Monday, Wednesday and Friday morning. He had little patience for Saturdays and Sundays, no matter what adventures Debbie had cooked up for them. He just didn't feel right. His body craved the water.

On Monday mornings, he was usually the first one into the pool, and this Monday was no exception. In the water, he could move freely, bending and turning, the arthritis finally releasing its hold on his hips and knees, letting him feel … well, not exactly young, but more like himself, anyway. On dry land, he could still walk unaided, but progress was slow and painful to watch. Osteoporosis had bent his back and bowed his legs but he often told his wife that he'd be damned if he ever resorted to sitting in front of the TV all day long. He'd been used to an active life. As a boy, he'd been known for his moves on the dance floor. Well into middle age, he'd played tennis, run a few miles after work, and rode his bike on weekends. He wasn't about to let a few aches and pains turn him into a helpless old man now.

Marlene Benson busied herself getting the exercise noodles sorted while Ken made his way towards the pool. She loved her job. As Activities Director, she got to know the residents and see what a difference her planning made in their lives. She enjoyed teaching her exercise and water aerobics classes, too. Sometimes, though, it hurt her to stand by and watch while the residents struggled to get themselves across a room. Her instincts were to rush in to help, but she understood how important it was to allow them their dignity. So she held back and tried not to see how hard it was for some of them.

Most of the class knew each other from having been attending sessions regularly for several years, and the noisy chatter of the twenty or so people already splashing in the pool's shallow end echoed off the tiled walls of the high-ceilinged room. It was sort of like being back in school, seeing each other most days.

"Natatorium," Ken recalled as he slipped carefully over the edge of the pool into the water. "That's what we used to call it at school."

"What's that?" asked Frank Howe, one of the three men in the class.

"Nothing, nothing," Ken replied. "Just thinking out loud. Natatorium. Remember that?"

"Sure," Frank said. "Boy, haven't heard that word in years. But that's what was carved into the stone facing of our swimming pool building when I was in high school."

"Mine, too," Ken said. "Wolfe."

"Wolfe. South Side, right?"

"Right," Ken agreed. He might have added something else, but Marlene blew her whistle just then. She started the music thumping, tossed enough noodles for everybody into the pool, and began counting out the routine.

Once in the water, Ken was like a different person. Most of his stiffness disappeared and he reveled in the feeling of freedom. He followed Marlene's instructions for a little while, but then he grew bored with the routine. He moved out of line, kicked up his legs, spread his arms wide, and floated luxuriously. Then he struck out towards the deep end of the pool, intending to swim some cross-wise laps. Someone else had the same idea but when she noticed Ken heading her way, she swam to the side of the pool and hauled herself out of the water. The deep end was all his. His arms sliced through the water, strong and confident. Back and forth, back and forth. When the class finished and most of the students headed for the locker room or the spa, Ken switched directions and kept swimming his laps, this time up and down the whole length of the pool.

"Natatorium, huh?" Ken ruminated as he swam. "That sure brings back some memories, doesn't it? High school. Wow, that was a long time ago. Who could ever have imagined ...?"

Ken might have been surprised to know that his wife was thinking along the same lines while she waited for her painting class to begin. Debbie also looked forward to Mondays. The week-ends seemed so long, these days. Monday meant painting class and re-connecting with her week-day routine and forgetting, for a little while, that she and Ken were getting old.

Bella always put on music while her class worked on their paintings. It helped the paint flow, she said. *It's funny how one art form leads so easily to another,* Debbie mused. *It's all connected.*

Music definitely helped the paint flow. It also brought back memories. Especially music from the 60's. It seemed, looking back, that most of life's important moments happened to music back then.

Soft summer nights, slow dancing in somebody's finished basement, the lights very low.

"Hold me close…" Debbie crooned under her breath.

"Never let me go…" Connie Marks joined in, coming up to grab some coffee before class.

"That Johnny Mathis" she reminisced. "We used to call them make-out songs. You'd put one of his albums on the record player, and that was it. So-o-o romantic! He sure could set a mood, couldn't he?"

"I know," Debbie agreed. "And I just can't seem to get that tune out of my head, since the other night."

That's not the only image I can't get out of my head, she thought but didn't say. She remembered it like it was yesterday. Dancing, dreamy, slow, the lights low and the music soft. Her head against his chest, warm and cozy. Then feeling cold, as he let her go. Let her go because of …her.

She shook her head. *Stop being silly*, she told herself.

"What happened the other night, Connie?" Joanie Passarelli asked, coming up to join them.

"Oh, you should have been there, Joanie. It was so much fun. We had a … I don't know if you'd want to call it a talent contest, or a karaoke night, or a dance … it was kind of a mixture of everything. And one of the girls started singing that old Johnny Mathis song, you know …."

"Chances are …," Connie warbled.

Joanie laughed. "I'm sorry I missed it. Sounds great. Who was singing?"

"Oh, just one of the girls. I don't think I know her, do you, Debbie?"

Debbie stirred cream into her coffee, seeing the woman on the stage, seeing the shocked recognition in Ken's eyes. Recognition, and something else, too.

"I haven't seen her at any of the meetings or anything," Debbie said.

"Well, you can't know everybody, can you? This is a big place," Connie noted.

Chapter Ten

Police procedure dictated that detectives should interview every person who was present at the location of a homicide, so Len Carlson and his colleague Ron Pepper proceeded to do just that. All the time they were conducting the interviews they were fully aware that the murderer could have already been long gone before they got there. There were people coming and going constantly, with absolutely no way to keep track of who was in the building at any given moment. There were multiple entrances and exits. It was a hopeless task, but the groundwork needed to be done.

"If it was me, sure wouldn't be hanging around here, would you, Len?"

"I doubt it. But on second thought, maybe I would. I mean, if that person was supposed to be here for some reason, maybe they thought they'd better stick around as if everything was normal."

"True, Len, good point. Well, so far we're doing terrific, huh? We've talked to everybody we can find and nobody saw or heard anything out of the ordinary. Interesting group of people. They've got all kinds here. Retired teachers, lawyers, engineers, doctors, even a couple of retired cops."

"I know. One thing kind of surprised me – lots of them are from out of town."

"That surprised me, too," Pepper agreed. "Except, now that I think about it, it makes sense. I think the out-of-towners are here because this is where their kids live and they want to be closer to them in their declining years."

"Not so declining, if you ask me. They're not kidding when they call them 'active adults.' I never saw so much going on in one place. I think you have a point, Ron. But lots of others have always lived in the area. There's a good chunk of them seem to be from Chicago, especially Bridgeport. I'm surprised they don't seem to know each other, I mean, from before, when they were young."

"Yeah, you'd think it would be more like old home week, wouldn't you? But Bridgeport is a good-sized neighborhood, and don't forget, they're not all the same age, either."

"True. Well, I'll tell you one thing, Ron. If any of them killed this woman, they're sure hiding it well. She moved in to this community about a year ago, but she doesn't seem to have involved herself in any of the clubs. A few of the water aerobics people say they've seen her swimming, but they didn't know her name. If she made any friends here, they haven't turned up yet. I don't see any kind of clues, do you?"

The SOCO team hadn't found a murder weapon anywhere, but the ME thought it must be something like a scissors. The team had found plenty of prints in the locker room, but as Carlson had thought in the first place, even if they could identify any of them, so what? Unless they found a murder weapon with prints on it, they were nowhere. Just to be on the safe side, they rounded up all the scissors and other sharp objects they could find, to bring them in and test them for blood. Considering that there was a quilting group cutting fabric squares, a painting group using palette knives, a fully-stocked kitchen at the back, and an office with its usual array of scissors, letter openers and so forth, it made quite a pile. Each item had to be bagged and labeled, naturally.

"And all of it useless," Carlson said aloud.

Ron Pepper knew what he meant. "You said it yourself, Len. It would be a miracle if we found anything usable on that pile of sharp objects. We have to find a motive, and for that, we need to know more about the victim."

"Let's get over to the victim's house," Carlson said. "If we want to know who she was, the information's going to be there."

Aside from draping police tape across the front door and back doors, the police hadn't yet done anything with Shirley Roger's house. They were still busy working the scene of the crime. Carlson had the key from the security office, but he didn't use it immediately. First, he and Pepper walked around the house and grounds.

Shirley Rogers had bought the townhouse in Martingale Manor about a year before she was killed. It was in a group known as a six-pack, consisting of six one-story houses connected to each other, arranged in an open rectangle, two on a side. A common driveway formed the center, with the garages facing each other across it. Each house had a small patio and garden area at the back, and a small strip of grass lining the walkway up to the front door. It was tidy and neat and looked a lot like an army barracks, especially since the parkway trees were still spindly and spare.

Inside, Rogers' house was unexpectedly warm and welcoming, with high ceilings and plenty of light coming in through the large windows of the sunroom and kitchen. Colorful rugs lay on the wood plank flooring. The walls were painted shades of warm yellows and ochres, framed landscapes adding greens, blues and reds to the color scheme. Well-upholstered sofas and chairs were arranged in several seating areas, and the whole impression was of openness and comfort. Carlson could see the entire space as he stood just inside the front door.

"Pretty," Pepper commented. Carlson nodded.

"Could be a model home, couldn't it?"

Pepper had put his finger on what was bothering Carlson. "It's too perfect," he agreed. "Looks like some decorator came in and put the whole thing together at one time. Where are the family pictures? Where are the little tchotchkes?"

The coffee table sitting in the middle of one of the conversation areas held a glass bowl of silk flowers, with a small pile of books carefully arranged by size and color near a corner. The lamps on the end tables matched, brass bases with plain white shades. Nothing was out of place. Nothing called attention to itself.

To the right of the dining area a short hallway led to the rest of the house. The two detectives turned into it. On the right was a bathroom, clean and spare. No shampoo in the shower, no damp towels on the rack. They kept going. Beyond the bathroom was a bedroom. The door was standing open. They moved inside, glanced around, and smiled.

A king-size bed occupied the middle of the room, covered by an old-fashioned looking quilt. The bed was flanked with bedside tables, each holding a lamp. One of the tables also held a clock radio, the time correct at two p.m. A long dresser stood against the far wall, and at last, here was an indication that a real human being had lived in this house.

The top of the dresser was covered with small photos in a variety of frames. There were several photos of a little boy, evidently the same child in each, as he grew older. There was a photo, somewhat faded, of a group of children wearing the typical parochial school uniforms of the 1950's. They stood in rows, the girls with braids, the boys with slicked-back hair, gazing earnestly and hopefully into the camera, faces scrubbed and bright across the years. A sign placed at the foot of the grouping helpfully indicated *Our Lady of Cherubim, 4th Grade, 1956.*

There was a photo of a young man and woman, arms around each other's waists, eyes squinting against the sun. There was a formally posed picture of an older couple, the man seated, the woman standing next to him, hand on his shoulder, wearing the clothes of the turn-of-the-century, solemn, unsmiling. The last photo Carlson picked up was one of the few in color. It showed a young man wearing a graduation cap and gown. His expression also was serious, eyes steady, no hint of pride in his accomplishment.

Carlson opened the top dresser drawer. It seemed to contain only a pile of underwear and he started to close it again, but then felt underneath the stack of panties and pulled out a pile of papers bound with a rubber band. The papers turned out to be cardboard report cards, documenting the academic progress of Peter Rogers at Our Lady of Cherubim School in Chicago. He'd done pretty well there, apparently. Mostly A's and B's.

"This is interesting, Ron. Take a look."

Pepper came over to see what Carlson held in his hand. He whistled. "Interesting, indeed. Judging by the dates of these report cards, I'd guess this Peter is probably the victim's son. Looks like they went to the same school."

"It might not mean much, though."

"Still, we better check it out."

They moved across to the room across the hall, which Shirley Rogers evidently had been using as an office. There was a wide desk, bookshelves, a rolling, upholstered desk chair. On the desk was a laptop computer. Pepper had lost no time in opening it.

"Here's a lucky break, anyway," he told Carlson. "This laptop's not password-protected." He tapped a few keys.

"There must be a few thousand documents on this thing," he told Carlson. "Forensics is going to have a heck of a time sorting it all out."

Carlson looked at the screen over Pepper's shoulder. There were, indeed, a vast number of files listed. Most of them bore labels that must have meant something to Shirley Rogers but didn't convey a heck of a lot of information to the two detectives.

"What we need here is one of those accountants, you know?" Pepper said.

"I think you mean a forensic accountant. Someone who can comb through the files and see what's what. We don't have anybody like that on the force, do we? We have tech people, but …." Carlson's forehead wrinkled. "I wonder …" he began.

"Yeah," Pepper said, finishing Carlson's thought. "That guy who's been working in the store already. Ms. Sarver's friend."

"Leo Schaeffer," Carlson supplied. "Maybe we could take him on as a consultant."

"Yeah. I bet he'd love that," Pepper said.

Carlson glanced at him suspiciously, but Pepper's straight face was giving nothing away.

"I have to admit, Len. It does make sense. Seeing that he's already working on stuff. But in the meantime, do you see anything like a will? A file of personal correspondence? Names? Anything to give us a clue of what this woman was up to, to make somebody mad enough to murder her?"

Pepper shook his head. "Nothing obvious. We're probably just going to have to look at each file one by one. Maybe we'll have some luck finding this Peter Rogers. I agree it's most likely her son. Why else would she have all those report cards? I guess it'll be up to us to tell the poor guy his mom's been killed."

"That's the part of this job I hate. But we have to find him first. We just look for somebody named Peter Rogers who might or might not live in Chicago. No sweat, right?"

Chapter Eleven

"How are the wedding plans coming along, Bella?"

Bella grimaced. It was a few days after Bella had discovered Shirley Rogers' body, but she didn't want to think about that now. There was too much else to do.

"What?" Mollie persisted. "Is there a problem?"

Mollie had dropped by just to visit, a rarity, since most of their encounters were for the purpose of accomplishing some project or other.

"Not really," Bella said. "It's just that I'd sort of like to just quietly get married, without a lot of fuss, but Art wants to do the whole shmear. I don't know if I'm up for that. You know me, Mollie. I'm not what you'd call a party animal. And I'm involved with my classes, and with this new co-op gallery. When am I supposed to find the time to plan a wedding?"

"Can I help?"

Bella looked at her friend hopefully. "Really? Would you want to?"

"Sure. You know me; I love this stuff. First thing, we have to get organized. How many people are we talking about? Dinner? Dancing? What kind of clothes? Do you have somebody to do the invitations? Flowers?"

Bella's looked so dismayed that Mollie had to laugh. Bella could do anything at all for other people. She was just as good at planning as Mollie, but when it came to herself, for some reason she had trouble moving forward.

"Never mind," Mollie laughed. "I'll draw up a list, and we'll tackle one thing at a time, okay? By the way, how much time do we have?"

"Well, we haven't set a date yet, but we're thinking probably sometime around Passover, just before or after."

"Don't you think it might be a good idea to talk to Rabbi Klein about that? How can we plan anything if we don't even have a date?"

Bella nodded. "I know, Mollie. It's just that ...."

"What? It's just what? Don't tell me you're having second thoughts about getting married?"

Bella twisted the emerald ring on her finger. "Maybe a little," she admitted. "I mean, I love Art, you know that. I couldn't ask for a better man. It isn't him."

"Then what is it? Come on, honey, you can tell me."

"It's me. I'm not sure I really want to be married again. I tried it once, for thirty years. It didn't work out."

"I know, honey, but things were so different then, weren't they? I mean, we got married because that was the next step in life, wasn't it? We didn't even know who we were yet, let alone who we wanted to spend the rest of our lives with. And sex was such a big deal, too. And you certainly weren't going to just move in together, not in those days."

Bella laughed. "I can just imagine if I'd told my parents I was going to move in with Martin Lewis. I don't know if they would have killed me or just locked me in my room until I came to my senses.

Mollie laughed, too. "But things are different today, and we're different. We know who we are by now, don't we? And what we really want."

"True. But ...."

"Have you talked with Art about this?"

Bella shook her head. "I don't want to hurt his feelings, Mollie. I know he loves me. I know he wants more than just to live together. He's a serious man. He needs to know I'm serious, too."

"You are, Bella. Nobody would ever think you're not."

"Yes. And I do love him."

"Well, you have to think about this, you know. You need to be absolutely sure."

"I know. I'm thinking." She laughed ruefully. "I'm doing nothing but thinking. Like for instance, do I have to change my name again?"

"Do you want to change your name?"

"Not really. I mean, I already changed it once, and then back again. How many names is one person supposed to have?"

"So keep it, then. Women don't have to change their names anymore. Especially not for second marriages. There, that's settled." Mollie sat back, satisfied. "See how easy that was?"

Bella laughed. "You're right. You make it seem so simple. OK, settled. So - how's the co-op coming along?"

Mollie was quiet for a moment. She wanted to help, but she knew Bella was going to have to work through her doubts by herself. She felt in her bones that Art Halperin was the right man for Bella, and that marriage to him would make her happy, but until Bella knew it, too – until, and if - …. So Mollie followed Bella's lead and addressed herself to the question.

"The co-op's coming along great," she said. "It will be a ton of fun getting it together. Everybody's really excited about it."

Mollie was in her element. Her dumpy little body, topped by a mop of curly black hair, hid a wealth of talent when it came to getting projects off the ground. And now she had two of them to work on.

"You have a strange idea of fun," Bella noted. "But all right, tell me – what's happening?"

The two women were comfortably ensconced in the soft brown leather arm chairs that flanked Bella's fireplace, the gas fire warming the room nicely. They put their feet up on ottomans and relaxed, sipping herbal tea and munching on the oatmeal raisin cookies Bella had picked up that morning from her favorite bakery, two doors down from the Art League.

"We've got a plan all worked out and now we just have to put it all into place. Rahj is terrific, and Kasia and Ben are both going to be a big help. They're still working, of course, so they don't have a lot of time, but at least they can be flexible about their hours."

"There's a lot to be said for retirement. It gives you time to get things done."

Bella managed employee benefits for the county before she'd retired and started working full time on her art. She'd been good at her job and enjoyed it, but once retired, she'd never looked back. She was even busier now than when she'd had to go to a job every day.

"True," Mollie agreed. She'd been a school librarian, and she did miss the kids sometimes, but she didn't miss getting to work at seven in the morning in order to get her library ready, and taking home files full of projects to work on in the evening.

"But anyway," she continued, "we're meeting there tomorrow to get started. The place is pretty much a mess, so job number one is to get in there, get rid of the junk, and sort out what's left."

"Sounds exciting," Bella said, with a straight face.

Mollie and Leo's car pulled up to the curb in front of the store only a moment after Bella and Art arrived next morning, dressed in their grubbiest jeans and sweats. Mollie opened the hatch of the RAV4 and emerged with a box of rags, which she handed to her husband. Reaching in again, she removed mops and buckets and distributed everything to the others. Bella had the key so she unlocked the door and the four of them proceeded to cart in all their supplies.

"This is worse than I remembered," Mollie said, looking around. The place definitely was discouraging to look at, a jumble of discarded packing materials and so forth left behind by the previous tenants. She sighed heavily. "Oh, well, the job won't get done by itself. Let's get to work."

The four of them set to, bagging garbage and hauling it out to the dumpsters in the alley back of the store. They worked slowly at first, especially Art, who examined every item as he picked it up. He seemed to think even crumpled papers and broken bits of mirror could be put to some useful purpose someday. Mollie soon disabused him of that idea.

"Come on, Art. Into the garbage bag. Everything goes."

"You're ruthless, Mollie."

"That's me," she said proudly. "Ruthless."

When the last bag had been hauled out, they stood sweaty and disheveled in the middle of the space and surveyed it. There wasn't much to see – just some scuffed and streaked walls and a floor that had once been nicely tiled but was now rough, a lot of the tiles broken. A half wall behind the counter separated the back of the premises from the front. Several bare light bulbs hung from the ceiling, but plenty of light streamed in from the big picture window facing the street. There was a door set into one of the side walls towards the rear of the store.

"I wonder where that door leads," Leo said.

"We explored that a little the other day, Leo," Mollie said. "It's just the basement." Leo nodded and headed down, Art following close behind.

"There's something about men and basements, I've noticed," Bella commented.

"You're right. I've noticed that, too."

"I heard that," Art said. "What you girls don't understand is that the basement is the foundation for everything else. If you learn the basement, you learn all about the rest of the structure. It's a lot like life."

"Looks like the previous tenants probably didn't use this much," Bella said, when they reached the bottom of the stairs. "I mean, there's hardly any mess here at all. Pretty dusty, though. Look at the footprints we're leaving."

Leo walked slowly around the perimeter of the space, trailing his hand against the wall. Suddenly he stopped, faced the wall, and looked closer. He ran his hand up and across.

"What have you got there, Leo?"

"Come here and take a look, Art. Feel that? It's sort of a notch or something?"

"Yes, you're right. We need more light over here. Anybody have a flashlight?"

"Just a second, I've got the app on my phone." Mollie fussed with her smart phone for a minute, until she got it to light up. "Here you go."

Art took the phone from her and shined it on the wall. Now they could all clearly see a line defining a rectangular shape. Leo pushed against it, and it moved inward a bit.

"Give me a hand here, Art." The two men pushed hard and the section of wall gave way, opening into another space.

"I think you've found a secret passageway, Leo".

The two men grinned at each other. Art shined the light into the space and moved forward, waving the phone around in front of him. He found a wall switch and in a moment the entire basement was lit up, revealing a place filled with storage equipment of every kind.

"We must be right under *Ruffles and Flourishes*," Art realized

"We really shouldn't be in here, guys," Mollie cautioned.

"I know, you're right," Leo agreed. He followed Art deeper into the room.

The basement of *Ruffles and Flourishes* couldn't possibly have provided a greater contrast to the basement of the store the co-op was renting. It was obviously a well-used adjunct to the main level. The large desk in one corner was flanked by several file cabinets, each drawer neatly labeled. Ranks of steel shelving were stacked with boxes, each one of those labeled, too. The floor was plain concrete, but swept clean.

Bella's eye was caught by an easel occupying a space opposite the desk. A completed canvas was propped on it, next to a table holding a jar of brushes, tubes of paint, and a paint-encrusted palette. Bella moved in for a closer look, touching the surface gingerly in case the paint was still wet. It wasn't. In fact, the canvas wasn't even painted.

"This is just a giclee," she announced, "not a painting. I wonder what it's doing down here."

"What's a giclee?" Art asked.

"A fancy name for an inkjet print. It's a way to produce copies of an original work on canvas, or on almost anything you choose, really. You can sell them for a whole lot less than an original, but then - it's not an original."

"Is that what Shirley was doing?"

"I guess she must have been."

"Is there something wrong with that?" Mollie asked.

"No, nothing. It's perfectly fine. Unless you try to pass a giclee print off as an original. That would be a problem. And judging by this set-up," she indicated the paints and brushes standing ready, "it looks like Shirley might have been planning to paint over this print. Not a lot, probably, just enough to put a film of oil paint on it, just enough to show some brushstrokes. We should take a look at what she has upstairs and see if there are any others."

"Whose painting is it?"

"I don't know, Mollie. I can't read the signature. It's down here in the bottom right corner, but it's just a scrawl."

The four friends looked at each other speculatively.

"It seems our Shirley had hidden talents," Mollie commented. "I've never known her to pick up a paint brush, have you, Bella?"

"Now that you mention it, no, I haven't. She was a member of the Art League, but she listed herself as an 'art appreciator' rather than as an artist. As far as I know, she never submitted any paintings or took any classes."

"Interesting. A closet painter." Mollie giggled.

"You mean, a basement painter," Bella elaborated. "Who knew?"

"Hey, girls, come here," Art called. "I think we've struck gold."

Leo had already pulled up a chair and was clicking away on the laptop he'd found on the desk. Leo Schaeffer had once tried to explain to his wife that being a CPA was sort of like being an anthropologist or archeologist or something. Always digging for buried treasure, trying to unearth secrets. Nothing excited him more than finding a previously unknown computer, with lots of files to explore. A few more clicks, and there on the screen popped up a spreadsheet from Quickbooks, accounts detailed in a way any accountant could be proud of.

"Aha!" Leo said. "This is more like it! I knew there had to be something like this around. When Mollie told me that Shirley was known for her organizational skills, it just didn't gibe with the mess she gave me to audit. I figured those papers couldn't possibly be telling the whole story. No business person could keep such terrible records and stay in business very long. So let's see what we've got," he continued, settling himself into the chair.

"I don't know, Leo, do you think you should be doing this?" Mollie looked warily into the dark corners of the space. Their little adventure was suddenly making her nervous. "I mean, now that Shirley is dead, murdered apparently.... I mean, the police will probably want to seal the place off, won't they?"

"Right. All the more reason to get to work right away, hon," Leo agreed. "Who knows how much time I'm gonna have here?"

He pulled out a pencil, rummaged around until he found a legal pad, and started making notes.

"Leo, we can't stay here," Mollie objected.

"Just a little while," he said, busily scrolling through computer screens, jotting down interesting items as he came to them. Then he raised his head as an idea struck him.

"You know what, guys? I could use your help," Leo Schaeffer told his friends. "I need you to take an inventory of what's down here." He turned back to the screen without waiting for a reply.

Leo was in his element. He called up one spreadsheet after another on Shirley's computer, scanning each one quickly, printing some of them out. Not for nothing had he been practicing accounting for his entire career. He knew what to look for, knew when things were out of place, and loved nothing better than uncovering the secrets that could be hidden in financial records. And *Ruffles and Flourishes* had secrets. He could smell them. He just didn't know how it all added up yet.

"I give up," Mollie said. "When he gets like this, there's no stopping him. Maybe if we help, we can get out of here faster."

Art, Bella and Mollie each grabbed a notebook and headed off to a different section of the basement, quickly noting down everything they found on the shelves.

"Listen," Bella hissed. They'd been working about an hour, each concentrating on a different section of the basement.

"What?" Leo looked up from his legal pad.

"I heard something."

Now the others heard it, too. The floorboards creaked above their heads.

"Somebody's up there," Bella whispered. "We've got to get out of here."

Leo was sorely tempted to pick up the laptop, but he told himself that would be theft, and foolish. He shut down all the windows and turned off the computer, but it hurt him to think he was leaving precious information behind. Not everything, though. He gathered up the sheets he'd printed out so far before slipping through the secret door to the other side behind the others. Art had already ushered the women up the stairs.

"Whew, we almost got caught," he said, when they were all safely back in the co-op.

"Who was that?" Mollie asked.

"No idea," Art said. "All I know is, if we'd been caught there, we'd have been in trouble."

They looked at each other and burst into giggles.

Chapter Twelve

Rita Cutler dawdled over her breakfast, indulging in a second cup of coffee while she read the Times, but finally she couldn't stand it another minute. She knew she was out of a job, now that Shirley was dead, but still, the business wasn't dead. Not yet, anyway. Not until the powers-that-be figured out what was going to happen to it. She couldn't do anything about that but she could at least keep things going in the meantime. Besides, what was she supposed to do all day if she didn't have a job to go to? She put her cup in the dishwasher and left her apartment.

Detective Carlson expected to find *Ruffles and Flourishes* closed when he got there, yellow police tape across the entrance. He was not at all happy to find the lights on and the door unlocked.

"Didn't anybody think to seal this place up? Do I have to do everything?" He yanked the door open angrily.

"What are you doing here?" he demanded of the woman standing at the counter.

"I work here," Rita Cutler said. "I mean, I guess I still work here. Nobody said not to come in to work."

Carlson sighed heavily. "Don't you know the owner of this place has been murdered?"

"Yes, I know. But the store is still here, isn't it? Shouldn't somebody be running it, at least until the new owner comes in to change things?"

"What new owner?"

"I don't know," Rita admitted. "I just suppose there must be one, isn't there?"

"Not to my knowledge. But whether there is or not, this place has to remain locked for now. I'll take your keys, if you don't mind."

Rita's mouth set stubbornly, but then she seemed to realize that Carlson held all the cards. She retrieved her purse from the back room, found the store key, and handed it over.

"Is this the only one?"

"Well, Shirley has one, of course. I have this one. If there are any others, I don't know about them."

"Okay," Carlson said sourly. "Thank you." He wrote out a receipt and handed it to Rita. She stuffed it into her purse. She returned to the back room for her coat and slipped it on. Reluctantly, she moved towards the front door.

Can this woman move any slower? Carlson thought impatiently. *Hold on, though. What are you doing? Dummy!* He berated himself for a fool. *Here I've been trying to get a handle on the victim and ignoring the one person who must have known her intimately.*

"Just a second, Ms. Cutler. I'm sorry. Let's sit down for a minute. Any chance for a cup of coffee?"

Rita turned to look at him. Clearly, she was wondering what to make of Carlson's changed demeanor, but then she shrugged. "Sure. There's a coffee machine in the back." She led the way.

Carlson sat at the small table while Rita busied herself at the little kitchenette. It took only a couple of minutes, and then she joined him at the table, a mug of coffee in front of each of them.

Carlson didn't waste any more time. "Ms. Cutler, as long as you're here, what can you tell me about Shirley Rogers?"

Rita pursed her lips. "I don't know much about her, really. You'd think that working together all day, we'd get to know each other, but we never talked much. When I was in the store, she usually kept to herself in the back room."

"What did she do in here?" he asked, looking around curiously. "There doesn't seem to be any office-type equipment. No stock or anything, either."

"I don't really know. Sometimes I'd see her working on her laptop, if I came in for coffee or something."

"Ok. But you must have talked sometimes," he pressed. "For instance, what about her personal life? Did she ever talk about her son?"

"Peter? I only found out about him by accident, sort of. I don't remember how it came up. Maybe I was talking about my kids or something, but I remember being surprised to find out she had a son. I think she wasn't very happy about their relationship. I overheard her talking to him on the phone once or twice."

"Yes? What about?"

"I don't know, Lieutenant," Rita said indignantly. "I don't make a habit of listening in to people's phone calls."

"Of course not," Carlson agreed. "But maybe she let something slip?"

"Well – I might have heard money mentioned. But I don't know what that would have been about."

Carlson nodded. "What about men? Did she ever talk about any men in her life?"

Rita shook her head. "I think she must have been divorced. There could have been some men since then, I suppose, but she never said. Not really."

"So what made you think that was possible?"

"I don't know," Rita said slowly. It might have been more the way she dressed or maybe the way she held herself. We don't get a lot of men in here, you know. Mostly women. But once in a while a man comes in to look for a gift, and whenever that happened, Shirley would be right there, kind of … what's the word? You know. One hand on a hip, the other fluffing her hair. Things like that."

Carlson nodded. "Did you know any of the men yourself?"

"No. Like I said, there was just the occasional male customer. That's all. It was nothing, really."

"Did you ever meet the son?"

"Oh, no. Well, I wouldn't, would I? Although, now that you bring it up …."

Carlson waited.

"I had a feeling once."

Carlson nodded encouragingly.

Rita looked up at him, her face squinched together. "Well, it's just that, I was leaving the store for the day, when a man came to the door. I told him we were just closing, but

Shirley heard me and told me to go home, that she'd see to him. So I left, and he went in. I asked her about it afterwards, but she said it was just an old customer."

"But you didn't believe that?"

Rita frowned. "It seemed to me there was more to it. The man was young, nicely dressed. I just had the impression ...." She shook her head. "I'm imagining things. It's nothing. I shouldn't have said anything."

"Ok. What about the business itself? Has it been going well?"

"I suppose so," Rita said. "We didn't seem to have a lot of customers, but Shirley never seemed to worry about that. I asked her once if we shouldn't put an ad in the Deer Creek Gleaner or maybe some coupons. But she said she was doing fine, and didn't want to bother with anything like that. So I let it go. None of my business, is it?"

Why is this victim so elusive? I almost feel like I'm getting a handle on her and then it slips away. What am I missing here? Sometimes, you just have to ask the right questions, he thought. *If only I knew what they were.*

Carlson let Rita Cutler leave. When she'd gone, he roamed around the store for a bit, idly considering the various little giftie things on the display shelves. The back room held a Formica-covered counter with a sink set into it, a small fridge underneath, and a microwave on top. There was a table and a few chairs. A tiny bathroom completed the set-up. Nothing about the place spoke of the person who worked there. Not unless you counted some mismatched mugs with various logos on them, and the box of Oreos Rita had left lying open on the table. If Shirley Rogers had done anything in this room but snack, she'd left no sign. Her business premises weren't giving away any clues. Yet ….

"Melanie," Carlson said when Officer Jennings picked up at his ring, "come on over to *Ruffles and Flourishes.* Bring a team. We're going to have to tear this place apart. There has to be something to find here. This woman ran a business, owned a car, bought a house. Somebody hated her so much they killed her, brutally. Why?"

As he spoke, Carlson continued pacing the room. When he came to a door set into one of the side walls near the back, he opened it. There were stairs leading down, and he took them two at a time.

"Well, well, well," he said, taking in the basement office set-up, the painting studio, the many well-filled shelves. "This is more like it."

When the other officers arrived fifteen minutes later, they found Len Carlson whistling to himself as he flipped through boxes of cellophane-wrapped prints and stacks of notecards.

"Look at this, Melanie," Carlson said. "It's like two entirely separate businesses. There's the nice little store upstairs, and then here it looks like some sort of studio. Plus enough inventory to stock a Wal-Mart or something. What was she doing with all this stuff?"

Melanie Jennings pursed her lips and let out a low whistle. "This'll keep us busy for a while," she said. "We'd better get started. Any idea what we're looking for, Len?"

Carlson shook his head. "Not really," he admitted. "But we'll recognize it when we see it. While you guys are working on this mess, I think I'll get back to Martingale Manor and talk to some people again. Somebody's got to know something."

Rita Cutler was thinking along those same lines as she slowly walked back to her car. She'd been in the business world all her life. She'd started right out of high school, taking a job as a clerk-typist for a small insurance company. Eventually, she rose to the position of office manager as the insurance company expanded over the years. She knew what it was like to see the same people every day, for years on end sometimes. You got to know them. Often, you knew them better than their own families did. People talked as they worked, went to lunch, celebrated births and deaths and anniversaries. When she'd retired, Rita missed the everyday give-and-take of the office as much or more than she missed the paycheck.. She missed getting up in the morning and having a place to go. She even missed the people she thought she'd have been happy to never see again, the whiners and complainers, the back-stabbers. Yes, even them.

When she saw the ad in the local paper for someone to work the counter at *Ruffles and Flourishes*, she decided that would be perfect for her. Not too much responsibility, no decisions to make, but a place to go and something to do. Someone to talk with. But it hadn't turned out that way at all. Shirley Rogers had no interest in making conversation, in sharing her life in any way. The simplest questions got only short, uninformative replies. Rita felt that she might as well have stayed at home. Except for the customers, of course.

Not that there were a lot of customers. In fact, Rita didn't understand how the business managed to stay solvent at all. Oh, sure, people did wander in from time to time. They'd roam around the store, picking up this and that. Sometimes they'd buy a few little things. Once in a while, they'd even buy one of the paintings Shirley kept hanging in what she called the gallery, over on the far wall. Even then, though, it never added up to very much. *If I was in charge*, Rita thought, *I'd do things differently.* But it wasn't Rita's problem, was it? No, Rita's problem now was what to do with the rest of her life.

Chapter Thirteen

Fabio Gompers prided himself on his ability to paint flesh that was so life-like, people wanted to reach out and touch it to assure themselves it was only paint. He reveled in oil paint, mixing as many as ten values of every color on his palette, placing exactly the right color in exactly the right place, and then blending them so meticulously you practically needed a microscope to see the brushstrokes. Unlike most of the artist members of the Deer Creek Art League, he was not self-taught. On the contrary, he had studied at the School of the Art Institute of Chicago, and then gone on to a residency at one of the finest ateliers in Florence. His forte was portraiture, but he could turn his skills to landscapes or still lifes just as well. His work was carried in some of the best galleries in the country and sold for thousands of dollars. So what was he worried about?

It was getting harder and harder for Fabio to do the fine work he was known for. Even landscapes, which call for less meticulous detail than portraiture, left his arthritic fingers stiff and aching for days after only a couple of hours of work. He preferred to stand while he worked at the easel, so he could easily move back and forth to judge his progress, but his hips and knees were telling him this wasn't a good plan. Yet he loved painting. Besides, he needed to keep a roof over his head, and keep the electricity on. Retirement wasn't an option. There are no pension plans for self-employed artists.

Fabio had sat silently for the rest of the Co-op Committee meeting, after Mollie had shared Bella's announcement of Shirley Roger's murder. He didn't hear anything of the discussion that followed. He was ruminating about what to do next. What had he left behind that could give him away? Surely there was nothing. Was there? How could he find out?

Art Halperin brought a glass of white wine over to Bella and sat down beside her on the comfy leather sofa. She took it from him and sipped at it, frowning.

"Is something wrong, hon?"

Bella shook her head, but her nose squinched up, turning her frown into a grimace.

"Something's bothering you, obviously. Come on – tell me," Art said.

"It's just that, you know when we were in the basement?"

"Y-e-s," Art said.

"Well – while you and Leo were poring over the accounts or whatever, and I found the painting on the easel? And it wasn't a painting, but a giclee being painted over? Why would Shirley be fiddling around with one of the giclees? I mean, if she was framing it, fine, of course. And if it was her own work, she could do whatever she wanted with it, naturally. But if it was another artist's work, or something she'd bought from a supplier, why was she painting over it? Was she going to try to pass it off as an original instead of a print?"

"Oh, I see. And then sell it for a lot more money than it was worth."

"Exactly. I don't like it, Art. I wish we'd been able to take more time there."

"Maybe you should mention it to the police."

"I would, except – how could I explain how I knew about it? We're probably guilty of breaking and entering, or something."

"True," Art agreed. "Although we didn't exactly break in. The door between the two basements wasn't locked."

"Splitting a few hairs, are we?"

Art grinned, unrepentant. "It probably doesn't matter much, anyway. Whatever shady business practices Shirley Rogers might have been up to, it can't be important now. After all, the woman is dead."

"You could be right," Bella admitted, but her expression was doubtful.

He took a thoughtful sip of his wine. "Maybe Leo will come up with something interesting to report. Let's see how he makes out with his little audit. He sounded excited about it."

Bella laughed. "Leo missed his calling, I think. He should have worked for the FBI."

Art chuckled, too, then took another sip of his wine, and cleared his throat.

"So – about our wedding…," he began.

"Were we talking about our wedding?"

"Not exactly, but while we're on the subject, don't you think it might be time to get the ball rolling? Like set a date, for example?"

Bella and Art had been seeing each other for more than a year by the time Art popped the question. He might have done it sooner, except that he could sense Bella's reluctance to get involved, and didn't want to scare her off. Finally, he couldn't hold back another minute. He held his breath after he'd asked her, afraid to say another word. When she said 'yes,' he was beyond ecstatic. He'd been willing to run off for the license that very second, but she needed more time.

How much more time? he wondered.

"Mollie said the same thing the other day," Bella told him. "She's offered to help make all the arrangements, the flowers and such. You sure you want to go through with this?"

Art's eyes widened in alarm. Hastily, Bella clarified, "I mean, with the big party, invitations and flowers and all that."

Art's marriage had been everything he could have wanted. If his wife hadn't died on him, he'd be married to her still. But more than five years later, he was ready to move on. He loved Bella and wanted to make their relationship official.

"I'm too old to be a boyfriend, honey," he said, when he'd proposed, more than a month ago. "The very word makes me cringe."

Bella smiled up at him. "How about 'lover?'"

"Even worse."

"Absolutely," he said now, responding to her question. "I want the whole schmear. Invitations, flowers, music. I want everybody to be there. I want a real wedding, with all the trimmings. So come on, what do you think? Should we say Spring? April?"

"April? Just before Passover?"

Art nodded. "We'll have to check the dates with Rabbi Klein."

Jewish law doesn't permit weddings during certain periods of the year, such as during the Sabbath, holidays, or periods of mourning. Additionally, the Sephardi, or Eastern, traditions and the Ashkenazi, or European, traditions, don't always agree with each other. It could sometimes be a bit complicated to find an acceptable date. The Passover season in particular has a lot of black-out dates for weddings.

"Yes, she'll be able to tell us. And then, what about the kids?"

"What about them?" Art asked.

Art's older daughter, Amy, lived in Evanston, not far from the house Art had shared with his wife. She was married and had two children of her own. Bella's daughter, Mindy, lived in Chicago, where she was an associate with the Chicago branch of an international law firm. Bella's son, Joel, lived in San Francisco. None of them had expected their parent to remarry, so Bella and Art's announcement in September had come as something of a surprise. None of them raised any objections, not exactly, but some had an easier time wrapping their heads around the plan than others.

Joel was fine with the idea, but he didn't spend a lot of time thinking about his mother these days. He was busy with his career as a software engineer and busy with his girlfriend, Michelle. If anything, he was relieved that he no longer needed to feel guilty about living so far away from Bella, in case anything happened to her.

Mindy had been surprised her mother had agreed to enter into another marriage. She knew all too well how miserable her parents had been together. She was proud of how strong and self-reliant her mother had become since that relationship ended. Art seemed completely different from her father, but you never know. Dating is one thing, marriage another. To outsiders, Martin Lewis appeared nice enough. It wasn't until you really got to know him that you realized what a bastard he could be.

Amy had always been the easy kid. She took after her mother, and nothing much set her off track. She missed her mother, but Sherry wasn't coming back, and life had to go on for the rest of the family. She fully embraced her father's engagement. She'd seen how miserable he was, alone and drifting without her mother, and she was happy he'd found someone else to share his life with.

"We'll have to find a date that works for them, won't we?" Bella asked. "Especially Joel, because he has the furthest to come." Then she remembered. "No, that's not true. What about Emily? Do you think she'll come all the way from Australia?"

"I'm not going to worry about that. She'll do whatever she wants, like she always does. Nobody told her to move so far away, so now she'll just have to deal with whatever comes up."

Bella knew the subject of Emily was painful for Art, but she wasn't one to avoid talking about something just because it was a little hard. At least, not usually.

Art's two daughters couldn't have been more different from each other. Amy was calm and steady. Emily was the exact opposite.

Emily and her husband, Ted Bernstein, had packed up their four kids, sold their house and most of the belongings, and taken off for Sidney nearly three years ago. The move came as a surprise to everyone who knew them. It seemed as if it might have been almost as much a surprise to Emily and Ted, too. One day somebody, maybe Ted, had brought up the idea of moving to Australia. A bare six weeks later, they were gone.

"Do you think she and Ted will stay there much longer?"

Art shrugged, trying not to show how much it hurt. "Who knows? Emily's not a great one for planning, you know. But whenever I hear from her, she seems to be happy down there. Ted's working, and Emily is home-schooling all the kids. She always was sort of a hippie type, you know. Would she want to uproot the whole family again to come back home? Your guess is as good as mine."

Bella reached for Art's hand and squeezed. He turned to her and wrapped his arms around her, pulling her close. There was nothing he could do about Emily. He was just happy Bella was finally willing to discuss a date, and one not far in the future. It felt like a big hurdle had been surmounted. "Let's worry about that after we get the Rabbi's opinion, okay?"

Len Carlson found himself driving through the gates of Martingale Manor again. He hadn't expected to come back there, but he kept feeling like he was missing something. They still hadn't found the victim's son, if indeed Peter Rogers *was* her son. None of the people he'd interviewed so far seemed to have a handle on Shirley Rogers as a human being. Could a person be so much alone that even people who knew her didn't actually know anything about her?

And yet, someone hated her enough to kill her. Someone was so enraged by the very sight of her that they took a pair of scissors and viciously stabbed her in the throat. But so far, Shirley Rogers was an almost complete cipher to the police. They were following up on those old black and white photos. He had high expectations of the business records, too. But what he hadn't turned up yet was somebody who could tell him who she really was.

Marlene Benson looked up distractedly from her computer screen when Carlson knocked on her open office door. The office, one of three off an all-purpose area in the administration wing of the building, was never quiet. People kept coming in to ask questions, sign up for various activities, or post information about their own projects on the bulletin boards. She had a tough time trying to concentrate. Her husband told her she should just keep the door shut, but she never did that except as a last resort. She considered being accessible an important part of her job.

She was trying to get the calendar filled out for the coming month. Marlene loved being the Activity Director. It was challenging to find interesting activities to offer to the residents, trying to provide a nice variety that included theater outings, sports events, and concerts plus anything else she could come up with. It wasn't easy to meet everyone's needs. The residents of Martingale Manor might be getting on in years, but that didn't mean they were all alike. Some loved exercise classes, some enjoyed learning new things, some liked to go to restaurants and theaters. Getting the mix right was like solving a new puzzle every month.

"What can I do for you, Detective?" she asked, trying not to let her annoyance show.

"I need your help, Ms. Benson," Carlson told her bluntly. "Shirley Rogers was a member of this community, and apparently a long-time resident of Deer Creek and yet nobody really seems to have known her. I can't find a record of a husband. We think she must have a son but so far, we haven't found him and we don't know where to start looking. The woman who worked with her every day doesn't know those most basic things. You're my last hope. What can you tell me?"

Marlene pushed her hair from her face, sat back in her chair, and sighed. "I thought you might be coming around, so I had a look through my sign-up sheets, but I couldn't find much information about her, either, Detective. This isn't an institution, you know. It's just a regular community where the residents happen to be of a certain age. I think she hasn't lived here very long. Her name doesn't start appearing in my records until about a year ago, and then, she only signed up for a couple of things. The last thing I have her down for was karaoke night. Honestly, I don't know if I ever spoke with her. I can't say I even remember what she looks like."

Len Carlson's shoulders drooped. He looked so disappointed that Marlene Benson forgot to resent the interruption in her day. She sorted through the pile of papers on her desk and pulled one out. "I did find one thing that might help. It's the list of people she's approved to let through the gate without the security guard needing to call for an okay."

"That's something, anyway. At least whoever's on that list will know her, right?"

She handed the paper to the detective. "Here you go," she said. "It's a pretty short list."

Carlson glanced at it hopefully, then turned it over as if he thought there might be something else on the back of the page. The list, if that's what it could be called, consisted of one name, and one name only.

Since Martingale Manor was a gated community, the residents had each been asked to supply the security staff with a list of people who could be allowed free entry into the complex. If a person wanted to come in but their name wasn't on the list, the guard would call the resident to see if they wanted to admit that person. The name Carlson read on Shirley Roger's list was Martha Ashton. Relationship: attorney.

"I don't suppose you'd have an address or phone number for this attorney, would you?" Carlson asked, not expecting a positive answer.

He wasn't disappointed in that, because Marlene shook her head. "Just what you see there, Detective."

"You don't keep a record of next of kin, or emergency contacts? The son? What about him?"

Marlene shook her head again. "As I told you before, this is simply a residential community, Detective. It's not any sort of institution. We don't provide any sort of care. Everyone who lives here is one their own, just like anywhere else."

Carlson took another look at the paper in his hand. "Martha Ashton, attorney. All right. I guess I better go track her down. Thanks."

Chapter Fourteen

Lily Turner sat by herself in the sewing room, bright-colored squares of fabric on the table in front of her. The squares were about four inches on a side, cut from remnants and scraps of cloth left over from various other sewing projects, plus lots of new cloth specially purchased. Harold used to say that Lily was obsessed with those squares. She spent hours sorting through them, making patterns, pinning and unpinning the squares together. He used to like to tell people that Lily didn't even know if he was around or not, as long as she had her bags full of scraps.

She was a familiar presence at the local fabric store, rummaging through the bolts of cloth, selecting different colors and prints at random, whatever caught her eye. She had a talent for putting them together in such a way as to create something spectacular. Lily's quilts were known for their originality. They had won prizes at fairs and contests all over the Midwest. The other women in the sewing club all looked to her for advice and inspiration.

Lily and her husband, Harold, had bought their brand-new, state-of-the-art, small ranch-style home in Martingale Manor three or four years previously. Taking care of the sprawling house they'd raised their kids in, with its half-acre lot, had become a lot more work than they felt like doing, now that they were getting older. Lily remembered how excited they'd been to buy that big house years ago, such a far cry from the urban bungalows they'd both grown up in. But it had done its job. The kids were long grown and gone, and it was time for Lily and Harold to move on. They both figured this would be their last move before the grave. It's just that neither of them had thought the grave would come to meet Harold quite so soon. But *c'est la vie*.

Whatever Harold believed, Lily had always known when he was around. Now that he wasn't anymore, the new house, small as it was, seemed enormous. She had everything she needed in her sewing room at home but she couldn't seem to settle there. She liked being in the clubhouse's sewing room. It felt comfortable, even when she was the only one there.

She held up a length of fabric for inspection, decided its colors might work with the pattern she was making out of the squares on the table in front of her. She searched in her bag for her favorite pair of scissors but only managed to find the rotary cutter. She didn't care for the cutter. She used it only reluctantly. True, it was more efficient, but she missed the feeling of the shear's long, sharp blades slicing through the material with a satisfying *whoosh*. *Well, can't be helped.* She folded the fabric carefully, aligned a template on it, and sliced it into squares.

Harold Turner hadn't actually been the love of Lily's life, but he'd filled the bill well enough for some fifty years. She hardly ever thought of the boy she'd once considered her one true love, but hearing the old songs the other night brought it all back. She remembered how they used to dance to those tunes and hum the words as they moved together. "Oh, my, was I ever really that young?" Lily sighed.

Harold came later, after high school. He seemed like a good catch, as they used to say. Somebody who'd be a good provider, steady and reliable. The spark wasn't there. Not like with that other one. But maybe he wouldn't have turned out so well, anyway. At least Harold never looked at anybody else. She wished she could tell him the latest. He would have enjoyed hearing about it.

Leo Schaeffer pushed his chair back from his desk and rubbed his face.

"Tired, honey?" Mollie asked. "Why don't you take a break? It's not like you're getting paid for this, you know."

"I know, but none of this is making any sense. I don't see how that woman could have been in business for ...what? Five years or more? Her sales records don't match her inventory records, her accounts payable don't match her inventory records or her accounts receivable – it just doesn't add up. It's crazy, but it looks like she was selling items she didn't have in stock, and not selling much of what she did have. When I found these QuickBooks records, I thought I'd be able to figure it out, but it still doesn't add up. I'm going to have to go over that list again."

"The inventory list? It's not finished, you know. Remember, we had to quit when we heard somebody walking around upstairs. But Leo, it's really not any of our concern, is it?"

"Actually, it is. Or at least, it's *my* concern. But until I can get into Shirley Rogers' other laptop, there's not much I can do."

"When do you think that'll happen?"

"Pretty soon, I guess. Detective Carlson said that their tech guys are still going over it, and they'll want to back up the entire hard drive, but once they're done, I'll be able to do my thing. 'Forensic accounting.' Who knew?"

"That's a whole new specialty for you, isn't it, Leo?"

"That's not exactly the right word, I suppose," he replied. "Forensic accounting generally implies fraud, or it's for use in litigation. I think what Carlson is looking for is more like anything that might have been a motive for Shirley's murder. Detective work, really. But I'm hoping there might be something on that other laptop that might fill in the blanks about all the discrepancies I'm turning up. We'll see."

"Brilliant job, Jennings," Len Carlson said.

"Thanks Detective, but anybody could have done it, you know. I just Googled Martha Ashton and up it came. Address, phone number, marital status, you name it. Are you just going to show up at her office, or are you going to call her first?"

Martha Ashton had an office in a small business park several blocks east of downtown Deer Creek. Two identical three-story concrete block buildings flanked a parking lot that served both buildings. Ashton's office was on the second floor of the one on the west side of the lot. Carlson by-passed the staircase in favor of the elevator, even as he reminded himself he needed to get over to the gym. He'd had to let his belt out a notch that morning. Time to get himself back in shape.

Ashton's suite was about midway down the corridor, indistinguishable from all the others in the row except for the neatly lettered name on the door, *Martha Ashton, Attorney-at-Law*. Carlson opened it and let himself in. The small waiting room was completely generic, from the unoccupied receptionist's desk opposite the door to the non-descript painting on the windowless wall. The lawyer must have heard Carlson enter because she stepped out of the inner office to greet him almost immediately.

Martha Ashton was probably in her late forties, tall, with lots of dark hair piled carelessly on top of her head. She was casually dressed in pressed gray slacks with a striped sweater on top.

"Detective Carlson?" she asked, extending her hand in a firm shake. "My receptionist is out to lunch," she said, waving a hand toward the empty desk. "Come on back."

Ashton seated herself at a conference table in the center of the room and nodded Carlson toward the opposite chair. "What can I do for you, Detective? The police officer who called me just said you needed some information, but she wouldn't tell me anything else. It all sounds so mysterious," she said, leaning forward. "What's going on?"

Martha Ashton had been practicing family law for most of her career. She'd tried the corporate route, right out of law school, but the dog-eat-dog atmosphere never suited her. She liked being on her own, drawing up wills and real estate contracts, negotiating divorces and child-custody cases. Most of her clients were perfectly ordinary, respectable people whose needs were also respectable and ordinary. A nice, quiet law practice, not very challenging maybe, but it earned her a decent living without a lot of trauma. She was perfectly happy working regular hours and sleeping soundly at night. If one of her clients got arrested for something, which occurred once in a while, she referred him or her to a criminal attorney. She couldn't remember the last time she'd had a visit from the police.

Carlson took a minute to consider his answer. The lawyer was curious but not worried. Her expression was relaxed, confident. She wasn't going to need kid gloves.

"I think you know Shirley Rogers," Carlson began.

Ashton nodded. "She's a client of mine. Has she done something wrong?"

"You might say so," Carlson agreed. "She's got herself killed."

"Killed?"

"Murdered," he clarified. He gave Ashton a moment to absorb this.

"Murdered? Really? When did that happen? Was it here in Deer Creek? How come I didn't see anything about it in the paper?"

"Well, that brings me to the reason I'm here. We don't usually release a victim's name until we've had a chance to notify their next of kin. We think she might have had a son called Peter, but we have no other information about him, so far. She was killed a couple of days ago and I've been having a hell of a time trying to find him or anybody else who knows anything about her. Finally, I discovered that you're on her list of visitors to Martingale Manor. The only name on the list, as a matter of fact. So I need to know what you can tell me."

"Me? I think I'm going to have to disappoint you, Detective. I don't know very much, either. But let me see if ...." She rose, went to a file cabinet, and pulled an accordion file folder out of a drawer labeled "Q-R-S". Coming back to the table, she slid off the elastic binder and pulled out several smaller manila folders, which she laid on the table.

"I helped Shirley with her legal business papers. She's the sole owner of her business, you know, so that wasn't complicated. And then I drew up a will for her. I suppose that's what you'd be interested in?"

Carlson pulled his chair closer to the table. "Yeah, let's start with that. We need to notify her next of kin."

"That's going to take some doing, Detective. She told me she had a son, but they've been estranged for years.

There wasn't anybody else. I'm the executor of this will, and I'm directed to wind up her business affairs, pay bills and taxes and so forth, and then sell everything that's left and donate the proceeds to her alma mater."

"Alma Mater?"

"Our Lady of Cherubim Catholic School. It's in Chicago. Bridgeport, to be exact."

"Our Lady of Cherubim?"

"That's right. She said it was where she got her start."

"Her start? Her start at what?"

Ashton spread her hands and shrugged.

"Did you ask her?"

"I did, Detective. She came right back and asked me if she needed to expand on her reasons for legal purposes. I said no. So she didn't."

Carlson smiled. He was beginning to get a sense of who Shirley Rogers had been. He had a feeling he might have liked her. But she wasn't making things easy for him.

"All right, then, what about this son? Is his name Peter? Do you have an address?"

"Yes, I do," Ashton said, leafing through her papers again. "She didn't want to give me that information, either, but I insisted. I made sure the will specifically stipulates that her son is not a beneficiary. I don't want to be confronted at some point with a living relative contesting this will. Here it is. Peter. Peter Rogers. He lives in Chicago. At least, he did when the will was drawn up." She wrote the information on a post-it note and handed it to Carlson.

"I'm going to need access to her business records, financial records, and so forth," she said.

"You'll have to get in line, Ms. Ashton," Carlson told her. "We have somebody looking into all that. Once we evaluate the information, we can probably release it to you so you can do your thing, but not until then. I'll keep in touch."

If America is a country of immigrants, Chicago is a city that perfectly exemplifies that fact. During the mid-nineteenth century, people started pouring into the little settlement by Lake Michigan from every corner of Europe, and the flow hasn't stopped yet. Not so much of a melting pot as a stew, every group of newcomers established their own neighborhoods, with languages and foods and churches and customs of every kind from home. There were, and are, Polish neighborhoods, Lithuanian neighborhoods, Italian neighborhoods, Jewish neighborhoods, Greek, Chinese, and neighborhoods founded by immigrants from countries that have long ceased to exist. Bridgeport is one of those places.

Bridgeport, on Chicago's south side, is best known for being the home of five Chicago Irish mayors and countless other politicians, from aldermen to fire chiefs. Somewhat less generally known is the fact that it was also home to many other groups besides the Irish, such as Poles, Lithuanians, Czechs, Germans, Bohemians and others. What most of these people had in common was their Catholic heritage, and the churches and schools they established in the neighborhood reflect this. Although there are plenty of public schools in the area, about half the children of Bridgeport attend parochial schools, each to their own ethnic preference.

"And once a Cherubim, always a Cherubim, I guess," Carlson commented to Detective Ron Pepper as they reviewed the case together in Carlson's office.

"I guess," Pepper agreed. He was a country boy, from somewhere out in Iowa, and to him, Deer Creek, with its population of 150,000, seemed like a city. Chicago, with its population of nearly three million, was almost beyond imagining. But he'd been in the area quite a while, and the fact that Chicago was a city of neighborhoods helped him cope with the idea of the vast numbers. It was easier when you could break it down into Lakeview and Little Village and so forth. "It becomes your identity while you're a kid, and you never outgrow it, do you? Still, it's pretty unusual for somebody to leave their entire estate to their former grammar school. There's got to be a story there."

"Has to be," Carlson agreed. "You want to go dig it out? I'd like to get over to Martingale Manor one more time, talk to some of these people again. It seems to me that some of them said they were originally from the South Side. Maybe they know something about this Cherubim school."

"I'll do my best, Len. What are the odds the school is even still there? The Archdiocese has closed a lot of these schools, you know. They can't afford to run so many of them anymore. And even if it exists, how many people do you suppose would remember Shirley Rogers? It must be fifty years since she was there."

Fabio Gompers typically spent hours on the internet every day, searching for material he could use in his work. He would have preferred to spend that time in his studio, developing his own ideas, but the arthritis was a fact of life that had to be acknowledged.

He'd figured out a long time ago that there were hundreds - no thousands – thousands, yes. Thousands of excellent artists who would never impose much of an impact on the art world. Even Fabio, successful as he was, would never find his paintings on the walls of the Met or the Art Institute of Chicago, let alone the Prado or the Louvre. Yet, he'd found a way to do what he loved and still pay the bills.

The problem had come about when one of his gallerists had accidentally stumbled upon his secret, and used that knowledge for her own profit. Yes, Fabio profited, too, but …. It was definitely an awkward situation. Which was about to come to a head. Unless ….

Ruffles and Flourishes fronted on Main Street but backed on an alley that ran behind the stores on Main and on Wright Street, just east of Main. A multi-level parking garage backed on the alley also, behind the block that the new co-op was on. Gompers didn't bother trying the front door of the shop, but he thought the back door might be open. It was worth a look, anyway.

Gompers entered the parking garage off of Wright Street and walked all the way through it, emerging into the alley from its rear exit. There was a row of dumpsters back there. He walked past them into the small concrete-paved yard behind the store. He pushed at the back door, not very hopeful that it would yield to his effort, so he wasn't disappointed when it didn't. He pulled a couple of thin-bladed levers out of his pocket and studied them for a minute. He'd seen countless TV shows where crooks break into places they weren't supposed to be by using a thin blade to pick the lock, but he didn't have a lot of faith the trick would work in real life. To his astonishment, when he inserted one of the tools into the lock and turned it, he heard a click. He tried the knob. The door opened.

The lights were on in the store's front windows. The glow of the street lamps outside provided a bit of illumination, too. Gompers could see at a glance that the place was empty. His eyes automatically went to the wall where he was used to seeing his paintings hang, but other pictures hung there now.

Apparently, Rita Cutler hadn't lost any time filling the empty spaces after he'd removed his work from the gallery. But there'd been no way he could do the rest of the job with her standing there watching him. He hoped it wasn't too late, now.

Gompers slipped back to the basement door. He reached for the switch to turn the stairwell light on, but then he remembered that the basement was only half below ground, and the high windows were at street level. He stepped back to pull his cell phone out of his back pocket. As he did so, he thought he heard something. Whispers, maybe, coming from downstairs. He held still, listened, heard nothing else. *Stop imagining things,* he told himself. *There's nobody there.*

He found the flashlight app icon and clicked it on, shading the light with his hand. In the dim light, he picked his way down the stairs.

Careful not to let any light show through the back windows, Gompers moved quickly to the studio set-up in the corner. He gathered up the tubes of paints and the brushes, and stuffed them into the tote bag he'd had the foresight to bring along. The easel was too large and awkward to move. It would have to stay. The painting that had rested on it was too large to fit into the tote bag. Regretfully, he took a knife from his pocket and ripped the canvas into pieces. With a couple of quick kicks, he managed to break the stretcher supports apart, and the pieces joined the bits of canvas in the bag. He looked around. He couldn't see anything else to scoop up. *That's it, then.* He left the building the way he'd come in.

Detective Ron Pepper hadn't visited the city for a long time, but Chicago is laid out in a grid. Once you understand how that works, it's easy to find any address, even if you've never been there before.

Bridgeport had seen plenty of changes over the years. Many of the original Irish and Poles had migrated to the suburbs, but the influx of Hispanics and Asians made up for the loss. Some of the parochial schools were indeed closed now, but Our Lady of Cherubim Elementary School still stood, and still served the children of the Parish. It was a sturdy red brick building, three stories tall, with a small church at one end. A paved concrete forecourt held some swings, a climbing structure, and a slide, but no one was using them at the moment. School was in session, and all the children were inside. Pepper pushed the front door open but he didn't go further into the building. Not right away.

Getting his bearings, Pepper inhaled a familiar odor of chalk dust, old mold, and sweat, the well-remembered smell of his Iowa childhood. This wasn't a good memory. He'd hated the place. He could never live up to the nuns' expectations, and he was forever getting his hands rapped with rulers as punishment for various infractions of the rules. Somehow he'd managed to get through all eight years, but when it came time to go to high school, he announced to his parents that he was going to the public school in the neighborhood, and not the Catholic boys' school across town. They'd argued, but he said he'd run away if they tried to force him, and they believed him.

The nuns didn't wear their black habits anymore, but they still looked like nuns. When Pepper walked into the principal's office and saw her frown at him, stern and cold, he was taken back all those years. He was twelve years old again, and about to be told to stick out his hands. He pushed away the image and stepped forward.

"Nineteen fifty-six?" The principal took the photo Pepper handed her and studied it, intrigued. The kids probably thought she'd been a fixture at Cherubim since the beginning of time, but Pepper could see that she wasn't much over fifty, herself. She hadn't even been born when that photo was taken. Her expression softened, and Pepper thought she might have been attractive once. Might be again, with a little make-up and her hair styled, instead of scraped back into a thin bun at the back of her head.

"I think any of the sisters who were teaching here then would be long gone by now," Sister Claude said. "But I wonder …. You know, you could try Sister Joseph. She might know something. Anyway, it wouldn't hurt to ask her."

Pepper followed Sister Claude's directions and walked down a long hallway, lined on both sides with gray metal lockers. By the time he reached the art room, at the very end, he was feeling claustrophobic. He remembered being intimidated the first few times he walked down similar corridors at his old school, which seemed so enormous and strange. Were they, in reality, just as cramped as this one?

The art room was aptly chosen, as it spanned the entire width of the corridor right at the end of the building. Tall windows across the outer wall let in plenty of light. Tables stood in ranks across the room, with several children hard at work at each one. They were busily piecing collages together. They chattered like a flock of little sparrows as they tore shapes from colored papers and glued them to backing boards. He stood at the threshold for a while, enjoying the scene, and no one seemed to notice that he was there. His policeman's mind told him this wasn't a good thing, given the things that go on these days. Before he left the building, he'd have to talk to Sister Claude about working on security.

Sister Joseph, at least he supposed that must be she, was engrossed in helping some of her charges with their project. She looked like somebody's grandmother, short gray hair brushed back from her forehead, jawline softly sagging a bit. But her movements were purposeful and her eyes bright. She might be getting on in years, but she was still up to dealing with a classroom of ten year olds. She looked up at Pepper calmly.

"Yes?" It was just one word, but this was clearly a woman who was used to command. Pepper smiled and introduced himself.

"Do you have a few minutes, Sister? I'd like to speak with you a bit."

Sister Joseph called to a young woman who was helping the kids at another table. A moment later, she took Pepper's arm and steered him to an alcove at the back of the room, furnished with a desk, a couple of chairs and not much else.

"I was hoping this might ring a bell with you, Sister," Pepper said, handing her the black-and-white photo he'd taken from Shirley Rogers' home.

Sister Joseph looked at it blankly, glanced back at Pepper, and then lowered her eyes to the picture once again. A smile slowly worked its way across her face. "Oh, my goodness," she said. "Doesn't this bring back memories? Where on earth did you dig it up?"

"So you do recognize this picture," Pepper said, not answering her question. "Can you tell me about it?"

Sister Joseph bit her lip. She pointed to a little girl in the front row on the right, hair chopped off in a classic Buster Brown, dark bangs thick and straight across her forehead. "I don't look much like this nowadays, do I?"

Pepper grinned, and looked back and forth between the nun's face and the child's. "I think I can see her in you," he said. "Something about the eyes, maybe."

"Maybe," the sister conceded. "A little. If you squint."

"Anything else look familiar?"

"Surely you can't be asking me to remember things from so far back? My goodness, it was more than sixty years ago, wasn't it? It was another world, school days, and plaid jumpers. The sisters seemed so forbidding then, until you got to know them, and then you realized they weren't so different from our mothers or our aunts. I'm glad we don't wear those habits anymore, though. I think maybe we're not as scary to today's children. Those black habits were such a barrier. Hot and uncomfortable, too."

"I bet you do remember, though, don't you sister? I bet you know the names of all the kids in the picture."

Sister Joseph bent her head to stare at the photo, and a smile started at the corners of her mouth. "You know, I think you're right, after all. It sounds like such a long time, but when I put myself back there in my mind, it seems like it could have been last week. Let's see...." She moved her finger along the rows, naming each child as her finger touched the image. "Shirley McCarthy, front and center, as always. I certainly remember her. Yes, and her son, too, although that was later, of course. What was his name? Yes, Peter. Not McCarthy, though. Rogers, that was it. Peter Rogers."

Pepper hadn't expected that, not at all. "How did you know him, Sister? He was years after your time."

"Of course, yes. Long after my time as a student. But I came back here after I took my vows. I've been teaching art here for fifty years. I just work part time these days, but I'm still here. I hope I never have to give it up. Little Peter Rogers was one of my students."

"How did you know he was Shirley's son?"

"How would I not know? This parish is just a small town, really. I didn't make the connection immediately, because the last name was different. But it didn't take long to realize, either. Poor little boy."

"Why 'poor little boy?'"

Sister Joseph raised an eyebrow, saying, as if Pepper should have already known, "Well, his father, of course."

"His father? What about his father?"

"He killed himself, poor man."

"Did he? While Peter was a student here?"

"Yes, that's right. While he was in my class, as a matter of fact. We were all so shocked. What a terrible, terrible thing to do. Terrible for the man, and perhaps even more terrible for his family. I remember Peter. He didn't say much, and we didn't know how to talk to him about it. These days we have counselors and such, to help the children through such traumas. But then, all we could do was offer sympathy, and he didn't want sympathy. He wanted his father back. And he wanted his mother, too."

"Didn't he still have his mother?"

Sister Joseph sighed, and shot Pepper a sharp glance. "Shirley was – what should we say? Shirley was missing in action a lot of the time. We didn't know the details, but we heard the rumors."

Now it was Pepper's turn to raise an eyebrow.

"Oh, yes, Detective. Do you think that just because we nuns hid behind our black habits, we didn't hear or see what was going on around us? No, I assure you. We still live in the world. We do now, and we did then, too. But we didn't know how to help Peter. We could only offer sympathy, and prayers."

"Do you know why the father committed suicide?"

Sister Joseph nodded. "Yes, I think so. I think it had to do with his having had to declare bankruptcy, when his business failed. He had a small business, some sort of store, I believe. And he couldn't make a go of it. He lost all his money. I think he had some idea of killing himself so his wife could have the insurance or something, but of course, life insurance doesn't pay in cases of suicide. So after he was gone, Shirley had just about nothing. She lost the house, and they had to move."

"Couldn't she have got some sort of job?"

"Yes, I believe she did get a job. But she wasn't really trained for anything. Most of the girls of that time at least took a secretarial course, or learned to be lab techs, or maybe nurses. But Shirley was too busy fooling around with boys to be bothered to pay much attention to school. She married poor Frank Rogers right after high school. Peter was born soon after, and I don't think Shirley ever held down a job. Not until she absolutely had to, and then she could only find a sales clerk position somewhere. She would have had to take Peter out of Cherubim and send him to public school, but our principal at the time, Sister Juliana, wouldn't hear of it, even if Shirley couldn't pay the tuition any more. I don't know where Juliana found the money, but she did, one way or another. So Peter finished eighth grade here. I lost track of both of them after that, though. Funny, how it all comes back, isn't it? I haven't thought of any of it for so many years. But you seem very interested, Detective. Why?"

"I'm sorry to have to tell you this, Sister. Shirley Rogers was killed recently. I'm investigating her murder."

Sister Joseph rapidly crossed herself. "Murdered! How terrible! What happened?"

"Well, that's what we're trying to find out. What happened, and who's responsible."

"I hope you do."

"I plan to, Sister," Pepper affirmed. "And you've helped fill in some of the blanks."

Chapter Fifteen

"I'm worried about Leo," Mollie told Bella, over coffee at the Starbucks down the street from the new co-op.

The two women were taking a break from their responsibilities at the Deer Creek Art League. "Are you? I'm worried about us," Bella retorted. "It seems like we're spending all our time working at the Art League lately. I haven't had any time to paint in weeks. Have you?"

Mollie shook her head. "This being retired business is hard. I'm busier now than when I was going to my job every day. Looking back, I don't know how I found time to work, what with everything else I have to do. But seriously, it's different with Leo."

Bella stopped fussing with her tablet, on which she had been busily making notes for her to-do list while she drank her coffee. She sat back and looked straight at her friend, ready to listen.

"He's taking all this business about the accounting pretty hard," Mollie said.

"I thought he'd be out of it, now that Shirley Rogers is dead. Why is he still working on it?"

"You know that lawyer the police dug up? She found out that Shirley had asked Leo to audit the books for her, to straighten things out for the IRS, so the lawyer asked Leo to keep on with it. She was pretty interested in the fact that he'd already started looking into the files on the computer we found in the basement, and she wants him to act officially as her accountant for this case."

"Her accountant?"

"Yeah. You know, she's the executor, so it's up to her to make sure all the bills are paid, and the taxes. Especially the taxes. She needs to have a CPA take care of that part of it."

"Sure, that makes sense. But wait, I thought we weren't going to tell anybody about being in the basement."

Mollie glanced away. "Well ... Leo sort of made it sound like Shirley let him in there before she got killed. He didn't happen to mention that we got in afterwards. No point in stirring things up unnecessarily, is there? And he really was working for Shirley, so.... "

Bella nodded. Maybe breaking and entering *Ruffles and Flourishes'* basement wasn't strictly legal, but she didn't think it rose to the level of a major felony, either. Anyway, they hadn't actually broken in. More like, found a loophole.

"Still," she said, "I don't understand why Leo is so upset. He's done this kind of work his entire life. What's different about this case?"

"You know me, Bella. Accounting isn't really my strong point. But I gather that the main problem is that the inventory we compiled doesn't gibe with the records Leo's been able to find so far. I told him it's probably because we didn't have time to finish the job that day, but he's not buying it."

"Seems to me we need to get over there again and take another look. What do you think?"

"Sounds like a plan," Mollie agreed, smiling conspiratorially.

The latest session of Bella's course at Martingale Manor was in full swing, but the ladies weren't as into their paintings as they had been earlier. To their credit, most of them had tried to follow Bella's instructions on how to begin a basic landscape painting, but habits of a lifetime were hard to break. They tried to understand the concept of building a painting from front to back, top to bottom, but they were in too much of a hurry to get to the main event and so their houses and trees tended to look pasted on instead of being integrated with the backgrounds.

"This is so much fun, Bella," Joanie Passarelli said. "I hate to see the class be over. Can't we keep doing it?"

"I'm glad you're enjoying it. I'm enjoying it, too. But I'm just running out of time, and driving over here with all my stuff adds almost another hour to the class time. You know, I teach the same class at the Deer Creek Art League, if you'd like to sign up for it. It's not far from here, and we have better equipment and some specialized lighting over there. Plus, we don't have to set everything up from scratch each session."

"That might be a good idea," Connie Marks said. "To tell the truth, I feel a little nervous about coming here lately. I sure wish they'd solve that murder, so we could all get on with our lives."

"True. It's just like her to spoil things," Debbie Wilson muttered under her breath, as she put the finishing touches on her trees. Nature had never seen anything quite like the vegetation sprouting on the small canvas, but the colors were bright and cheerful. She'd applied the paint with abandon and that was half the battle. Lots of beginning painters were awfully tentative with their brushes.

"Just slap it on, ladies. It's only paint. Don't be afraid of it," Bella always counseled. "Look, Debbie," she said now, moving over for a closer look, "if you just take your round brush in your fist and whoosh it around, your leaves will look a lot more convincing."

Taking Debbie's brush from her hand, Bella swirled it a pile of yellow paint, then dipped the tip of it into a pile of ultramarine blue. She lightly mushed the two together, creating several different shades of green. She applied the loaded brush to the canvas, moving it in circles around and over the tree trunks Debbie had drawn in. Immediately, the previously painted leaves softened and melted, appearing a lot more like the blur of greens to be seen in any forest and a lot less like individually pasted-on leaf shapes.

"Oh, I see what you mean, Bella. Thanks."

"Yes, good. Try to relax. This is supposed to be fun, right? You were on the right track the other day, but now you're all tensed up again. By the way, what did you mean? Who spoiled what?"

"Just talking to myself," Debbie said, concentrating on her painting.

"But you said 'she.' Did you know Shirley Rogers?"

"Not really," Debbie said. "Well, I used to know her, years ago."

"Used to? But not anymore?"

"No. I hadn't seen her for years and years, until I saw her here not long ago. She wasn't Rogers then. Her name was Shirley McCarthy. We went to the same schools, in Bridgeport."

"No kidding? It's such a small world, isn't it? But you didn't like her then?"

"Not much, no. She was one of those girls who thought they were something special, if you know what I mean. But that was a long time ago."

"In a galaxy far, far away...." Bella finished.

Debbie smiled. "Seems like it, doesn't it?"

"Sometimes, yes, it does. But then sometimes it seems like it was yesterday."

Connie Marks had a point, Bella mused a little while later. She could definitely sense a difference in the atmosphere of the Clubhouse at Martingale Manor. Whereas when she'd first started coming there, everyone was casual and friendly, now people seemed more reserved. They still smiled and greeted each other, but there were shadows that hadn't been there before.

"It's a shame, really," Bella commented to Art that evening, as they walked down Main Street. "I hope things will get back to normal soon over there."

"It will, eventually. I think the murder has brought a little dose of reality to the place. From what you've told me about it, it seemed sort of fairyland-ish before. But once this murder is solved, it'll probably be fine."

"I don't know," Bella commented doubtfully. "I hope you're right, but I think this sort of problem has a long life. Well, here we are."

Bella unlocked the door of the co-op. Work had progressed since the last time she'd been there. Ben Goldberg and Rahj Patel had evidently been busy, because there was a new counter across the back of the space, with open shelving that could be accessed from the rear while presenting a nice clean sweep of color to visitors. The new laminate flooring looked almost as good as the real thing and had the advantage of being a lot cheaper than wood. The project's cost was definitely a consideration, since Penny Pearson's legacy would only go so far. Bella walked towards the back and reached for the light switch, but Art stopped her, saying, "Let's not attract any more attention than we absolutely have to. We can see well enough by the light over the front window."

Bella and Mollie hadn't wanted to involve any other members of the Deer Creek Art League in their plan to search the basement of *Ruffles and Flourishes* again, so they agreed to meet at ten o'clock at night, when all the Main Street stores were closed. Getting into the spirit of things, when Mollie and Leo joined their friends a few minutes later, they were both wearing black turtlenecks over their dark jeans.

"Any trouble getting in?" Mollie asked.

"No, I have the key, remember?" Bella said. "Come on, let's get on with it."

The four of them went down into the basement and Art found the secret door connecting the co-op's basement with that of Shirley Rogers' store. They each came prepared with a flashlight, but they were careful to shade them with their hands, mindful of the fact that light could be seen in the alley through the basement's windows.

"So what exactly are we looking for?" Art asked Leo.

"Look," he said, pulling some papers from his briefcase. "I printed out some of the records. I was trying to tally the inventory against the accounts payable, and it just doesn't come out right. I want to go over the inventory again and see what we're missing. It looks to me like there's stuff on the shelves that wasn't purchased through any of the suppliers on record here."

The police had already been in the basement; that much was evident. They hadn't left too much of a mess behind, but there were some boxes on the floor instead of on the shelves and some loose papers scattered around, too.

The easel was in the corner where it had been before but there was nothing on it.

"The paints are all gone, too," Bella noticed, looking around. She stooped to pick something up. It was a small strip of canvas, roughly cut, paint peeling from its surface. Bella scratched at the paint. The canvas wasn't white underneath. It was imbedded with color that looked more like ink than paint. She put the scrap in her pocket.

It took most of the night, but by the time they finished systematically itemizing every item on every shelf, a pattern had become clear, at least to Leo.

"There are invoices for all the little giftie things," he noted. "Office supplies, boxes, ribbons – all that sort of thing is accounted for. But there are no suppliers listed for these boxes of notecards or for these giclee prints. This makes no sense. How am I supposed to know what she paid for them? How can I know what she was selling them for, or how many have already been sold?"

"Could there be other records somewhere?" Art asked.

"Must be," Leo agreed. "But it beats me where they could be. I downloaded everything I could find on her computer. We haven't come across any sort of records on these shelves. There wasn't anything in the store itself, either. There's some shady business going on here. Damned if I know what it is, but I'm going to have to tell that lawyer I can't certify the books as is. I don't know what she's going to want to do about that."

Chapter Sixteen

Bella Sarver and Mollie Schaeffer surveyed their work. They'd just finished hanging the new monthly show on the gray felt-covered walls of the Deer Creek Art League, a thankless task since few of the participating artists were ever happy with the results. The next step was even worse. The person they brought in to judge the show, a different judge each time, was faced with the job of trying to determine the best works among a huge diversity of paintings and sculptures on display. How do you say a painting is better than a fiber piece or a ceramic? Not exactly apples to apples. More like apples to elephants. Yet that was what was required. The issue came up at the board meeting every month, but no one had managed to find a solution so far.

"I think our members are getting better," Bella commented. "I remember years ago, some of the paintings weren't bad but lots of them were pretty awful. Not so anymore. Many of these are up to professional level. Look at this landscape by Fabio Gompers, for instance. You can just about step into it and disappear."

She moved close to the wall for a better look, but then frowned. Gently, she touched the edge of the canvas, which wasn't framed, but which was wrapped around thick stretchers, giving the work almost a sculptural appearance. Her finger came away with a flake of blue paint. She touched the piece again and more paint came away from the canvas. She scratched at the surface lightly, and the paint flaked off like dandruff from a scaly head of hair.

"What are you doing, Bella? Fabio will kill you!"

"Why will I kill you?"

Bella jumped at the question. "I didn't hear you come in, Fabio. We just finished hanging the show. What do you think?"

Fabio stepped back, folded his arms across his chest, and examined the exhibit, frowning critically. "Not bad," he said. "Not bad at all. I like how you girls varied the sizes and shapes, so that the eye moves from one painting to the next automatically. Interesting."

"Yes, thanks, but look at this, Fabio." Bella pointed to the corner of the picture where the paint had disappeared. "What happened there?"

Fabio bent for a closer look, touched the canvas experimentally, and then gently scratched at it. Another flake fell to the floor.

"Damn! I really thought it would be okay. It was such a long time, I was sure the paint would have completely dried."

"You're going to have to explain that, Fabio," Mollie told him.

He sighed deeply. "Right. Well, you know how you can't paint acrylic over oil, only the other way around?"

Mollie nodded. "Sure, that's pretty basic. Bella explained it to us at one of our first classes."

Oil paint takes an extremely long time to dry thoroughly. Even though it feels dry to the touch, the layers underneath slowly lose their moisture over time, and as they do so, the top layer tends to crack a bit. Acrylic paint dries much more quickly, and so oil paint can go right over without a problem, but if you paint acrylic over oil, the more slowly drying oil paint will cause the top layer of acrylic paint to crack and flake.

"Okay, so I thought, since I painted this oil a long time ago, it must have dried thoroughly enough so that it would be fine to paint over it with acrylic. Obviously, I thought wrong. I should have known better."

"I see. Well, what do you want to do about it?" Bella asked.

"I don't see any way I can fix it now. Can I just leave it up, but write NFS on the card?"

Bella and Mollie consulted with a look. "Not for sale? I guess that will be ok," Bella told him. "It's a shame, though. It would be a really nice painting if it hadn't been for that."

"I know," Fabio admitted. "I was trying to salvage a canvas. Penny wise and pound foolish, isn't that what they say?" He shook his head ruefully.

"That's what they say. So, Fabio, was there a reason you came in here? You *do* know the gallery is technically closed just now?"

"Yeah, right, but I saw the lights on and thought I might as well drop in and check on my sales for the month. I like to keep tabs on things. Do you mind?"

Bella gestured to the desk. "You know how to find the records on the computer, don't you?"

While Fabio looked up the records, she and Mollie put the finishing touches on the exhibit, making sure the labels were correct and placed at eye level and straightening some of the jewelry on the shelves.

When Fabio had gone, having discovered exactly no sales at all for the previous month, Bella returned to his landscape on the wall. She touched her finger so the bare spot and yet another flake of paint came loose.

"Look at this, Mollie. This paint is coming right off the canvas. I know we just agreed we could leave it up, but this is ridiculous."

"Is it still wet?"

"No, it's dry. It's flaking off. And look at what's underneath."

Instead of a white canvas, the lost paint revealed a small section of blue sky. Bella tapped at it experimentally, and frowned again.

"Well, I know," Mollie said. "It's the underpainting. Nothing unusual about that."

"It's not an underpainting. Take a close look. This image is printed on the canvas, not painted. Look, you can see the textures are different all over. There's some paint, but mostly not. And what there is, isn't even sticking very well. This isn't old oil he painted over. Fabio knows better than to make a mistake like that."

Mollie leaned in for a closer look, and touched a finger gingerly to the canvas. "So what is it then? A giclee? But why would he do that? What's the point?"

"I guess he thought he could fool people into thinking this was the original, instead of one of his prints. He wasn't even careful about it. But as you said, Mollie, what's the point?"

Bella thought for a second, then pulled a scrap from her jeans pocket. She was still wearing the same jeans she'd had on when they'd all revisited the basement of *Ruffles and Flourishes*. "I'll bet you anything that's what this is, too," she said, holding it out for Mollie to see. "Somebody was taking giclee prints and putting a thin layer of paint over it to make it seem as if it were an original painting. That's what was on the easel we saw when we were in the basement the first time. Somebody came back and removed it. Not only that, they must have ripped it right up and got rid of it entirely."

The women looked at each other, not sure what to make of their discovery.

"There could be an entirely innocent explanation for this," Mollie said.

"And that would be...?"

Mollie had no answer.

Fabio Gompers congratulated himself on a job well done. He'd got himself into a miserable situation and now he was out of it. The evidence was gone. No one would ever know that he'd been doctoring giclee prints and passing them off as originals. He never really understood how Shirley Rogers had discovered his little game, but somehow she had, and she roped him into working his scam for her. Thank goodness, that problem was over. Now he was in the clear.

He'd hated doing it. He hated the grubby basement space Shirley had set up for him. He resented the time he spent there. It took time away from his real work. And yes, even the giclees were his real work. His own choice. Not dictated by anyone else. Not until she threatened to tell the world that he was a fake.

Fabio wasn't a fake. He was an artist. He could paint anything. At least, he used to be able to, before his fingers seized up and holding a paint brush became an endurance test.

Fabio stretched his hands out before him. He used to be so proud of those hands. They would do whatever he told them to. They could make strong, broad sweeps of a brush, filling a canvas with color. They could make delicate little movements, bringing out the most subtle nuances of a subject's complexion. He had only to think *soft here* or *a little more pink* and it would be done. He was like a violinist, creating beauty and magic with his brushes. He examined his fingers, the joints swollen, the fingers skewed sideways, more like claws than fingers these days. No amount of ibuprofen could straighten them. And yet, he was a painter. He needed to paint as much as needed air.

He could work on the small paintings all right. But the broad, strong brush strokes he used to cover large canvases were harder to manage these days. The wealthy collectors had giant spaces to fill in their enormous homes and offices. They paid the big bucks for paintings that impressed with their size as well as the originality of the art. Fabio's galleries hadn't much use for fiddly little pieces that had to be approached close up in order to be seen, no matter how beautifully painted. Yet he still had bills to pay, didn't he?

And he was smart about it. He only repainted the giclees of a few artists, ones he admired, ones whose work was similar to his own. He was a specialist, and he was picky. That's why he spent hours poring over the artists' websites, looking for images that he could download properly and make into good giclee prints. A little paint, expertly applied, and whammo! A brand-new original oil painting.

What harm did it do? The artists never knew about it. It wasn't like stealing, for crying out loud. It was more like sharing. He was actually doing them a favor, bringing their artistry into more homes than they could reach on their own. They still had their original paintings, or the collectors who'd bought them did. If only that busy-body hadn't found out and made such a fuss. Well, that was all in the past.

Fabio looked around his studio. He *lived* in a condo in Martingale Manor. It was perfect for his needs, a man on his own. There was plenty of room for his books and what little furniture he'd rescued from the remnants of his marriage, a small kitchen, bedroom, bathroom, no mess, no clutter. He'd hesitated a long time before making the move. The thought of living in an 'over 55' community didn't match with his image of himself as young, macho, strong. But when he looked in the mirror, he had to admit that the image looking back at him was a little different. There was this bald guy, kind of stooped over, grey bristles dotting the lined cheeks. Worse than that, his once-powerful shoulders were cramped with arthritis, to the point that he could barely raise his arms anymore, let alone apply his brushes vigorously to the large canvases he'd favored. The fact that there was an indoor pool in the clubhouse where he could participate in the Water Movement for Arthritis classes three mornings a week settled the deal.

He'd once had a lovely studio in the big house he'd shared with his wife, but the divorce had taken care of that. So now he rented a large, sunlit space over a strip of stores along Forest Avenue, at the edge of downtown Deer Creek. He had a nice view from the south-facing windows, which overlooked the park. But best of all were the high ceilings and large, north-facing windows that allowed him to work by natural light most of the day.

A small kitchenette stood at one end, next to a tiny bathroom. There was room for a desk and some files, also a large industrial printer. The rest of the place was filled with easels, flat files for holding large sheets of paper, a couple of drafting tables, and several rolling taborets to store paints and brushes in, and to hold his palettes. It was an ideal set up. And now he could resume his work without having to supply Shirley with her extra-curricular merchandise. He'd never enjoyed working over the giclees she ordered from such places as Fine Art USA, anyway. She had lousy taste.

Chapter Seventeen

Ron Pepper shared what he'd found out about Shirley McCarthy Rogers from Sister Joseph with the team as soon as he returned from the city.

"It sounds like our victim wasn't much to write home about, was she?" Carlson noted.

"Guess not. According to Sister Joseph, she didn't seem to be cut out for marriage or motherhood. She played around after her husband killed himself, and probably before, too."

"That doesn't mean she deserved to be killed. I wonder what the son will have to say for himself. There's got to be a story there. The lawyer, Martha Ashton, says Peter Rogers was specifically disinherited. She made a point of putting that in the will, to make it clear that leaving him out wasn't just an oversight."

"Pretty drastic move, wasn't it?" Pepper said. Jennings nodded, biting her lip thoughtfully.

An interview with Peter Rogers was next on Carlson's agenda, but first he wanted to make sure his team was all on the same page with the information they had so far.

Carlson, Jennings and Pepper went over the interview notes again and made a chart of their findings, noting the demographics of each person and their location at the time of the murder. The ME had been able to pinpoint time of death pretty closely, based on the fact that the body was still warm when it was found and rigor hadn't yet set in.

"The problem with location is that just about anybody in the building could have slipped out from whatever else they were doing and gone into the women's locker room to kill Rogers," Jennings said.

"True, and there's access from both the pool and the clubhouse lobby," Pepper pointed out.

"Well, it probably was a woman, right? I mean, somebody would have noticed a man going into the ladies' bathroom, wouldn't they?"

"Maybe," Carlson interjected, "but also, maybe not. It would have been taking a chance, but it's possible a man watched for his moment and then slipped in and out."

"It was taking a *big* chance, don't you think? What if somebody had come in right after him?"

"It would have been easy enough for him to slip into the next shower stall and draw the curtain. Or slip into one of the toilet stalls and close the door. Who would know?"

The three studied the chart again. "Think, guys," Carlson exhorted. "There has to be a link here. This wasn't a random killing. Somebody murdered this woman for a reason. It was a crime of opportunity. Someone had a grudge against her, someone hated her enough to wish her dead, but they didn't plan the murder. They just saw their chance and took it. Why?"

"Okay, so – Martingale Manor is a fairly new subdivision, right?" Pepper said. "Everybody moved there from someplace else in the last five years. Did we ask them where they came from?"

Carlson shook his head. "No, we didn't get that." He made a note on his pad.

"Another thing," Jennings added. "This is an over-55 community. There's a pretty wide range of ages, but look, the majority of residents cluster around 70 years old, between about 67 and 75."

"Not the population you'd be expecting to include a murderer," Carlson said.

"Not the first place you'd look, no," Pepper agreed. "There's the matter of strength, too. Lots of these people couldn't have done it, physically."

"I guess that eliminates anybody in a walker or a wheelchair, doesn't it?" Jennings commented.

"Probably. But most of them can get around pretty well. They might not be that strong, but how strong do you really have to be, if you're furious? And this wasn't a random murder. There was hate involved."

Peter Rogers' cell rang as he was walking out of his office on the 27th floor of the Merc. He glanced at the screen, didn't recognize the number, pressed 'ignore,' and slipped between the elevator doors before they closed. He didn't usually leave the office this early in the evening, but trading was over for the day and he had a headache. All he wanted to do was head home and lie down.

The Mercantile Exchange Building is located on Monroe and Wacker, with its wide back porch overlooking the Chicago River. Rogers generally cabbed it home. His South Loop apartment was a hefty walk away, but he decided the fresh air might do him some good. It had been a difficult day, another in a string of bad days. He was ending it quite a bit less wealthy than he'd been in the morning. He might recoup his losses tomorrow, if the derivatives market recovered. Or he might not.

The market had its ups and downs. Everybody knew that. Rogers prided himself on his cool head. When the market was up, he soared with it. When it turned the other way, he held on tight. He had a system. It had been working for over twenty years. He just had to hang on now, and everything would be fine. He just wished this headache would go away.

Peter Rogers lived by himself in the South Wabash high rise, in a condo he'd bought with the proceeds of his first big trading year. It was one of the highly desirable apartment buildings in the South Loop that had begun rising in the nineties, adding a new chapter to the history of the neighborhood. He'd once shared the apartment with a wife, but she'd found someone she liked better and left. Thank goodness there hadn't been any kids, so now it was just him. He didn't mind. He had female companionship when he wanted it, and didn't need to bother pleasing anybody else if he didn't feel in the mood.

He'd decided quite a while ago that he was one of those people who were better off alone. No ties to anyone. That was the way to do it. He learned that lesson as a kid, and it was still valid. Depend on yourself and you won't be disappointed.

It was already dark when Rogers reached home, but his head felt a little better for the half hour walk in the chill air. He threw his coat on the living room couch as he headed past it to the bar at the other side of the room. He poured himself a Jameson Irish, no ice. The doorbell rang before he got to the second sip. He pressed the intercom. "Yeah?"

"Detective Len Carlson, Deer Creek Police Department. Can I come up, Mr. Rogers?"

"Police? What's this about?"

"I'd rather tell you in person."

"Will this day never end?" Rogers muttered to himself. He pressed the buzzer to let the lobby door open and went to unlock the front door of the apartment. By the time Carlson stepped off the elevator on the thirty-second floor, Rogers was already sprawled on his couch, drink in hand, head thrown back against the cushions, nearly asleep.

Carlson knocked on the door and was surprised when it swung open at his touch. He called out, but there was no answer, so he pushed the door the rest of the way and walked in.

Directly across from the front door were floor to ceiling windows offering spectacular views of the Chicago skyline. The lights of the city shone into the apartment, making it bright as day despite the fact that no lamps were lit. The condo was furnished very simply, with a couple of black leather sofas, several glass and stainless steel tables, and not much else. A large steel sculpture, looking vaguely like a ship's figurehead sailing into the wind, graced an ebony sideboard against an inside wall.

Rogers never stirred, though he must have heard Carlson enter. He was trim and fit, the gray strands in his close-cut hair the only clues to the fact that he might be older than he looked. His clothes were well-cut, but somewhat rumpled, the once-crisply ironed shirt untucked

"Mr. Rogers," Carlson said.

Rogers opened one eye and peered up at the Detective. Carlson was about his own age, in his mid-forties, with plenty of medium brown hair and an athletic build. He stood in the middle of the room, calmly waiting for a response.

Rogers heaved a sigh and sat up, reluctantly. He rubbed his face, sipped his whiskey, and waited.

Carlson took a seat on the sofa opposite Rogers. He expected a question, but none was forthcoming. Rogers' expression spoke only of fatigue or maybe boredom. Not anxiety. No curiosity. Interesting.

"I'm afraid I have some bad news for you."

No reaction.

"I tried your phone a while ago, but didn't get through."

Still nothing.

Carlson considered a couple of different approaches, but in the end, he decided to just come out with it. "Your mother, Shirley Rogers, was killed yesterday."

Rogers blinked. He took another sip of his drink. "What's it to do with me?" he asked.

Carlson kept a straight face. "I take it you and your mother weren't close. When was the last time you saw her?"

Rogers rubbed his hand over his face again and leaned his head against the back of the sofa. Finally, he said, "Look, Detective. I've been having one hell of a day, and this is the last thing I needed. You want to know about my mother? Shirley? I haven't seen or spoken to her in more than twenty years."

"Is that so?" Carlson said.

"Yeah. How the hell did you find me, anyway? She didn't leave me anything, did she?"

"Since you ask, no, she didn't. Why? Were you hoping for an inheritance?"

"You don't hope for anything from Shirley Rogers, Detective. That way, you won't be disappointed."

Carlson waited, but Rogers didn't add to his statement.

"Right. Well, your mother seems to have left everything to charity. But she listed you as next of kin in her will. Her lawyer gave me your name, and we tracked you down."

"Ok, then. We're even. She never gave me anything when she was alive, and now she's dead, still nothing. No problem. What do you want from me?"

"Somebody killed her, Mr. Rogers. I was hoping you might have some idea who."

"Nope. No idea. None. Most anybody who's ever known her might have done it. It was just a matter of time. I'm kind of surprised she lasted this long, if you want to know the truth. Somebody should've taken her out years ago."

Rogers looked at Carlson defiantly, as if expecting him to argue the point. Carlson had no intention of doing that. His expression gave nothing away, but as he watched, Rogers' thoughts chased themselves across his features, one after another. Carlson sat relaxed. If he was getting impatient, it didn't show.

Eventually, Rogers rose from his sofa and started pacing around the room. "I suppose you think that's terrible, don't you?" he began. He shook his head. "You didn't know her. She was about nothing but herself. Not my Dad, for sure. He killed himself when I was eleven, and she drove him to it. Flirting with anything in pants, out drinking and fooling around when she should have been home taking care of her family. She always had a man. There were lots of different men. When I got older, I started to realize she didn't actually like men much. She just enjoyed knowing she could reel them in. She liked the excitement, but after a while she'd get bored and kick them out. Then things would settle down a little, and she'd pretend to be a model mom. Until the next time. I left home just as soon as I could get away. I joined the Navy when I was seventeen and never looked back. I didn't need her then, and I for sure don't need her now. I hope you're not expecting me to pay for the funeral, are you?" he asked, glancing at Carlson suspiciously.

"Not necessary," Carlson told him. "According to the lawyer, that's all taken care of, pre-paid and everything."

"No kidding?" Rogers showed some interest for the first time. "Where'd she get the money?'"

"Did you think she was short of money?"

"She was always short of money when I knew her, Officer. Or so she told me, if I ever asked her for any. Somehow there always seemed to be enough for her, though. For her fancy clothes and her fancy hair-dos. For her partying all around town. Somehow she managed to get by, didn't she?"

"Did she have a job?"

"My mother? A job?" Rogers laughed, but he wasn't amused.

"She must have supported herself somehow. Where did her money come from?"

Rogers shrugged.

Carlson opened his briefcase and pulled out the old black-and-white photo. He handed it to Rogers without comment.

Rogers took it from him, glanced at it, and handed it back. "It's not mine," he said.

"No. It was your mother's. We found it in her house."

"Okay. So what?"

"You remember Sister Joseph?"

Rogers shook his head.

"She remembers you," Carlson told him. "She remembers your mother, too. In fact," Carlson said, pointing to the little girl at the end of the first row, "this is Sister Joseph. And this," he said, pointing out the little girl smiling out from front row center, "is your mother."

"Nineteen fifty-six, huh? Before my time."

This was getting to be hard work, Carlson reflected. He knew some of the story of what happened to the Rogers' family, but he'd been hoping Peter could fill in some of the blanks. Obviously, the scars from childhood had never healed.

"You and your mother both went to Our Lady of Cherubim School, though. And your mother cared enough about that to keep this picture. She also left her entire estate to the school. So obviously, it meant a lot to her. Why?"

"How should I know? It didn't mean much to me. I was glad to get out of there. Glad to be rid of those nuns, with their mealy-mouthed prayers and fake sympathy. When my father killed himself, they wouldn't even give him a Catholic funeral. They don't do that anymore, but at the time …." He broke off, and looked away.

"Your father killed himself because he went bankrupt, didn't he?"

"Who told you that?" Rogers demanded.

"Sister Joseph. As I mentioned, she remembers you very well. And your mother."

"Yeah, well, maybe she doesn't know as much as she thinks about that. Sure, he went bankrupt. But if he'd had a decent wife, somebody to support him when he was down, he never would have done it. He just couldn't see any other way out."

"He had a store, didn't he?"

"That's right. It was a children's clothing store, right in the neighborhood. I don't know what he could be thinking. It was just a little place. There was no way he could compete with the big department stores, Sears and Carson's and such. He had to pay top dollar for everything he stocked, but he couldn't charge top dollar. Not in Bridgeport, for God's sake! He put everything he had into that place. He worked there day and night. I probably never would have seen him at all, except I used to go over there after school, and on Saturdays. I'd help him out. Not that I could do much, but he let me wait on customers sometimes, or maybe wrap up a package or something."

"Did you mother help out, too?"

Peter shrugged. "I guess she did. Sometimes. If she didn't have anything better to do. Mostly, it was just me and Dad. And then, after he died, it was just me."

"Just you?"

"Just me, yeah. I had some crazy idea of running the store by myself, but I was only eleven years old. I remember, I ran over there when I heard what my dad had done. I was going to keep the place going. My mother followed me. She had to drag me out of there, kicking and screaming. She closed the place right after that. I guess she didn't have any choice. My dad had already declared bankruptcy, and the creditors were lined up to get what they could."

"What happened after that?"

Rogers looked at Carlson, eyebrows raised.

"I mean, who took care of you, after."

"I took care of myself. My mother showed up every once in a while, mainly to change clothes, I guess. Sometimes she brought a guy with her. Never the same one twice. Then she'd split again. I'd hear her come in sometimes, after I was in bed. She'd still be asleep when I left for school in the morning. When I came home in the afternoon, the apartment would be empty. After a while, I stopped caring if she was there or not. I don't know how, but I managed to finish school. Then I joined the Navy, and that was that."

"You stopped keeping in touch – when?"

"I heard from her every now and again. She'd call me sometimes, but mostly she left me alone. After a while, I stopped hearing from her. I put her out of my mind."

Carlson waited. Rogers poured himself another Scotch. He walked over to the window and stood looking out at the city. He didn't seem to remember that Carlson was still there.

Finally, Carlson asked, "So what did you think she's been living on all this time?"

Rogers turned around, slowly. "I didn't think about it. I told you, Detective. I didn't have anything to do with her. She wasn't part of my life."

"So then you'd be surprised to find out she owned a successful business, right?"

"A business?" Rogers asked suspiciously. "What kind of business?"

Carlson told him.

"What did Shirley know about business? How could she start up a business?"

Carlson shrugged. "I couldn't tell you how, but she did. It seems to have been going pretty well. A good location, right on Main Street."

"What Main Street? Where?"

"Deer Creek. It's west of the city. Do you know it?"

"I never leave the city, Detective. Well, not true, I guess. I travel some. But never to the 'burbs. I'm a city boy; I'm allergic to the 'burbs. So is Shirley. Or she was."

"Not any more" Carlson told him. "She was living in Deer Creek when she was killed, and she had a business there."

"I'll tell you something, Detective. If Shirley was running a business, there was something wrong with it. Guaranteed."

"Do you think so? What?"

"I have no idea, but take my word for it. If you start digging, you'll find something."

"Maybe so," Carlson agreed. "Anyway, your mother's lawyer is taking care of the funeral, wrapping up the business, selling the house, and such." He set his briefcase down on the coffee table, opened it, and handed Rogers a card. "Here's her contact info, in case you want to talk to her."

Rogers took the card and stuffed it in his pocket.

Carlson reached into the briefcase again, pulled out a stack of papers bound with a rubber band, and handed it to Rogers. ."We found these when we searched your mother's house."

Rogers glanced at the bundle in his hand, then looked again, more closely. The papers were his old report cards from grammar school.

"We found these, too." Carlson handed him the photos they'd found in the search, the ones of the little boy, a bit older in each successive picture.

When Carlson left, Peter Rogers was still sitting on the couch, the photos and report cards in his hands. He didn't look up when Carlson closed the door. But after a while, he took the business card Carlson had given him out of his pocket. He studied it for a few minutes. Then he picked up his cell and called Martha Ashton.

Chapter Eighteen

Carlson stared out the passenger-side window, ruminating about the results of that earlier meeting. According to the store assistant Rita Cutler, her boss talked with her son from time to time. She thought he might even have visited the store. So why the lies? More important, what, if anything, did that have to do with the murder? They were accumulating information about the victim, no question, but so far, nothing was adding up.

Melanie Jennings piloted the car the short distance from the center of Deer Creek to Martingale Manor. The two of them planned to re-interview the people who'd been at the clubhouse at the time of Rogers' murder, about thirty-five people. The department staff had made appointments with most of them, and the investigative team had divided up the names into manageable sections, assigning a detective and an officer to each section.

The label "active adult community" was pretty accurate. The residents didn't tend to be home a lot. In fact, a fair number of the thirty-five potential witnesses had already split for places as far away as Chile and Bulgaria. But there were enough remaining to guarantee a full day of interviews.

"Pretty here," Carlson noted, as they drove past wide swaths of undisturbed prairie, interspersed with copses, mostly bare now, the remaining leaves turned red and gold.

"I know, that's what I like about living here. It's close enough to Chicago to be able to take advantage of everything the city has to offer, and there's plenty going on in Deer Creek itself, but look at this," Jennings said, waving her hand in an arc. "Don't you love how they're letting a lot of the land go back to prairie? For a while there, it felt like we were going to be paving over every inch of earth."

Housing developments, having taken a breather during the financial crisis of 2008, were again sprouting up like crazy, and the outer edges of Deer Creek, previously home to soybean and corn fields, were now a-buzz with steam shovels and cranes and every kind of truck, delivering cement and pre-fab walls, floors, and roof trusses to the countryside. It indeed was beginning to feel like there wasn't going to be any stretch of unbuilt-upon land left.

Jennings flashed her badge at the attendant, who pressed a button, letting the gate rise. She parked in the clubhouse's lot, with the rest of the team coming in behind her. Marlene Benson met them with maps of the subdivision she'd copied for the police. Carlson distributed the maps to his team. They left their cars in the lot and each team took off in a different direction. None of the homes was more than a ten minute walk from the clubhouse.

"It's a good thing you're here now, Detective," Benson told Carlson. "Another couple of weeks, and they'd all have been off to Florida or Arizona or maybe Mexico. This place really empties out in winter."

"Must be nice," he replied. "I wouldn't mind getting away to the sun for a while. What do you do with yourself if nobody's here?"

"Well, it's not quite as bad as all that. There are still plenty left. It's just that I think a lot of people moved here just in order to feel safe leaving their houses for months at a time. They know there's limited access to this community."

"Yeah," Carlson agreed. "Except for the occasional murderer."

Bella stowed her supplies in her car after class, slammed the hatch shut, and started to get in the driver's seat when she noticed Debbie Wilson leaving the clubhouse, struggling to balance several bags, a wet canvas, and her purse. "Let me take some of this," Bella offered. "You live nearby, don't you?"

"Thanks, Bella. Yes, I'm just down the block here."

"Down the block" turned out to be two or three blocks from the clubhouse, a small, neat ranch house. They were both slightly out of the breath by the time they'd arrived at the front door.

"How did you think you were going to manage all this, Debbie?"

"I guess I didn't think about it. It's a nice day and I didn't want to drive such a short way, especially since Ken didn't come with me this morning. He wasn't feeling too well, so he decided to skip the water aerobics for once. But I forgot I was going to have to bring the wet canvas home, as well as all these other things. Anyway, we're here now. Come on in, I'll make some coffee."

The walls of the entry hall were lined with framed paintings. Debbie walked right past them on the way to the open kitchen at the other end of the house, but Bella took her time, studying each painting as if it were hung in a museum. Most of them were classical still-lifes, various arrangements of bowls, vases, fruits and flowers. They weren't bad. They weren't particularly inspiring, either. Bella was still examining them when Debbie returned with the coffee.

"Thanks," Bella said, taking the cup from her. "These paintings really brighten up the foyer, don't they? But I can definitely see a difference in the work you're doing lately. Look," she said, holding up the still-wet canvas. It was just another little still-life, but the brush strokes were looser, fresher – not so tight. "This one is so painterly. You've really got some nice texture here."

"Well, I've been trying to follow your advice, Bella. I still have a long way to go, though."

But Debbie looked pleased. She led the way into the sun room beyond the kitchen, where there was a comfy-looking sofa and a couple of chairs. Ken was already there, sipping some coffee and reading a newspaper.

"I hope you're feeling better," Bella said, taking a seat on one of the chairs.

"I'm fine, thanks. I think I just needed to take it a little easier this morning. How was class?"

When Jennings knocked at the door of the Wilsons' a while later, Bella opened it. She wasn't surprised to see the two police officers. Debbie had mentioned that they were coming.

"Come on in," she said, moving away from the door. "The Wilsons are expecting you."

"What are you doing here?" Carlson asked, not sure he wanted an answer. This was the second murder in Deer Creek this year, and the second time Bella Sarver had something to do with it. Cause and effect?

"Just leaving," Bella said. "Debbie needed some help with her supplies, so I walked back with her."

"Did you? Find out anything interesting?"

"Why, Detective," Bella smiled. "I was just trying to be helpful."

"Watch your step, Ms. Sarver. One of these people is probably a murderer."

"Do you have any suspects yet? And what about the murder weapon? Was it a knife?"

"The ME thinks it must have been a scissors. Seen any suspicious scissors lately?"

"I see a lot of scissors around here, Detective. People use them in all sorts of ways. There are the quilters, and the painters, and the kitchen, of course. Plenty of sharp things in the kitchen."

"Too many suspects, in other words. Like I said, watch yourself."

"Everyone is so nice, though. I don't think I've ever been in such a friendly community. Everybody always smiles and says hello when they see you."

"And yet …."

"Well, as you know, people don't change their spots, do they? They just get older and more wrinkled."

"If you know something, I'd appreciate it if you'd share it with me, Ms. Sarver."

"Not really. It's just …. I have a feeling there's some history here. Goes back quite a while, I think."

"What kind of history?"

"I don't really know," Bella admitted. "It's just a feeling I'm getting. It might be nothing. It might have to do with some past relationship."

"Not real helpful, Ms. Sarver," Carlson told her. "Can't you be more specific?"

Bella shook her head. "I'm sorry. It's probably nothing."

"Hmmm. All right. Just take care, will you?"

Bella walked back to her car, paying no attention to her surroundings. She was thinking about scissors. They weren't anything she'd given much thought to, before.

Ken Wilson rose painfully from his chair when the police officers entered the house and led them slowly down the hall to the living room, leaning heavily on his cane. Light poured into the house from the large north-facing windows taking up almost the entire back wall. The house was built on an open plan, with only the two bedrooms, one at each end, closed off. It was the same model as Shirley Rogers', but it couldn't have looked more different.

There was nothing generic about the Wilson's house. It seemed clean enough, but there were books and magazines scattered everywhere. The walls were covered with all sorts of paintings and family photos, and collections of china and glassware were displayed in several cabinets. An open shelving unit held an array of music boxes, some enameled, some with inlaid wood patterns. Several had little ballerinas dancing on their tops. The living room held an arrangement of over-stuffed couches and chairs, and the sun room at the back was similarly furnished, and filled with baskets and pots of houseplants. No decorator had designed this house.

Ken lowered himself carefully into one of the overstuffed arm chairs and indicated the couch under the facing windows for the visitors.

"My wife will be out in a minute, officers. She's just cleaning up after her painting class. Would you like some coffee?"

"Is it ready?" Jennings asked, but then noticed the full pot on the kitchen counter, along with several mugs. "I'll get it." She'd seen how difficult it was for Wilson to maneuver his bent body into the chair.

Bella Sarver had given Carlson his opening. He waited until Jennings had supplied them all with coffee, then said, "I understand you and your wife were originally from Chicago."

"We were," Wilson agreed. "Bridgeport, in fact."

"So how did you happen to come out to Deer Creek?"

"Oh, we've been here for ages. We raised our kids here, you know. Bridgeport was a long time ago."

"Why bring it up now, Detective?" Debbie Wilson asked. She'd come into the room from what must be a bedroom, and taken a seat beside her husband.

Instead of answering, Carlson asked, "Did you ever hear of Our Lady of Cherubim parochial school?"

The Wilsons smiled at each other. Ken patted his wife's hand. "That's where we met," he said.

"Really? So you two have known each other since ....?"

"Since forever, yeah. But why are you asking about Cherubim?"

Carlson pulled a sheet of paper out of a folder he'd brought with him and handed it to the Wilsons. On the paper was a copy of an old black-and-white photo: *Our Lady of Cherubim, 4th Grade, 1956.*

"Does this ring any bells?"

Debbie and Ken looked at the photo. Ken's eyes lit up as he spotted the little girl in the second row on the left. Even in black-and-white, you could see her freckles. She was trying to look solemn and serious for the photo, but a little smile teased the corners of her mouth. Behind her and to the right, a little boy stood frowning at the camera, his hair slicked down except for one unruly hank standing on end. Grinning, Ken handed the photo back to Carlson, pointing out the two children with a forefinger. "That's us," he said. "Here and here. Boy, that really was a long time ago, wasn't it? Where on earth did you find it?"

"This, or I should say, the original of this picture, was standing on Shirley Rogers' dresser. We found it there yesterday when we searched her house. Is one of these girls her?"

"Why in the world would she have kept that photo all these years?" Debbie wanted to know. "That's crazy."

"But you knew Shirley Rogers, right?"

"Shirley McCarthy."

"What?"

"Shirley McCarthy. That was her name, Detective," Debbie said. "Here she is. In the front row. Of course." Debbie pointed out a little girl with short braids and a gap-toothed grin.

"So you did know her?"

"Yes, obviously. Why?"

"Did you know she lived here in Martingale Manor?"

The Wilsons glanced at each other, but Ken was the one who answered. "Not until we saw her the other day at the karaoke party. I think we both recognized her then."

"She didn't look much like this little girl here, did she?"

Ken shook his head. "It wasn't her looks, so much. She'd changed quite a bit since the last time we saw her, back in high school."

"She got old," Debbie said bluntly.

Ken smiled at his wife. "Yeah. You and I look exactly the same as we did then, of course. No, it wasn't her looks. It was more something about the way she stood, or the way she was singing. I can't really put my finger on it, but it sure brought back memories."

Carlson raised an eyebrow, but nothing more seemed to be forthcoming.

Jennings wondered if Carlson was going to push it. He showed no signs of impatience, but finally Jennings couldn't stop herself. Patience seemed to her an over-rated virtue. She said, "Funny how you lose touch with people isn't it? I'm from Bridgeport myself, but I haven't seen any of my old classmates in years."

"Really? Where did you go to school?"

"I went to Our Lady of Cherubim, both grammar school and high school."

Carlson coughed and choked on his coffee, splattering some on the front of his shirt.

"Are you okay, Detective?" Debbie asked. She handed him a napkin to mop at the stains. She was glad he'd managed not to spill any coffee on the couch.

"Fine, fine," he muttered. "Went down the wrong way."

"No kidding," Ken said to Jennings, oblivious to Carlson's difficulty. "Neither of us went to the high school, but we were at Cherubim for the first eight years. But you're a lot younger than us. You couldn't have even been born when we graduated."

"No, I'm sure it was different when you were there," Jennings said. "The neighborhood's changed a lot, even since I was a kid. It's still really diverse, but not so many Irish as there were then."

"True. There were plenty of Irish in those days. Most of them went to parochial school. We both did, too, as I said, for grammar school, but high school was more expensive, and our parents couldn't afford it then. So we went to public school."

"Which one?" Jennings was genuinely curious. Nothing like revisiting old history.

"Wolfe. Do you know it?"

"Sure. Some of my friends went there. My parents made sure that my brother and I got a Catholic education through high school, but the fees were high and lots of my friends' parents weren't able to manage it. It was hard for my parents, too, but they wanted to make the effort. I know Wolfe, though. It's still there. Still a pretty good school, too, I think."

Debbie was about to comment, but Carlson interrupted. "Sorry to butt in on your reminiscing, but how well did you know Shirley Rogers?"

Debbie looked up at him, reminded of the purpose of this visit. "She was just one of our classmates, you know. She was never really a friend."

Ken nodded confirmation.

"So you wouldn't have any theory as to why somebody killed her?"

"No. Like we said, Detective, we hadn't seen her in decades. I have no idea at all what she's been up to for most of her life."

"I see. What was she like then?" Carlson persevered.

"She was just a girl," Debbie shrugged.

"She was pretty," Ken put in, and then looked guilty for having mentioned it.

"Was she?" Carlson asked, after a beat.

Debbie tightened her lips, but had nothing more to say.

"She wasn't very pretty when I saw her, of course. Her throat was torn open."

Jennings looked at her boss in surprise. It wasn't like him to be crude.

Ken blanched, but he answered quietly, "She was a pretty girl when I knew her. Even in grammar school, there was something special about her."

Debbie laughed shortly. "Shirley was special, all right. She was a little flirt. She had all the boys running after her, always giving them the 'come on,' and she loved it. She especially enjoyed going after other girls' boyfriends. That really gave her a kick."

Ken bit his lip, but he said nothing more.

Carlson had known girls like that back in school. The kind of girl who could leave a guy all hot and bothered just by a little twist of their hips. It worked on boys. It worked on grown men, too, even old ones. Carlson wondered if Shirley Rogers had still had the knack.

Jennings smiled. "I guess you didn't care much for her, Mrs. Wilson."

Debbie shrugged. "It was all a long, long time ago. I hadn't thought about Shirley in years."

"Okay. But what did you think when you saw her the other day at that party?"

"We were surprised, naturally," Ken said. "What else?"

"Did you speak with her? Reminisce about old times?"

"No. We told you, Detective. We'd never been friends, only classmates. Anyway, she left the party right after she finished singing. She didn't stick around to talk."

"And then the next thing you knew, she'd been murdered in the clubhouse."

It was a statement, not a question. Nevertheless, Carlson hoped for a response, but he didn't get one.

"Yes," Debbie said, finally. "I think that's all we can tell you, Detective. If you're through...? I have an appointment to get ready for."

Carlson wasn't satisfied. But any more questions might have seemed like harassment. After a long minute, he nodded to Jennings, rose, and left the house.

"So, Officer Jennings, you didn't think to share that little bit of information with me earlier?"

"I didn't think it mattered, Detective. It may have been the same building, but it certainly wasn't the same school, you know. Those people are probably forty years older than me. I doubt if anything is the same, or was when I was a kid. But you're right. I could have mentioned it, anyway."

"Hmmph."

"I think you ... surprised...," Jennings said, searching for the right word, "Mr. Wilson when you told him the victim's throat had been torn open." She glanced curiously at Carlson as she unlocked the car door. "He didn't expect to hear it that way. Neither did I, to be honest."

Carlson slid into the passenger seat and buckled his seatbelt. "Sometimes people need a little shaking up."

"I guess. Seems a little ..." she shook her head. "You know, Mrs. Wilson confirms Peter Rogers' account of his mother's personality. Do you think Shirley Rogers was still a big flirt? Could she have been involved with one of the men here, for instance?"

"I was thinking along those same lines, Melanie. Maybe she was up to her old tricks."

Chapter Nineteen

"How do you like teaching over at Martingale Manor?" Kasia asked. Bella and Kasia were both used to wielding paint brushes, but they were generally smaller than the four-inchers they were using now to apply paint to the walls of the new co-op. Kasia was up on a ladder, trimming the wall where it met the ceiling, while Bella worked on the bottom edge of the wall, along the baseboards. Her back was starting to ache as she struggled to find a comfortable position, a struggle she was sure she was losing. She wondered if she should ask Kasia to trade, although she wasn't too fond of ladders, either.

"I like it," Bella said, trying to ignore the pains creeping down her spine. "My students don't really pay a lot of attention to what I say, but they seem to be having a good time, which is all that really matters. I'm not expecting any of them to suddenly become expert painters, not in this time of their lives."

"True. My mom says there's so much going on over there, it's like living at summer camp, all year round."

"Your mom? Oh, that's right, I met you there that day."

"Yes. She and my dad moved in about two years ago, and they love it. My kids love it, too, especially the kid's pool. I took them over there a lot during the summer and it was great. And now that it's getting cold out, I'm glad of the chance to swim in their indoor pool."

"Don't you have to be a resident to use the pool?"

"You can be a guest, and my mom got an extra pass for me, so I can get in even without her. I think you're not supposed to do that, but...." Kasia shrugged. "Oh, damn," she said suddenly.

"What's the matter?"

Kasia pulled a rag out of her back pocket and began dabbing at the ceiling with it. "I got some paint on the ceiling just now. I must not have taped off the edge well enough."

She got down from her ladder and began rummaging through the duffel bag she'd brought with her. "I think I have some more tape in here."

She tossed aside a swim suit, a towel, a paperback book, a scissors, a make-up bag and a few more items before emerging with the roll of blue tape she'd supplied herself with earlier. "I'm going to have to clear out this bag one of these days. Stuff goes in but doesn't ever seem to come out again."

Bella laughed. She stood up from the wall and stretched. All this crouching and creeping along the floor was beginning to take a toll on her body. She hated to admit defeat, though. So what if Kasia was thirty years younger? If Kasia could climb up and down the ladder, she could just keep going, too. She loaded her brush once again with the thick vanilla-spice ice-cream color paint and bent down to apply it to the next section, trying to take satisfaction in how smoothly it covered the wallboard.

"I like this color, don't you, Kasia? It will be just the right background for hanging the paintings. Speaking of which, have you guys come up with a name for this place yet?"

"No, didn't Mollie tell you? We're having a contest. All the members of the Art League are invited to submit names, and then the committee will vote on them. The winner gets a free year's membership in the co-op. Wasn't that a brilliant idea?"

"Absolutely," Bella agreed. "I'll have to try to think of something. It should be catchy and upbeat. I'll get Art to brainstorm with me. By the way, I love your notecards," she added. "Are you going to be putting them in the co-op?"

"What notecards?"

"The ones you've made from photos of your paintings," Bella replied. "I saw them in *Ruffles and Flourishes* a while ago and I just love how you took some of your paintings and created notecards from them. You must have seen them when you dropped in there, didn't you?"

Kasia looked at her sharply. "Who told you I dropped in to that store?"

"Didn't you mention it?"

Kasia shook her head.

"Oh, sorry. I thought you did. Maybe Rita told me, when I was in there recently. But anyway, how are they selling? Or anyway, how were they selling? It's a shame the police had to close the store. I hope whoever the new owner is will be able to get in there soon."

"Bella, I have no idea what you're talking about. I never made any notecards. It's not a bad idea, but I never thought of it. I just do my paintings. I did put some photos of them on Fine Art USA for them to make giclees on demand, but that's not going anywhere. There's so much competition, it's a wonder anybody ever sells anything on that website."

"Really? But I was sure I saw your .... Well, never mind. I must be mistaken." Bella frowned. She'd been so sure.

"Looks good, ladies," Ben Goldberg said, breaking into Bella's concentration. He and Rahj Patel had been painting in the back room, but Ben decided it was time for a little break and came out to survey the front.

Kasia and Bella had nearly finished the trim work. The rolling would go much faster. "Teamwork," Ben said, satisfied. "We'll get this job done in no time."

The store front was beginning to look like a place that might eventually host an art gallery. Rahj and Ben had created a design involving moveable walls and counters, the idea being to make the gallery flexible enough to accommodate all sorts of different exhibits. To avoid the problem of ruining the walls with multiple nails, they'd decided to invest in a sleeve-and-rod hanging system. It was expensive, but it offered a lot of flexibility, which was what was called for to handle frequently changing displays of wall-hung art. They'd ripped out the old tiles from the floor, intending to replace them with laminate strips after the walls were painted. It would look like wood, but at a fraction of the cost.

"You know, I think we really might be able to open by Christmas, the rate we're moving along here," Bella said. "It's a shame we can't do it sooner, but even if we can make it by the first of December, that will still be in time for people to find some last-minute gift items here."

"I hope so," Ben said. "I'm a little worried about having a conflict of interest, though. I mean, what about the Art League's holiday show? How are we going to deal with that?"

"We should discuss it at the next meeting, Ben. But I'm thinking that with this co-op we'll be establishing a sort of critical mass that's going to bring more customers to both places. Sort of an arts district, instead of just one little gallery slash classroom slash meeting place and so forth."

"You could be right, Bella. I hope the others will see it like that, though, instead of just competition."

"That's what I was trying to explain to Shirley Rogers before. She was worried about the competition, but I argued that competition is actually good for business. I wonder what's going to happen to her business now, though. I wonder if anyone will be able to take it over. I'd hate to see it close down."

"I know she didn't have any partners. What about heirs? Can you bequeath a business, though? I mean, doesn't it depend on who signs the lease and so on?"

Bella shrugged. "I have no idea, Ben. I guess we'll find out soon enough."

Chapter Twenty

"It's beautiful, Mom. He must really love you."

Mindy Lewis held her mother's left hand and admired the emerald and diamond ring that graced the third finger. She'd inherited her mom's red hair, but otherwise didn't resemble her in the least. She was inches taller, a legacy from her father, as was her surname. She'd been twenty-six when he ran out on Bella, taking half the furniture in the house with him. Mindy was already an attorney by then, having passed the bar just a year earlier.

"He does," Bella agreed. "He's a good man."

"But?"

Bella looked at her ring. She wasn't as close to her daughter as she would have wished. Sometimes weeks went by when terse texts were their only form of communication. Mindy was immersed in her work as a patent attorney and Bella had immersed herself in art after retirement. Their lives followed different paths.

Bella had taken the train into the city in order to meet Mindy for a long-overdue lunch date, wanting – and needing - to forget about painting and murders and myriad other obligations for a while. It had been over a week since Shirley Rogers had been killed and as far as Bella knew, the police were no closer to making an arrest than they had been that day. But she didn't want to think about that now. She and her daughter were enjoying coffee and cannoli after pasta and salad, at a lovely Italian place Mindy had found on the riverfront. Chicago can be chilly in Fall but today was an exception, and they were taking advantage of the unexpected warmth to enjoy dining al fresco while they watched the river traffic floating past.

"But nothing," Bella replied. "I love him, too. I can't believe how lucky I am to have found him." She drank some coffee.

"But?" Mindy questioned again.

"It's just ... he wants to get married."

"Obviously."

"And ... I do love him, you know. But after your father, I'm just not sure I'm ready to take that step again."

"Why can't you just live together for a while? In fact, that's what you *are* doing, isn't it? What's the hurry about a wedding?"

"I know, but it's Art. He likes to have things settled, all the 't's crossed and the 'i's dotted. He wants to put his Evanston house up for sale. It's just sitting there empty, with all his things still in it. As you said, he's living with me now, but feels like it's my house and he's ... he's not sure what he is. It's uncomfortable for him. And then there's his daughter, Amy. She'd like to see him settled, too. He's so good for me. We're so good together. But I just don't know."

"Well, clearly, you need to be sure. It's no good getting married if you're going to be miserable about it. Can't you just tell Art you need to put things on hold while you think it all through? You're a brave lady, Mom. Don't let him push you into something you're not ready for."

"How will I know when I'm ready?"

Mindy squeezed Bella's hand. She wasn't used to feeling older and wiser than her mother. The sudden role reversal didn't sit well with her. Suddenly, she gestured to the waiter for the bill. She looked at the total only long enough to calculate a tip, added it to the credit card slip, and signed it.

"Come on, Mom, let's walk. It's a beautiful day."

The sun was shining and the Magnificent Mile, North Michigan Avenue, was crowded, hundreds of people rushing past the shops, taking in the sights. There was so much energy; Bella could almost feel the vibrations. They crossed the bridge over the Chicago River, heading north, matching their strides to the rhythm of the city.

Bella had always been a great walker, and she'd made a habit of walking with the kids even while she still had to push them in a stroller. There was something about moving along, moving forward, that made it easier to talk, especially when there was something really important to say. Mindy and Joel learned early that 'let's go for a walk' meant 'let's talk.'

"So – how did you know you were ready to marry Dad?"

Bella grimaced. "How did I know? Oh, honey – things were so different then. If you got to a certain age, like twenty or twenty-two or so, it was time to get married. It's what everybody expected you to do. So if you met somebody, and there was a spark, you didn't know it was only sex. You thought it had to be true love."

"What about the sexual revolution? Didn't that change things for people?"

Bella grinned ruefully. "I guess it did, over time. Things are really different now than they were when I was young. But it didn't happen right away, you know. And your father and I were still operating under the old rules."

"So you got married, just like that."

"Just like that," Bella agreed. "You didn't move in together, God forbid. My parents would have had a stroke. You got married. Sometimes, it worked out fine. Sometimes, not so much."

Mindy glanced at her mother, and then looked down at her shoes. Bella didn't understand how she managed to walk in them, but Mindy favored four inch heels most of the time. However, in concession to the fact that she knew she'd be walking a bit, she'd left the stilettos under her desk and changed into a colorful and sturdy pair of Reeboks. They were cute, but there's only so long you can look at the pair of shoes on your feet.

"I can't even imagine what that would be like," she said finally. "There's so much to see and do in the world, why would you want to tie yourself down to one man, a house, kids – all that? I mean, maybe someday, but ...."

Bella smiled. "Like I said, it was so different in those days. Most girls, and most boys, too, I think, couldn't wait to be grown-ups. And being grown-up meant marriage, family - the whole shebang. It's what you saw in the movies and magazines, and what you watched on TV. The sitcoms all showed the standard family, with Dad working at the office and Mom in the kitchen, and two or three cute kids getting into all sorts of predicaments, but nothing that couldn't be solved in half an hour. So that's what we thought was normal, and that's what we wanted. Things started to change about the time I came of age. Betty Friedan wrote *The Feminine Mystique*, and we started to question, and to want something else, something more. But it didn't happen overnight. I was so glad that you had more choices. I still am."

"Is that why you're having second thoughts about getting married again?"

It was Bella's turn to look at her shoes. "Of course," she argued, "it would be so different now. Art and I have both been married before. We know who we are, what's important, what's not. It might be really nice. In fact, it is nice," she emphasized, as if to convince herself. "I love having Art around. I love knowing I can count on him."

"But?"

"But nothing," she said firmly. "I'm just being silly." She turned to her daughter. "So – what's going on with you?"

Len Carlson reassembled his team at the station after they returned from the Martingale Manor interviews. They grabbed coffees and found seats at the big conference table. It had been a long day and Carlson knew he should let them go home, but he wanted to get their impressions while they were still fresh.

Most of the residents of Martingale Manor who had been present in the Clubhouse at the time Shirley Rogers had been killed had been re-visited and re-interviewed. When the police officers compiled and compared their notes, they found the story that each resident told remarkable only for their consistency with their original version and their lack of illumination of the situation. Yes, they were present, and no, they didn't see anything unusual.

"One thing I found out," Detective Ron Pepper began, "is that hardly anybody admits to having recognized Shirley Rogers, and yet it turns out that quite a few of the people here grew up in the same neighborhood, in Bridgeport. Now I know you and I both grew up in small towns, not cities, Len, but Chicago is a city of neighborhoods, and each one is like a small town, too. Everybody knows everybody else, or they know their brother or their uncle or whatever. So if they're all the same age group, and they all grew up in the same neighborhood, they had to have run into each other, either at school or at church or just hanging out at the same school playground. So somebody knew Shirley Rogers."

"We know at least a couple of people did. Apparently, Lily Turner and the Wilsons both recognized her at karaoke night. Do you think they'd seen her before that? But why wouldn't they just say so?" Carlson asked. "Likewise for anybody else who recognized her. Do you think they're all covering up for something?"

"Who knows?" Melanie Jennings said. "Debbie Wilson thought Shirley was quite a hot little number in high school. And she didn't like her. Maybe there were others with the same opinion." She held up a finger, struck by an idea. "What if ..., no that's just too silly. It was all a lifetime ago."

"What?" Carlson demanded. "Come on, spit it out."

"Well, I just wondered, what if there's some history there. I mean, more than just observation. What if Debbie Wilson had a reason to hate her?"

"Sister Joseph seemed to think there are a few people who could have had a good reason," Pepper noted.

Jennings smiled. "I can't believe Sister Joseph is still at Cherubim! She must be 100 years old by now," Jennings exclaimed.

"Did you know her when you were there, too?"

"I sure did, Ron. She taught me art. She was already pretty old then."

He nodded. "Well, she's still going strong. I don't think she's 100 yet, but she's definitely past her use-by date. And there's nothing wrong with her mind. She remembered all the kids in the picture I showed her. She remembered the son, too, Peter Rogers. Not that that really gets us very far. I mean, how long ago was it? Must be close to fifty years by now. An awful lot of water under the bridge since then, as they say. So – fill us in on Cherubim, Melanie. What was it like?"

"Well," Jennings began, "Sister Joseph was there, as I said. She taught art. I remember she always liked to gossip. Whenever us girls were giggling about something or somebody, you could see her nearby, keeping her ears stretched. She didn't say a lot, at least to us kids, but she knew everything that went on at that school." Jennings smiled, remembering.

"And...?" Carlson prompted.

"And nothing. It was just school, you know. Nothing special. You have a good point about the neighborhood thing, though, Ron. When I was there, the district covered a wider area, but there were more schools when Shirley Rogers lived there. So most of the kids, if not all of them, were from the same relatively small area. But people change a lot in fifty or sixty years you know. And Shirley changed her name, too. So even if some of these people knew her then, I could certainly believe they didn't recognize her now. Actually, I'm pretty surprised that Debbie Wilson did. Do you remember kids from back in grammar school?"

"Sure, don't you? Maybe not all of them, but a lot still stick in my mind. I'm still friends with a couple of the guys. Of course, I remember how they looked then. They could have changed a little, since. It hasn't been fifty years for me, but long enough."

Lily Turner remained at her worktable, still piecing together her squares. The two officers who'd wanted to ask her questions had left a while ago, but they'd sure stirred up a bunch of memories.

"Do I remember Shirley Rogers? No, never met *her*, but I sure remember Shirley McCarthy. So what if it was fifty years? Some things you just don't forget."

Of course, that's not what Lily told the police officers. Not exactly. No, she'd answered them politely. "Yes, I knew Shirley a long time ago. No, I hadn't known she was living her at Martingale Manor until I saw her not long before she got herself killed. I have no idea what she was doing in the years in between."

After the police left, Lily poured herself a cup of coffee and brought it over to her workroom. "Fifty years," she said aloud, although the room was empty. "It was a lifetime ago, but I still remember."

Everything *mattered* so much in those days. What you wore and how you did your hair. Whether that all-important *He* liked you. Did you know the latest song? Could you dance the Mashed Potato? Why did everything matter so darned much? And yet it did. The pleated plaid skirts rolled up at the waist so they'd look shorter. The hair, teased and sprayed so it stood up inches above your scalp and flipped perfectly just above your shoulders. The abject mortification if the whole package wasn't just right.

Shirley McCarthy was always just right. She was perfect. Lily hated her. All she had to do was smile in that certain way and cock a hip, and the boys fell all over themselves to please her. When she came into a room or walked down a school hallway, she might as well have been the only girl there, as far as the boys were concerned. Lily saw it happen, more than once. It happened to her.

At least, it happened to her boyfriend. Shirley stole him out from under her, and then, once she hooked him, she let him go. He was devastated. He walked around with his eyes on the ground for weeks afterwards. But he never came back to Lily.

She shook her head, sorted through some squares, pinned four of them together experimentally into a larger one. She could follow a quilting pattern all right. She had books full of them. But Lily preferred the challenge of making up her own patterns, her own designs. She held the new square up to the light in order to see it better. Yellow flowers against a purple ground. Very pretty, she decided. It would do.

Art Halperin wasn't giving any thought at all to Shirley Rogers. He'd been wondering how best to advise the Northwestern student in physics he mentored, who was trying to make a decision about grad school. But the student canceled at the last minute, after Art had already driven all the way to Evanston. Might as well not waste the trip. There was a bookstore he liked over on Sherman Avenue, and he walked there from the parking lot.

Evanston is a very pretty old town, home to Northwestern University, north of Chicago near the shores of Lake Michigan. Art had lived there with his wife for most of their long marriage, and he still owned the house they shared. He'd have to sell it, now that Bella Sarver had finally agreed to set a date and they were planning to live in her townhouse in Deer Creek. It was going to be hard to let the house go. It was so full of memories, mostly good, a few, painful.

The painful part had come in the last couple of years, when Sherry was fighting her losing battle with breast cancer. For a while, they thought they'd had it beat, but then it came back. It spread everywhere, and finally, the doctors admitted there wasn't anything else to be done except try to make Sherry comfortable. Comfortable! Right! Like that was really possible.

Art didn't think Sherry would mind that he was going to marry Bella. She hadn't been the jealous type. She wouldn't begrudge him happiness now. Even so, he felt a little bit guilty, as if he was cheating on her, something he'd never even thought of in all the years they were together. But Sherry wouldn't have wanted him to spend the rest of his life by himself. He knew that.

Bella was so different from Sherry. She was a lot more independent-minded, for one thing. It was what had first attracted Art to her, on that painting trip to Tuscany. Well, the spiky red hair and the turquoise sneakers she favored also had something to do with it, but no -.... It was a lot more than that. He just hoped he could make her as happy as she made him.

All six members of the Co-op Committee were present when Rahj Patel called the meeting to order. "We're right on schedule," Rahj began. "The place is cleaned up, the walls are painted, and the hanging system's on order. Now we just need to recruit members, set up a work schedule, and do some publicity. I think we're definitely on track to open for Christmas. Great job, everybody."

"We're doing fine about getting members to exhibit," Kasia said. "In fact, we're going to have to limit how many pieces each member can hang, because so many want to be a part of this." Kasia Novik, in charge of Education, had been writing articles for the Deer Creek Art League bulletin, plus posting information on the League's Facebook page. As a result, she'd been fielding tons of phone calls from members wanting to sign up.

"Have we created a form for them to fill out?" Mollie Schaeffer wanted to know. "Because I'm going to have to know who they all are and when to schedule them. Have we definitely decided on the hours yet?"

"I think we're agreed on that," Rahj said, looking around the table. "To fit in with the other businesses on the street, we'll plan to be open six days a week, Tuesday through Sunday. We'll do noon to eight Tuesday, Wednesday, Thursday and Friday, and ten to six on the week-end. So," he continued, scribbling quickly on a pad, "if we have four hour shifts each day, with two people on each shift, we're going to need four people every day during the week, plus four each on Saturdays and Sundays. So that means we need twenty-four people to commit to working four hours a week. Can we do that?"

"Absolutely," Ben Goldberg said. "Right, Kasia? We have at least forty people who said they'd be interested."

"Yes, except – lots of them have day jobs. We're going to need to depend on a lot of retired people for the week-day staffing."

"True," Ben agreed, "Will people be willing to give up that much time? Remember, they're not being paid for this."

"You guys figure it out, okay?" Rahj interrupted. "And they are being paid, sort of. I mean, if they don't agree to take their shifts, the co-op won't carry their work."

"So it all depends on sales, doesn't it, guys?" Bella Sarver put in. "If we're successful, that'll be an incentive for the members to put in the time. We'll just have to try it and see what happens, right?"

"Yes, you're right, Bella," Kasia said. "I've been thinking about this a lot, and one of the things you said struck a chord with me. You said you liked the notecards I had at *Ruffles and Flourishes*. Well, I never had any notecards, there or anywhere else. But it's a good idea, isn't it? It's a lot easier to sell a box of notecards for a few dollars than an original painting for hundreds, or even thousands. So we should encourage our members to supply a good mix of work, and include smaller, more saleable items in addition to their main pieces."

"Good idea," Mollie said. "Although I could have sworn that Shirley Rogers was carrying notecards with prints of some of your paintings on them. I saw them myself. Your work is so distinctive. It's hard to believe somebody else could be working the same way, with your beautifully lit still-life paintings. Your colors just glow, you know."

"Thank you, Mollie. But, yes, of course I'm sure. I never printed any cards from my work."

"Unless," Mollie began.

"Unless what?"

"Remember what you and I found before, Bella? Those giclees?"

"Well, but notecards aren't giclees."

"No, but they could be reproduced by a similar process, couldn't they? Kasia, do you have a website? With images of your work on it?"

"Well, yes, of course I do."

Bella nodded, satisfied. "Another piece of the puzzle filled in, then."

"What do you mean?" Kasia said. And then, "Are you saying Shirley Rogers downloaded photos from my website and had notecards made from them?"

185

"Exactly, Kasia. Wow, that was really taking a chance, wasn't it? What if you'd gone in the store and seen them yourself?"

"Except I never did."

Fabio Gompers listened to this discussion with interest. Another piece of the puzzle, indeed. He kept his thoughts to himself.

Chapter Twenty-One

"So according to her son," Carlson told Ron Pepper next day, "his mother was a real party girl. He blames her for his father's suicide. He says he pretty much raised himself after that."

"You believe him, that he hasn't seen her for years?"

Carlson shrugged. "Her assistant, Rita Cutler, seems to think they'd been in touch. She thinks she might even have seen him once, in the store, as she was leaving for the day. She strikes me as a pretty reliable person. I have no reason not to believe her. Why would Peter Rogers lie about that? What's he hiding?"

"What did he say when you pointed out the lie?"

"I didn't bother," Carlson said. "I couldn't prove it, either way. Not yet. But obviously, the childhood wounds are still raw. I couldn't get much out of him on specifics, but it sounds like she left him alone a lot while she was out dancing and drinking and who knows what else."

"She was probably hurting, too. A woman doesn't behave like that without a reason," Melanie Jennings put in.

"Don't tell me you're feeling sorry for her," Pepper said.

"Well, actually, I am," Jennings said, pushing a wayward strand of dark hair behind her ear. "I mean, if even her own son had a pretty poor opinion of her, that's pretty sad, don't you think? Look – the poor woman has been murdered, and I haven't heard one person express any grief over it. She doesn't seem to have had a single person who cared about her."

Carlson sat back in his chair and listened. Melanie Jennings was shaping up to be a good cop. She did what she was told. She got along with her co-workers. She never fussed about an assignment. Carlson realized he'd been taking her for granted, but now he considered she was becoming a valuable member of the team. He thought some of that must be down to him. Suddenly, he felt old.

Pepper seemed surprised, too. Surprised, and a little ashamed of himself. He'd been so focused on the *hows* and *what if's* that he hadn't given much thought to the victim as a human being, either. "I see what you're saying, Melanie. She couldn't have been very happy."

Jennings nodded. "From what we know of her, she was pretty attractive and she saw that as her ticket to good times. She was used to men panting after her. But really, she must have had awfully low self-esteem, too, to use herself that way. I wonder what her childhood was like. I'll bet it wasn't pretty."

"You think she might have been abused or something as a child?" Carlson was thinking along the same lines, but it was Pepper who asked the question.

"It's possible, Ron. Who knows? That could explain a lot, couldn't it?"

"Maybe," Pepper conceded. "But that was a long time ago, wasn't it? She might have been attractive when she was young, but not anymore. You saw her body. Ignore for a minute the fact that her throat was cut. Did she look sexy to you?"

"Not really, but then I'm not a seventy-five year old guy, am I? Maybe it's all a matter of perspective. Maybe it's not about what's actually reflected in the mirror as much as what a person thinks she sees when she looks into one."

"Could be" Carlson agreed. "But is this getting us anywhere? What does it have to do with her being murdered? This was a spur of the moment thing. Somebody got really mad, an opportunity presented it itself, and whammo. Nobody planned it. Maybe there wasn't even a really good reason. We need evidence, not speculation. I wish we could find the murder weapon. I don't see how it could have disappeared. We searched the whole club house, didn't we?"

"Sure, but whoever did it could have left before we got there, taking the weapon with them. I think our best bet is to look for motive. Right now, we're working blind," Pepper said. "The most likely suspect would have been the son. It sounds like he could have had a motive."

"Yeah, maybe, but if he'd wanted to kill her, why wait all these years? He claims he didn't know anything about his mother's life these days, not even where she was living. But even if he did, why now? Did circumstances change somehow? And besides, how would he have just happened to be in the clubhouse's locker room when she was taking a shower? No, it's like I said before. It was an impulse."

"Pity. Did the house search come up with anything we can use?"

Carlson shrugged. "Maybe. We'll have to see. So far, it's just what you'd expect. The guys found some papers in a fire-proof box – insurance policies, the deed to the house, a car title. The photos and report cards she'd kept from when her son was small."

"So she wasn't completely heartless, then?" Jennings asked. "I mean, why would she have kept those things if they didn't mean anything to her? What did Rogers say when you showed them to him?"

"He didn't say anything. I left him to think about it."

"What about the victim's laptop? Anything on that?" Pepper asked.

"Which one? There were two, remember? One in the store, in that basement office, and one in her house."

"Right. I wonder why she had two."

"I don't know. Maybe one for business and one for personal stuff?" Carlson speculated. "We've got that CPA, Leo Schaeffer, working on it. The tech turned the computer over to him after she figured out the passwords and stuff, so hopefully, he'll be able to make some sense of what went on. There were a lot of business records on the laptop we found in the store, but there didn't seem to be anything personal on it. Between him and the lawyer, maybe they can come up with something. The son seems to think there must have been something shady going on with the business."

"What does he mean, 'shady'?"

"He didn't specify, Ron. He just said that if Shirley Rogers was involved, there was something wrong with it. Guaranteed. But he doesn't think much of his mother, so who knows?"

"Nice," Jennings commented.

"Yeah."

Peter Rogers stared out his window for ages after Carlson left him. Far below, the lights of cars moving along Lake Shore Drive formed an unbroken chain, the lake dark and silent beyond them. It seemed a long way from Bridgeport.

Rogers generally tried not to think about his mother. Not his father, either. He'd trusted his father, at least. Frank Rogers was always there to make sure he had decent meals every day. He took him to Sox games sometimes, in the summer. In a lot of ways, he made up for the fact that Shirley had checked out. Until one day, Frank let him down, too.

Rogers remembered his father's funeral. Not many people were there, mainly the parish regulars. His parents didn't have a lot of friends. At least, his father didn't. His mother had all too many friends, the wrong kind, but Peter didn't know that then. He knew his mother was gone a lot, but he never knew where she was. His father never said, and somehow, Peter knew better than to ask. Anyway, as long as his dad was with him, everything was fine.

The priest intoned the ancient words of the funeral mass but Peter let them wash over him, unheard. He wondered who would take care of him, now that his father was gone. He knew he wasn't going to be able to depend on his mother. He'd never depended on her. And now she was gone.

She hadn't even left him anything in her will. What was the story with those old photos, and the report cards? Probably just didn't get around to throwing them away. She owed him. She owed him big. And what did the cop say? There was a business? There was a house?

The phone rang for a long time and Rogers thought he was going to have to leave a message, but finally Martha Ashton picked up. She sounded as if she'd been asleep, but she woke up soon enough when he told her who he was.

Chapter Twenty-Two

Rosalie Klein looked like nobody's idea of a rabbi, but she had been ordained at Hebrew Union College-Jewish Institute of Religion in Cincinnati along with eighteen other women and thirteen men. Ever since Rabbi Sally Preisand was ordained in 1972, many other women had followed her trailblazing footsteps into the rabbinate. By the time Rosalie Klein came along, her right to study for and become ordained was taken for granted, at least by the Reform and Conservative movements. Even the Orthodox establishment accepted that women could be effective leaders in their communities, if not exactly full-fledged rabbis. The fact that she had no long white beard was a non-issue.

Rabbi Klein was younger than any of Art's and Bella's daughters, and looked younger yet, with her curly black hair in a bouncy pony-tail and her slim body clad in jeans and a sweatshirt that read HUC-JIR across the front. But the members of the Deer Creek Jewish Congregation considered themselves blessed to have found her. Her enthusiasm rubbed off on everyone, especially the kids she loved to lead in songs and games. She brought a new exuberance to the regular Friday night and Saturday morning Sabbath services.

"How's the art world coming along?" she asked Bella, when she and Art showed up at her study.

"Well, you've heard about the co-op, right?"

Rosalie, more comfortable with being called Rosie by her friends, nodded. She'd joined the Deer Creek Art League almost as soon as she'd arrived in Deer Creek. Before she began her rabbinical studies, she'd planned to be a high school art teacher. She was still a serious painter, and had been happy to find an arts community as well as a synagogue community to welcome her.

"Okay, so it's coming along. We're going to need members to exhibit there, as well as to work there. Any chance you'd be interested?"

"I'd definitely be interested," Rosalie said, "but I'm not sure I'd be able to commit to the time. Or especially, to the schedule. You know I'm on call twenty-four/seven. I've been working on my latest series for ages, but it's hard finding the time to finish it."

"A series? That's exciting, Rosie. What is it?"

The Rabbi waved her had dismissively. "Oh, it's just an idea I had. It's a group of collages, each piece dealing with the life of the women in the Exodus story. You know, the midwives, Moses' mother, Yocheved; his sister, Miriam; the Pharaoh's sister."

"I'd love to see it. How many have you done so far?"

"Oh, a few. But tell me about the gallery. It's such a terrific idea – to have our own gallery. It's so hard to try to do all the marketing yourself, and if you're not already well established, the good galleries don't want to hear from you."

"I know. That's why we thought that if we run our own place, we artists might have a better chance to make some sales. Anyway, it's worth a try."

"Absolutely. But – that's not why you're here, is it? You two are looking at Spring?"

Art nodded. He and Bella seated themselves on the couch while the Rabbi flopped into an armchair and sat cross-legged, facing them. She pulled out her phone, scrolled through her calendar, and frowned. "Spring is difficult," she told them. "Between the holidays of Purim, Passover, and Lag B'Omer, there aren't many available dates. How about June? Oh, wait, there's Shavuot."

Rabbi Klein punched in a query. "No, it's okay. Shavuot comes in May this year. So June, then. You can have the entire month of June to choose from."

The blinds over the window behind the Rabbi's chair were fully raised, allowing the day to come in. The sky was bright blue and very clear. *Sunny days like this are often the coldest in winter*, Bella thought, irrelevantly. She remembered what Mindy had asked her. *Is Art pushing me into something I'm not ready for? When will you be ready? Will you ever be ready? For crying out loud, you're old enough to know what you want, aren't you? What are you so afraid of?*

Bella's heart was pounding. She was surprised that neither Art nor Rabbi Klein seemed to hear it. Bella concentrated on trying to breathe. Inhale, hold it, exhale. Slowly. Again. Rosalie Klein was looking at her; she could feel it. *Come on, pull yourself together*, she told herself.

Art turned towards Bella, his eyes shining. He was so sure, so full of hope. He was a good man. Bella knew that. Sometimes you just need to take a leap of faith.

"June, then," she agreed. "The second Sunday in June." She held out her hand and Art took it in both of us, holding on tight. Bella looked at him then, and the knot in her chest began to unwind. *Trust your gut. Isn't that what you always told the kids? How do you feel about it?* Bella's gut was trying to tell her something. *Let go. This is going to work.*

"Mazel Tov!" Rabbi Klein exclaimed, jumping up from her seat. "The second Sunday in June it is." She typed in a few words on her calendar. "This calls for a celebration," she announced. She went over to her bookcase, removed a bottle of kosher wine from one of the shelves, and poured out a glass for each of them. "L'chaim! To Life!"

"What took you so long?" she asked, after they'd each taken a healthy gulp. "I was beginning to think you'd never get around to it."

"You can't rush into these things, can you?" Bella asked.

Rabbi Klein raised an eyebrow. "I don't mean to be rude, but you guys aren't exactly teenagers, are you? What's there to wait for?"

"Just what I've been saying," Art agreed. "Life's too short to fool around. We love each other, so let's get married. We have nobody to please but ourselves. If the kids don't like it, that's their problem."

"Your kids have an objection?"

"No, no – it's nothing. Actually, my Amy is just fine. She loves Bella. She's all for us getting married. And Emily … well, Emily couldn't care less." Art bit his lip.

Rosalie Klein looked a question at him, but it was Bella who answered.

"Emily doesn't object to our marriage. In fact, she's probably hasn't given it any thought at all. She's living her own life," she told the rabbi. "She and her husband Ted picked up their four kids and took off for Sidney, Australia a few months ago. She doesn't seem to care that it's literally halfway across the world from home."

"I hadn't heard about this," Rabbi Klein said. "What are they doing out there?"

"Emily's home-schooling her kids, all four of them. Ted does something with computers; nobody seems to know exactly what. So as far as earning a living, it doesn't matter where he lives. He can work anywhere. And for now, it's Australia. They never discussed it with Art, or with anyone else, as far as we know. Amy didn't know anything about it, either. By the time they told us, it was a done deal. Their things were already packed, tickets were bought, and that was it."

"I see. Well, it's no wonder you're so upset, Art. Anybody would be."

"Yes. It's not like they decided to make Aliyah and move to Israel or something. I mean, that, I could understand. I wouldn't be happy about it, but at least it would be for a purpose, to raise the kids in a Jewish country. "

Rosie Klein smiled. "Would that really make you any happier, though? They'd still be a world away from you."

"True. You're right, I know. But Australia? Where did that come from? They don't know anybody there. How am I supposed to get to Australia? How will the kids ever know me? I'll be lucky to see them once or twice in the rest of my life."

"I'm so sorry, Art. This has to be painful."

"Yes. Well - there's nothing I can do about it, is there? So let's just plan the wedding and get on with our lives, too. Maybe they'll come to the wedding, although I doubt it."

"We'll hope they can make it. After all, it's more than six months from now. That should give them enough time to work out arrangements. Maybe they'll even decide to come back home to stay. It could just be an adventure, you know. There's nothing to say it's a permanent commitment."

Art's head did a quick bob up and down. Bella squeezed his hand, but he wouldn't meet her eyes.

Rabbi Klein waited a bit, then straightened in her chair and asked, "What about your kids, Bella? Will they be there? Or are they having a problem about you two getting married? Is that what Art meant?"

"No, no, it's not a problem. It's just that Mindy isn't very pro-marriage in general. I think it's my fault. Well – mine and my ex's. After what she saw between us, growing up, she says she's not ever planning to go that route. But we'll see. She's still young."

Bella glanced up briefly and shrugged, then continued. "I think she'll come to our wedding, though. After all, she lives right here in Chicago. I'm not sure about her brother, Joel. He's out in San Francisco. It's not that far, not like Australia, so I hope he'll be able to come."

"So they're okay with your engagement?"

Bella and Art shared a look and smiled.

"As a matter of fact, we haven't exactly told them about it yet," Bella admitted. "Well, not the out-of-towners, anyway. But I don't think Joel really cares one way or the other. He's living his own life out west. He has his career, and his girlfriend. Mindy will be fine, I'm sure. She just has to get used to the idea. I've been on my own a long time, and I don't think she expected me to ever get married again." Bella laughed. "I never expected it, myself."

"Sometimes life surprises you, doesn't it?" Rabbi Klein smiled.

"Sometimes," Bella agreed.

"What about you, Rosie? We need to find somebody for you, now, don't we?"

"Why, Art, I didn't know you were such a matchmaker," Rabbi Klein teased.

A red flush moved across Art's cheeks, but he smiled, too. "I don't like the idea of being alone, not for me, not for you, either. A nice girl like you should be married."

Rabbi Klein shrugged. "That's what my mother tells me, too. But it's not so easy to find somebody these days, is it? Especially when I say I'm a rabbi. For some reason, that tends to turn a lot of men off."

"Then they're not the right kind of men," Art asserted firmly. "There's someone out there for you. We just have to find him."

"My mother's working on it. She's got all her buddies in Worcester, Mass going around with their antennas out. Every time she hears about somebody's nephew or cousin or whatever, she tells me about him. As if I could magically fall in love with somebody I never even heard of before." Rosalie shrugged. "In the meantime, let's concentrate on getting the two of you hitched, okay?"

They talked a bit about whether it should be an afternoon or evening wedding, and whether or not they wanted a traditional ketubah, or wedding contract. "I know someone who makes these absolutely gorgeous ketubot," Rosalie told Bella. "They have all the traditional legal wording, naturally, but then she embellishes them with ... well, with anything you'd like, actually. Maybe your favorite flowers, or some meaningful quotation, or maybe just a beautiful decorative design. She turns an ordinary ketubah into an absolute work of art. You frame them and .... Well, anyway, I think I have her card here, somewhere."

"That sounds great, Rabbi," Art said. "We should look into it, right, Hon?"

"Listen," the Rabbi said, hesitating a little, when Art went to get the car. "I hope you don't think I'm …. But it just seemed to me that you're … well, you're not quite as enthusiastic as Art is about this wedding."

Bella didn't answer her directly. But then she said, "It must be kind of hard for you to counsel people sometimes, isn't it?"

"You mean, because I'm young?"

Bella nodded.

"Actually, yes, sometimes it's a little awkward. Also, it can be frustrating, especially when I give people my best advice and they go on making poor decisions anyway," she said with a sudden grin. "Listen, I realize that being older means you have a lot more experience than I do about life, but even so, sometimes it helps to have somebody to bounce things off of, you know? And I'm a pretty good listener."

Bella smiled. "I can see that nothing much gets by you, that's for sure. But really, everything's fine. Everything will be fine."

Chapter Twenty-Three

Bella was late to class the next day. She'd been laying sleepless most of the night, thinking about the wedding and the kids and the rabbi, everything all jumbled together. She'd finally been able to let it all go and drop into sleep about the time the sun came up. When the alarm rang, she felt like she'd only just closed her eyes. Somehow she managed to wash and dress, spike up her hair, and grab a cup of coffee from the Keurig to take along as she raced out the door. By the time she arrived at Martingale Manor, she felt a bit more like herself and even managed to put on something resembling a normally alert expression. She hurriedly loaded props and supplies into her shopping cart and hauled everything into the clubhouse.

As she headed into the corridor leading to her classroom she found her way blocked by a fragile-looking woman standing precariously on a chair. The woman must have heard Bella's half-muzzled intake of breath, because she turned her head toward the sound and began to wobble. Bella had an instant to decide if she should rush forward to catch her or stand still and hope for the best.

While Bella hesitated, afraid to move either way, the woman on the chair found her balance again by supporting herself against the wall and continued what she was doing. She held one edge of a large quilt while her partner, another grey-haired woman who looked marginally more substantial than her companion, stood on a facing chair and stretched to pin the opposite end of the quilt to a rod fixed near the top of the wall. Job done, the two got down from their chairs. They inspected their work critically, standing as far back as possible. Given that the corridor wasn't more than five feet wide, this was a challenge.

The quilt was pieced together out of varying bits of fabric to form a star in the center, a very traditional pattern. However, the design was anything but traditional in its bold use of color, pitting bright blues against bright oranges and yellows, a perfect example of the use of complementary colors to force both colors to assume a vibrancy neither could have on its own. Instead of the little flowery patterns often found on quilting pieces, the designer had used strong solids interspersed with bold stripes, zig-zags, circles – almost anything but prissy little flowers. The entire design worked together to produce something unique, an ancient technique brought into the twenty-first century.

"This is marvelous," Bella exclaimed. "Who made it?"

"That would be me," the more delicate woman admitted, grinning from ear to ear. "Isn't it something?"

"It certainly is. You should be really proud of this. Hi, I'm Bella Sarver," she announced, holding out her hand. "I'm teaching painting here. I think I've seen you before, haven't I?"

"Lily Turner," the woman answered, shaking Bella's hand with a surprisingly firm grip. "And this is Bobbie," she added. "Bobbie Richards."

"Lily is our best quilter," Bobbie said, shaking Bella's hand in turn. "And she won't let anybody forget it, either. Modesty is not her strongest quality. But I have to admit, she may be entitled."

Bella fingered the edge of the quilt admiringly. "Do you teach quilting, Lily?"

"No, no, nothing like that. I'm just in the quilting club, that's all."

"That's not all," Bobbie said. "There's a bunch of us quilters, but Lily is always the one who comes up with the best ideas. I've learned a lot from her since I've started going to the club every week."

"How did you come up with this design, Lily? It's so unusual."

Lily shrugged and her face scrunched up with an 'aw shucks' expression. "I just do, I don't really know how. I set out my fabrics and play with them until something works."

"So – instinct, then. It's funny, but I've been experimenting with something like this in my paintings, too. I mean, working with shapes and colors, trying to focus just on the design of the composition. Would you like to come in to our class and explain how it's done?"

"Oh, I'm no painter," Lily said, waving her hand in front of her face. "Like I said, I just like to piece together fabrics, make patterns of them. I fool around until I get something going. I wouldn't call it art."

"Well, I would," Bella argued. "It's beautiful."

The seven painting students were all busy at their easels already, each working on a different composition, using photos they'd taken themselves as references. Somebody had plugged in their phone for music, and the bright room buzzed with energy.

"Hey, guys, can I have your attention for a minute?" Bella interjected. "You can keep working, but just listen. This is Lily Turner. Maybe some of you already know her?"

Debbie Wilson looked up, saw Lily, and frowned. Lily frowned back.

"Lily? You're Lily? I used to know somebody named Lily." Debbie moved closer, searching Lily's face for some tell-tale sign. "Wait, did you grow up in Chicago? South Side?"

"Sure did. Bridgeport. Thomas A. Wolfe High School. I wondered how long it was going to take you to remember me. I noticed you the other night. You're Debbie something, aren't you? Debbie...."

"Wilson," Debbie supplied.

"No, that's not it," Lily said, shaking her head impatiently. "Wait a minute." She looked up again, sharply. "Debbie Kowalski. That's right. Kowalski. You were a year or so behind me, weren't you? So was the woman who was killed. Shirley McCarthy."

"I didn't recognize her at first," Debbie admitted, "but when she sang with the karaoke that night, I suddenly knew who she was. We were in the same class. It was a long time ago."

"Yeah. She went after your boyfriend, I remember. He was in my class. She made a big play for him, and then when she caught him, she turned him loose. It was a big scandal in those days, wasn't it? I mean, you just didn't do that, not back then, if you were a nice girl."

"She wasn't a nice girl," Debbie said flatly.

Lily smiled reminiscently. "No, she wasn't a nice girl. She stole my boyfriend, too. When she was done with him, he tried to come back to me, but I didn't want him anymore by then. I wonder whatever happened to your old boyfriend."

"I married him."

"No kidding?" Lily laughed out loud. "You married him? After he left you for Shirley?"

Debbie shrugged. "I loved him. He apologized for being a fool, and he was so sweet to me, I forgave him."

"So you married him."

"Yes. Not right away, of course. We both had school to finish, and then college. But we stuck together. We've been married nearly fifty years."

"Fifty years?" Bella put in. "I can't even imagine. And you've been happy all that time?"

Debbie shrugged again. "We're married, what can I say? We raised a family and lived a life. It wasn't all moonlight and roses, but what life is? We chose our path, and we followed it. We're still following it. Ken is a good man. He's been a good husband and a good father. What more could a person want?"

"Excitement?" Lily asked.

"Excitement? Is that what you have with your husband?"

"Not any more. Harold passed away a while ago. To tell the truth, he wasn't too exciting in the first place. But as you say, he was a good man. No sense in wondering what life might have been like if you took a different road, is it?"

"No," Debbie said. "No sense at all. And look, Bella here is about to take another road. She's getting married again."

Lily turned to give Bella a long look. She opened her mouth to say something, changed her mind, and closed it. Instead, she said, "Congratulations. When's the happy day?"

"June," Bella said. "We just set the date."

"Did you? What happened to your first husband?"

"Nothing. He's just not my husband anymore."

"Mm-hmmm," Lily commented.

Bella knew what Lily meant. "It won't be the same this time," she said. "Art's a very good man. We're really good together."

Lily cocked an eyebrow, but she didn't add anything else.

"Right." Bella clapped her hands together. "So –Lily - I wanted you to explain how you figure out your designs. Hey, listen, everybody. Lily creates the most beautiful abstract designs with her quilts. I want us to try to do something like that with our paintings. Lily, why don't you start by telling us how … well, how you start."

Lily Turner was more of an observer than a leader. She watched and she listened. She was happy to let others take center stage while she stayed in the background. But she could step up if she had to, and she'd agreed to this.

She heaved her quilting bag onto the nearest table. This was a capacious sack filled with all kinds of supplies, half-started projects, notebooks and drawings. It was nearly as much an appendage as her actual arms and legs. She pulled it open and started rummaging, removing random items and piling them in front of her as she spoke. Her voice was so low she might as well have been talking to herself. If the class wanted to pay attention, fine. If not, she never minded her own company.

"I've been collecting fabrics as long as I can remember. I like to browse the fabric stores for interesting remnants, so I always have something to work with when my fingers get itchy. That's when I start sorting through pieces of cloth, laying them out, seeing what colors and patterns might work together."

"Do you always make the same patterns?" Joanie Passarelli asked, fingering some of the fabric. Several of the painters had moved closer, though a few chose to keep on working at their easels.

"Good question. And the answer is, no. I always start with the fabrics. I never think about a pattern until later. And then there are lots of different ones. Different sizes. Different purposes."

Seeing that several more women had gathered near, interested in what she was saying, Lily expanded a bit.

"Sometimes people make what's called a souvenir quilt, with scraps of materials from things like christening dresses, wedding dresses, and so forth. Sometimes quilts are made with a theme, maybe to celebrate an event, or a holiday or something. I've done a few of those myself. But mostly, I just like to make my own designs. I usually begin the work with four and a half inch squares. Once I get the basic pattern worked out, I fill in with smaller bits, or I cut the squares into triangles, even circles sometimes. But that comes a lot later. The overall design comes first."

"Just as I've been telling you, ladies, you start with the composition," Bella interrupted. "Same idea."

"Right," Lily went on. "So the first thing is to just choose my fabrics and cut them into the right size squares."

Lily took a few pieces and moved them around the table, trying a couple of different arrangements. She selected a blue and white striped cotton, paired it with a solid blue field speckled with black dots, and added a bright yellow sprigged with tiny white flowers. She was beginning to enjoy herself. "I don't often use these little fussy prints, but this one caught my eye, and I think it will set off the blues nicely," she explained.

"Ok, so let's begin with these three pieces." She rummaged in her bag again, pulled out a couple of cardboard squares, and set them aside. "I use these as templates," she offered. Sifting through the contents with a frown, she eventually pulled out a small trimming scissors and heavy pinking shears. She laid them on the table, and continued to search, her forehead wrinkling ever more steadily.

"Is something wrong?" Bella asked. "Can I help you find something?"

"My scissors," Lily mumbled, still wading through the bag. "I can't find my good shears. How am I supposed to cut the squares without my good shears?"

"Can I take a look?" Bella asked. Lily shoved the bag over to her. Bella opened it as wide as possible and began to look through it. After a few minutes, her hand triumphantly emerged with a pair of sewing scissors. "Here, is this it?"

Lily grabbed it away from her. "No, that's my other one. It's too small. I need my good heavy pair of shears."

"Are you sure you had it with you? When did you see it last?"

"I always have it with me," Lily retorted hotly. She glared at Bella. "I used it the other day, in class."

"Did you use it at home after that?"

"I don't remember. I guess I must have. You know, I'm always working on something. It gets to be automatic. I don't know if I even think about it, not really. It must still be there. How could I have done that? I always put everything back in the bag. Well," she said, her furrowed forehead smoothing out a bit, "I guess I can use this one, just to demonstrate." She picked up the scissors Bella had found.

"Right, then. So I take a piece of fabric, lay it out on the table, and take my templates and lay them on the fabric. Then I take a piece of marking chalk and draw the outline on the fabric. Then I cut out the squares. This scissors will work for now, but what I usually do is pin a couple of lengths together and cut out the pieces two or even three at a time. For that, I need my rotary cutter. I can use my good heavy shears, but the cutter is faster. Still, there's nothing like a nice strong shears to make you feel like you're really doing something."

The ladies watched Lily work. Somehow, in the course of the activity, her back straightened and she appeared strong and capable, all fragility disappeared. In no time at all, three piles of squares lay on the table in front of her, one pile for each of the three fabrics she'd selected. She surveyed them, satisfied, then removed a bright red pincushion in the shape of a tomato from her bag, placed it on the table, and pulled up a chair. "From now on, it's a matter of trial and error. You make a block of squares, pin them together, and see if it's good or not. If it is, you keep going. If not, you keep fiddling around until it works."

"I see what you mean," Debbie noted. "About like doing a composition for a painting."

"Exactly." Bella nodded. "That's what I was hoping to get across. No matter what you're creating, the composition matters. The shapes and colors need to support the overall composition. It wouldn't be any good to have a really nice corner if the rest of it didn't work. So try to ignore details until right at the end. First, make sure your shapes are good, right?"

While Bella gave the class their 'homework' for the next class, Lily Turner stuffed everything back into her bag. She was nearly out the door when Bella caught up and went out into the hallway with her.

"I really appreciate your taking the time to explain your process, Lily. Thank you. And isn't it funny how you and Debbie used to know each other years ago? It's such a small world, isn't it? Maybe you can be friends again now."

Lily shook her head. "Debbie Kowalski and I were never friends. I don't make friends with fools, and she was a fool. Still is, probably. Can you tell me why anybody would take back a boyfriend who'd left her for another girl?" she demanded. "Foolishness."

Chapter Twenty-Four

Fabio Gompers flipped through the pile of stiff paper, growing more irritated by the minute. "This is all garbage," he complained to himself. "What was that woman thinking? They wouldn't fool anybody for a minute."

He'd retrieved the giclee prints from *Ruffles and Flourishes'* basement the other night, along with his paints and other equipment. There are giclees and there are giclees. The best ones are printed on heavy canvas, and once framed, it's hard to tell them from actual paintings. Especially if they'd been touched up a little with some oil paint. The cheap ones are printed on so-called canvas paper, which is just textured paper that doesn't accept paint well at all. Those were the kind Shirley Rogers had purchased from her various internet suppliers.

Fabio was proud to have studied with some of the best at the Art Students League in New York. He was skilled in classical techniques and his large landscapes were lushly rendered.

He absolutely adored painting. He loved everything about it. He loved the way the brush felt in his hand as he wielded it. He loved mixing luscious piles of paint, blending and stirring until just the right color emerged. He loved the smell of turpentine and linseed oil. Their fumes never gave him a headache. He breathed it in as if the odors were the finest perfumes. The idea of earning a living doing anything but painting was anathema to him. It nearly killed him that arthritis left him without the strength to attack his large canvases anymore, and he needed to resort to deception. But it was either that or give up painting altogether, and he'd rather cut off his right arm than do that. He also needed to eat regularly.

It was surfing the internet that gave him the idea. He found a site that offered good quality giclee prints for sale at nominal prices. They were by various artists, in various styles, but some of them were close enough to his own style to pass muster. He ordered one, just to see if his idea would work.

When the print arrived, already stretched and mounted, he stood it on an easel and studied it for a while. Then he mixed some paint on his palette. Gingerly, he touched his brush to the print. He wanted to add enough paint to make it appear that the whole thing was an original painting, but not so much that he obliterated the print. It was a delicate process. His first effort wasn't bad, but he wasn't satisfied, so he ordered a few more of the prints and tried again. It took a while, but eventually, he arrived at just the right technique. The finished, doctored painting was everything he'd hoped it would be. To his eye, it looked terrific. Now to see if one of his galleries would accept it as his own. He sent it off to an establishment in Scottsdale, Arizona, and held his breath.

The Scottsdale gallery never questioned it. Fabio's new career was off and running. Until he got cocky. Until he got a little greedy. Until he started to get a little sloppy.

He figured he could pick up some easy prize money by submitting one of the small paintings to a monthly exhibit held by the Deer Creek Art League. It wasn't one of his best, but he didn't worry about being found out. The DCAL members were only a bunch of amateurs, after all. Fabio congratulated himself when he won Best of Show. His triumph was short lived when Shirley Rogers recognized the painting as having been done by a different artist. Fabio wasn't the only one pouring over art websites.

Just Fabio's bad luck, but Shirley was quick to take advantage of the situation. Suddenly, he found himself working for her.

Fabio bought only the best quality giclees to use as a basis for his embellishments. But Shirley was greedy. When she found out she could buy prints for a pittance, charge a very large mark-up for the 'improved' prints, and then pay Fabio a share, she chose that route. She refused to understand that their harmless little deception was only going to be successful if the paintings held up over time. Which they wouldn't do if the foundation was only cheap paper. And when the paint started peeling and the customers discovered they'd paid premium prices for prints they could have ordered from the internet themselves at a fraction of the cost, they were going to come looking for Fabio, not Shirley. He kicked himself for signing his own name to the paintings. At least, he should have blurred the signatures so they were illegible. "You were a fool," he told himself. "But that's over with now, thank heavens."

The useless papers landed in the trash bin with a satisfying thunk.

The police had finally removed the crime scene tape from *Ruffles and Flourishes*, at Martha Ashton's request. They'd already searched the place from top to bottom and conceded that Martha, as official executor of Rogers' will, had a legitimate interest in gaining access to the premises. And now that Leo Schaeffer was officially working for the Deer Creek Police Department as an accounting consultant, he had access to both of Shirley Roger's laptops, so between the two of them, Martha was confident that they'd be able to figure out how Shirley had run her business.

Martha was beginning to be sorry she'd ever taken Shirley Rogers as a client, though. She'd never bargained for having the responsibility of closing down a business, and a messy, disorganized one, at that.

"Are you sure about this, Leo?"

"I'm telling you, Martha, there are items on this inventory list Bella and Mollie made that don't appear on any of the records Shirley left. Likewise, lots of the entries for sales don't correspond to any of the inventory lists, whether Shirley's or my wife's. I don't know how this woman could have had any idea what she had in stock, what she'd bought, what she'd sold – nothing makes any sense."

It crossed Martha's mind that neither Bella nor Mollie should have been making any inventory list, but she decided to ignore the thought. After all, she was a lawyer, not an accountant. She definitely needed Leo's help.

"What about on the other computer, Leo? The one that was in her house?"

"Well, that's interesting, too. I can't find anything that looks like business records on that. No inventories or anything. But there are bank records and an investment account. The woman had an awful lot of money, some in cash and plenty in various mutual funds. I can't find any tax records, but I don't see how she got that much of an estate just from this little gift shop, or whatever it is. Any way we can get hold of her tax records?"

Martha shook her head. This was all getting beyond her. It seemed a lot more likely that the IRS would want info about the estate, rather than providing any sort of back records to the deceased's lawyer.

Rita Cutler had been summoned back to work when Martha realized she was going to need a lot of help. Rita was happy for the chance to work again and earn some extra money, albeit only for the time it was going to take for Martha Ashton to finish dealing with the store. She was a great help with sorting through the stock and such, but she couldn't supply much information about the workings of the operation.

"I wish I could, Martha," she said. "I told you before; Shirley never shared any of her business practices with me. I could have done a lot more for her. I mean, I used to manage a real estate office before I retired. But she only had me opening the store and helping customers. I know Leo was trying to work out the finances even before Shirley died. Maybe if she hadn't been killed, she could have explained things to him."

"Maybe," Leo said doubtfully. "All I can say is, we should just verify the inventory in stock, mark down the prices 50%, assuming there was a 50% mark-up in the first place, and get rid of everything we can. We can set a time limit, and after that, we take any merchandise that's left and donate it someplace. We could mark it down even more, if you'd rather do that. It's a loss either way, but so what? Then we pay any bills that come in, pay the taxes and if there's anything left over, donate the cash to that school, that Cherubim or whatever."

Martha cleared her throat. "There might be a complication about that. I'm not sure yet."

"What do you mean?"

"Apparently, there's a son involved here. He called me the other day to find out about his mother's estate. He wasn't happy to hear that her will makes everything over to Our Lady of Cherubim."

"Is he going to contest it?"

"I think he might. As a matter of fact, he called me last night and left a message. I spoke to him this morning. He's meeting me here later."

"Interesting," Leo commented. "Rita, do you know anything about this?"

Rita shook her head. "Shirley never wanted to talk about her son. I only found out about him when she accidentally let something slip one day. But I can totally understand him contesting the will, can't you? If I'd been disinherited, I'd sure be mad."

"Yes, it's a shame," Martha agreed. "I tried to ask her why she was doing it, but she wouldn't give me a straight answer."

"I know, that was just like her. She didn't talk much about anything at all. Like I said, she kept everything close to the vest."

"One thing we know for sure, we're going to have to pay taxes," Martha said. "So - what do we tell the IRS?"

"Simple," Leo said. "We tell them it looks like Shirley was selling things she didn't own, hadn't bought, hadn't paid for. Clearly, there was some sort of fraud going on. For instance, look at these notecards. Kasia Novik recognizes the pictures on them as ones she posted on the web, but she never made notecards out of them, much less gave Shirley Rogers permission to do it. Out and out theft. As of now, we have no way to know if she did that with any other artist's work, but it seems pretty likely, doesn't it?"

"It does," Martha agreed. "Maybe one of the artists whose work she poached found out, and murdered her."

Leo chuckled. "Maybe. They sure picked a funny place to do it, don't you think? I mean, a shower stall in Martingale Manor isn't exactly a nice, dark, back alley, is it? Anyway, how would they know she was there? It's a private clubhouse, residents only. In theory, at least."

"What do you mean, 'in theory'?"

"From what I hear, they have all kinds of guests running around loose over there, too. They're supposed to control who has passes to the place, but there seem to be a lot more of them than there are residents. Apparently, the former management just handed them out wholesale to anybody who asked. Bella tells me the new management is trying to rein that all in now, but it'll take a while. In the meantime, there's no sure way to know who's coming in to the community."

"Really? Well, whatever - it's not our problem, Leo. We just have to close out *Ruffles and Flourishes*. Neither of us was an officer of the company. There wasn't any company. Rogers was the sole proprietor. She's the only one responsible, and she's dead. So what will the IRS do?"

Leo shrugged. "We'll file the paperwork using the best documentation we can and send them whatever money seems warranted, at least as far as there is any."

"There's a nice hefty amount in the bank accounts we found so far."

"Right, and there are probably some investments, too. We'll need to get into her house and sort out whatever paperwork is there, as well.

Martha sighed. "I don't like it. This isn't the way I do things."

"Do you have another idea?"

Martha shook her head. She said, "Rita, didn't you ever suspect anything?"

"Well, I did kind of wonder sometimes. It seemed kind of strange that she spent so much time down in the basement. Some days, she spent most of the day there. I know there was extra stock and office supplies, because she'd bring those up from time to time. But she never let me go down to get them, even when I offered. So that was kind of weird, but like you said, Leo, it was her store. None of my concern, when you come right down to it. But I'm really sorry that the store has to close. It's a nice little business. I wish there was some way to keep it open."

Leo and Martha exchanged a speculative look. "How long does the lease have to run, Martha?" he asked.

She consulted some papers. "It has another two years. But the contract is null and void, now that the lessee is deceased."

"What if somebody else agreed to take it over? Is that a possibility?"

"It could be," she said slowly. "But whoever did that would have to pay the estate something for it. A sublet, if you will."

She eyed Rita dubiously.

Rita glanced from one to the other. "Do you mean me?"

"Would you be interested in doing that?"

For a moment, Rita's face lit up, but then it fell again. "I'd love to. I'd absolutely love to. But where would I get the money?"

"You don't have savings?" Leo asked.

Rita shook her head. "Not much. I just have a small 401K from when I was working, but they didn't do a match or anything, and I couldn't afford to put a lot in it. But that and Social Security is what I live on. That's another reason I was happy to get this part-time job, to help out a little."

"Hmm," Leo contributed thoughtfully. But Rita shook her head again. "No, I wish I could. But I don't have much money, and I wouldn't want to go into debt with a loan, either."

"That is a shame. Not only for you, but for the neighborhood. I hate to see a nice business close up."

"Well, speaking of closing up," Martha put in, "we still have some work to do, guys."

"Right. Well you can go down there now, and help us, if you don't mind, Rita," Leo said. I want to actually see each item on this list my wife and her friend Bella made, and check it off. Then we'll do the same with everything in the store."

When he locked the front door of *Ruffles and Flourishes* hours later, Leo was sure the three of them had accounted for every single item on the premises. They'd added a number of things Mollie and Bella hadn't had time to write down, but their initial list was fairly complete, given that they'd been so rushed.

"A funny thing, though," Leo commented, when he, Martha and Rita were seated in The Copper Kettle down the block from the store, enjoying a belated lunch. "There are a few things we found in our unofficial search earlier that seem to be missing now."

"Unofficial search?" Martha asked.

Leo opened his mouth, closed it again, and said, "Let's not go there, OK?"

Martha looked at him deadpan. She seemed about to ask something else, then told herself she was probably better off not knowing. She bit into an overflowing BLT, chewed slowly, swallowed. "OK. What's missing?"

"A pile of giclee prints, for starters. The painting studio in the corner is still there, complete with easel and taborets, but the paints and brushes are gone. Someone has been there. Did anyone else have a key?" he asked, looking at Rita.

"Not as far as I know. Although," she said thoughtfully, "now that you mention it, sometimes when I got there in the morning, things were moved around, you know? I mean, I might have left a stack of cards on the counter or something, and they'd be on one of the tables, instead. But I just assumed Shirley had moved them herself, for some reason. Do you think somebody else could have been going in there after hours?"

"Possibly," Leo said. "It's beginning to look like it." He spooned up some thick chili. It had been a really long time since breakfast.

Peter Rogers found a space for his titanium grey BMW 530-I on the third level of the parking garage off of Wright Street. He walked south on Brookline Street, and turned right when he reached Main Street. *Ruffles and Flourishes* sat at 228 Main, the third store from the corner.

The BMW spent most of its life in the garage under Rogers' condo building. He didn't have a lot of use for it in the city, but he sometimes took it out on the week-ends, for a long drive up I-94 to Wisconsin. Once north of the city, the expressway opened up, and he loved feeling its power under his hands. The lease was expensive, but it was one of the rewards he told himself he deserved, another one being the condo near the Lake. He'd been a little worried about how long he could keep either one, but maybe now there was a solution in sight.

Martha Ashton had been floored when Rogers called her the night before. It was late. She was already in bed, half asleep. She hated getting phone calls after hours. Late calls were never good news, in her experience. She nearly hadn't picked up. But then she thought it might be important, so she relented.

Martha understood from Shirley that she and her son had been estranged for years. In fact, Shirley hadn't even wanted to tell her about him, but Martha pressed her about any possible family members who might expect to inherit until she'd finally admitted she'd had a son. Knowing that, Martha had advised Shirley it would be best to at least notify him about the terms of her will, but Shirley refused. Martha was glad that at least she'd insisted on having his name, if only for her own records.

Peter Rogers stood on the sidewalk outside the store and looked up and down the street. As he'd mentioned to Detective Carlson, he didn't spend a lot of time in small towns. He was used to Chicago's towering skyscrapers lining streets that were packed with pedestrians rushing to their destinations; cars, trucks and taxis honking their horns and jockeying for space. What he saw now was a street lined with quaint-looking two-story storefronts. Mothers pushing strollers stopped to window shop. Teen-agers released from classes walked in groups of three or four, the girls giggling and gently pushing each other, especially if a group of boys was nearby.

So this is where Shirley Rogers had ended up, was it? He was having trouble picturing his mother in this setting. Like him, she'd been a product of bustling city streets. Not this. Did she ever feel comfortable here? He shoved open the front door of *Ruffles and Flourishes*.

Martha was working towards the rear of the store but she came forward when she heard the door open, hand outstretched to shake Peter's. She invited him into the back room so they could talk in private. "What can I do for you?" she asked, when they were seated, with mugs of coffee in front on them on the table.

"It's like I told you on the phone. The police said my mother left everything to Our Lady of Cherubim School. She was my mother. She should have left her estate to me."

Martha studied him for a moment. He was probably a little younger than herself, but he was an attractive man. Tall, smooth-shaven, bright blue eyes. She wondered what could have caused him and his mother to end their relationship. And who had ended it? Shirley? Peter?

"Should she?" Martha responded. "Why? I understand you haven't seen or spoken to her in years."

"I'm still her son."

"And ...?"

"And ... I must be entitled to something, aren't I? What are we talking about, anyway? Did she leave a lot?"

"She had a right to leave her assets anyway she chose. You're not automatically entitled to anything. And yes, the assets are fairly substantial. Our Lady of Cherubim School will be able to do a lot with their inheritance."

"Do they know about it?"

"Not yet, no. I still haven't determined exactly who needs to be notified. I'm waiting to hear from the Archdiocese. But I expect they'll be getting in touch with me soon enough."

"I bet they will," Peter said. "I bet they had a lot to do with getting my mother to sign everything over to them. I bet she didn't just think of it all by herself."

"Yes? Why do you say that?"

"Well, it's obvious, isn't it?" Peter asked, exasperated. "It's only natural for mothers to leave their estates to their own kids, not to some school they went to eons ago. Anyway, I want to contest it."

"Contest the will?"

Rogers nodded affirmatively.

Martha Ashton sat back in her chair, took a sip of her coffee, and sighed. "Listen, Mr. Rogers. I don't think you really want to do that. I'm your mother's lawyer, not yours, but I'll give you some advice for free. Do you have any idea how hard it is to contest a will? Ninety-nine percent of all wills that go to probate go through without a hitch. Practically none of those that are contested are over-turned. The odds against you are enormous. It will cost you a lot of money, and time, and may open up a slew of memories you'd rather leave closed. I advise you to think about this very, very carefully."

"I hear you, but I have grounds."

"What grounds?"

"Undue influence. Those nuns talked her into it. She didn't know what she was doing."

Martha sighed again. "I absolutely assure you, Mr. Rogers. Your mother was of perfectly sound mind when she instructed me to draw up this will. It was properly witnessed. There is no question whatsoever that she didn't know what she was doing. I can't say whether or not the nuns influenced her thinking, but if so, she was completely competent to decide in their favor. You have no hope of winning this suit."

Peter Rogers studied the lawyer's face, his own without expression. Abruptly, so abruptly that Ashton involuntarily jumped back in her chair, he rose. He held out his hand.

"Thank you for your time, Ms. Ashton," he said. "See you in court."

The BMW roared onto the Eisenhower, back towards the city. Peter Rogers was furious. He didn't want to admit it, but Ashton was right. It would cost a lot of money to bring this suit, and that was something he was short of just at the moment. *I'm her son, damn it. I'm entitled to whatever she had. Besides, I need it.*

Rogers' mind raced almost as fast as the car he would soon have to return to the leasing company. *There has to be way. There has to. This can't all be for nothing.*

Chapter Twenty-Five

Leo had both of Shirley Rogers' laptops open on his desk, with multiple files open on each screen. The police hadn't allowed him access to Shirley's house, naturally, so he had no idea of what papers it might contain. But there was plenty to work with just on the two computers. In fact, way more than enough.

"Leo, it's two in the morning. Don't you think you've done enough for one night?"

"Look at this, Mollie," he said.

She rolled her eyes, but pulled a kitchen chair around to the desk and sat next to her husband. After decades of marriage, she knew him well enough to understand he wasn't going to stop working until he fell over in exhaustion. Which she herself was about to do any minute.

She'd gone to bed around eleven, read for a little while, then turned off the light and tried to sleep. But it was no use. If Leo wasn't lying next to her, snuffling and snorting, there was no way she could get any rest, either. She'd thrown back the covers and got out of bed to go search for him.

"What?" she asked, wearily resting her cheek on her hand.

"Remember how Bella saw Kasia's notecards in Shirley's shop? Except they weren't actually Kasia's? Well," he went on, not waiting for her to answer, "that's not all there was. See – if you look at this history on Google, Shirley trolled all kinds of art websites. One of her favorites was Fine Art USA, you know, the one where artists can post photos of their work for people to buy prints of the original paintings? Except it doesn't look as if she actually bought any prints. I think what she did instead was download some of the photos, and then have them printed at other sites. She made notecards, using the work of other artists besides Kasia, and she had a lot of larger prints made, too. Giclees. Except – we didn't find any larger giclees, did we?"

"No," Mollie said slowly. "There's a gallery section in the store, but that has original paintings."

Leo could see the wheels turning in Mollie's mind. "Unless ...."

"We need to take another look at those paintings, don't we?"

Mollie nodded. "We better bring Bella along."

The next time the four co-conspirators entered *Ruffles and Flourishes,* they didn't need to sneak in via the basement passage in the middle of the night. Leo had the key, so he unlocked the front door and they all trooped in. The afternoon sun flooded the store with light through the large, west-facing windows, but Leo flipped the switches on anyway, just because none of them had anything to hide.

Art Halperin had never seen the store in its glory, but he knew it couldn't have looked like this, not if Shirley Rogers had planned to entice shoppers with her displays. Instead of the vignettes she'd arranged, with colorful scarves draped near tables of little figurines, which sat among small silver picture frames, which encircled key rings with imaginative designs and sayings on them, the merchandise looked as if it had been stocked by an obsessive-compulsive bookkeeper. Which it had, in a sense. Under Leo Schaeffer's direction, Rita Cutler had dedicated each table and display case to one type of merchandise only, every item prominently labeled with description, inventory number, and price. Large placards stood in holders all around the store, proclaiming **Everything Must Go. 50% Off the Entire Store.** A similar banner rested on the main counter, waiting to be hung across the front windows.

"Wow, Leo," Art exclaimed, clearly impressed. "You guys have really been busy here."

"No sense wasting time," Leo said modestly. "The sooner we can wrap things up, the better it'll be for everybody."

"It's a shame, though," Bella commented. "It was such a nice store. I used to like coming in here to browse, and Rita was always more than happy to point out the newest items. I hate to see a nice business like this go away."

"It's funny that you're saying that, Bella. We were just talking with Rita about that the other day. She said she wished she had the money to take over the lease and keep *Ruffles and Flourishes* going, but unfortunately ...."

"Hmmm. Well, so what did you and Mollie want me to see, Leo?"

"Over here." He led the way to the gallery alcove. "Take a look at these paintings and tell me what you think."

The gallery alcove held a variety of paintings with nothing much in common except that they were all representational in subject matter. Landscapes looked like landscapes; still-lifes looked like still-lifes. Bella did a once-around while the other three watched. "I don't know what I'm looking for, Leo. Can you give me a clue?"

"Just tell us what you see. Does anything strike you about these pieces?"

Bella took another walk through the gallery, taking her time, gazing at each one. "Well, none of these are particularly wonderful, are they? Nothing really stands out. There aren't any abstracts, or really, anything distinctive here. I know Fabio said Shirley carried some of his paintings, but I don't see his signature on anything, and anyway, none of these are his style."

"I don't know if any of these are his," Leo said. "When I ran into him that day, you know, Mollie, he said he was taking his paintings back, because they weren't selling."

"But you don't know if he actually removed them?"

"I didn't stay to see, but I assume he did. Rita Cutler would know for sure."

"I bet he did," Bella said. "Like I said, these don't look like something Fabio would do."

"Doesn't he paint realistic compositions, Bella?"

"Well, sure, Mollie, but most of his work that I've seen still manages to have something special about it. I don't know, maybe it's a certain light that comes through, the way he glazes thin layers over underpaintings until everything sort of glows. I'm not sure what is, except …."

"Except what?" Leo nudged.

"Speaking of thin glazes …." Bella turned back to the paintings in the gallery. She studied them, then scratched at a couple thoughtfully with her fingernail. "I think we found those missing giclees, Leo. Look here. These have a thin layer of paint, but you can see underneath are just laser-jet prints on canvas. She must have doctored each of them. I'll bet she just used a lot of medium with a little paint, enough to add some texture and brush strokes. That's what she was doing with the studio set-up in the basement. She was passing them off as originals, but they're only cheap prints. She was sure charging original oil painting prices, though, wasn't she?"

Leo nodded vigorously. "That's what I thought, but I wanted your expert opinion, Bella. It's the only thing that makes sense, under the circumstances. I mean, there's no record of any sort of consignment agreements with the artists, and no record of outright purchases. Just those giclees, like I said."

"The woman was a thief," Art stated bluntly. "No wonder somebody killed her."

"You mean it was one of the artists whose work she stole?" Mollie asked. "But how would they have ever found out?"

"I don't know," Art admitted. "But it could have been."

"What about a disgruntled customer? I know if I'd paid these kinds of prices and then found out my oil painting was just a cheap print, I'd be pretty upset."

"Yeah, Bella, but wouldn't you just ask for a refund? It's fraud, but it's not personal, right?"

"Whatever. I think Detective Carlson probably should know about this," Bella said.

"It's funny, you know," Leo ruminated. "That son of hers was here the other day, to talk to Martha."

"Shirley's lawyer?" Mollie asked. "What for?"

"He's planning to contest the will. He thinks he should get everything, not that school what's its name, Cherubim?"

"I suppose he has a point," Mollie said. "After all, he was her son."

"Yeah, maybe," Leo conceded. "But it was what he said that stuck with me. He said if this was his mother's business, there was bound to be something wrong with it. 'Shady,' he said. Looks like he was right.

Chapter Twenty-Six

Sister Joseph knelt and crossed herself, then repeated the familiar words, "Bless me, Father, for I have sinned." She normally confessed on Saturdays, but she felt the need to clear her conscience a few days early this week, so on Thursday, the day after she'd spoken to Detective Ron Pepper, she went into the church after school and waited until she saw Father Taber enter the confessional.

Sister Joseph chose her confessors carefully, not because she was afraid of being denied absolution, but because the priests who were assigned to Our Lady of Cherubim seemed younger every year, while she herself kept getting older. Her knees didn't want to bend anymore, so kneeling was painful. Getting up again was even harder. She didn't want to go through the exercise if she had to confess to someone young enough to be her grandson, though she might have enjoyed having one had her life taken a different turn.

She wondered about the fact that she had a choice of confessors. She knew there was a shortage of new priests coming into the Church these days, just as there was a shortage of nuns. But that particular situation didn't seem to be affecting Bridgeport.

It mattered that her confessor be a priest of a certain age. Sister Joseph had reached a time of life where she shared fewer frames of reference with others, simply because the young ones were living in a different world from the one in which she'd grown up. Often, she heard the children in her classes talk about various experiences that left her mystified. She was afraid the same was true in reverse. A similar phenomenon applied to priests as well as to children. And she not only wanted to be understood; she wanted some useful advice.

Father Taber wasn't as old as Sister Joseph. But he appeared to be in his late fifties, at least, if not even past his sixtieth birthday. He wasn't heavy, but he was what used to be called 'pleasingly plump.' She didn't care for priests who were too thin. She understood their desire to stay in shape but there was something comforting about talking to a priest who clearly enjoyed his food. And Father Taber had kind eyes, a nice, clear grey. His confessional always had the longest line in front of it on Saturdays.

"It's been less than a week since your last confession, Sister Joseph," Father Taber said now. "Surely you, of all people, haven't done anything terrible since then, have you?"

"It's not so much what I've done, Father, as what I haven't done."

The conversation she'd had with Pepper had been weighing on her mind. He'd asked about Peter Rogers, so she'd told him what she knew. But had she painted too harsh a picture of his mother? Maybe she should have told Pepper why Shirley behaved as she did. Then again, maybe it wasn't important any more. She considered bringing up the subject with Sister Claude, but the principal of Cherubim had a lot on her plate these days. Besides, she was young enough to be Sister Joseph's daughter, if she'd ever had a daughter. No, Father Taber was probably the better choice.

"It's like this, Father," she began. She filled him in on the earlier conversation.

"After he left, I realized that I hadn't told the detective about Shirley McCarthy as a little girl, back when we were all little girls together. Poor Shirley didn't end up being much of a wife or a mother, but then, she probably didn't know how, you see. She never had anyone to model herself after. In fact, I think our school might have been the one place she really felt safe. The sisters were a sort of surrogate mother for her. They were kind but the rules were firm and they didn't bend them for anyone. I think that gave her a sense of security. But it wasn't enough, not in the end."

Sister Joseph, or little Gail Elliot, as she'd been then, remembered well how Shirley McCarthy had always loved to show off. Her hand was always the first to be raised to answer questions, though she often enough didn't have the right answers. She smiled and primped, and on singing days, her voice rose high above the others. But it didn't make up for the fact that when she went home, it was usually to an empty house. Her mother worked hard cleaning other people's houses in order to put food on the table. Shirley's clothes were always hand-me-downs, even her school uniform. Still, it looked the same as everyone else's, so at least no one could make fun of her about that. Even if she did stick on bits of ribbon here and there, to try to make it a little distinctive.

"Did she not have a father?"

"The father was a drunk. I think he probably was a wife-beater, too, looking back. I didn't realize it at the time, but I remember I'd see Shirley's mother once in a while, if she came to school for parent-teacher conferences or something. She often had dark glasses on, and once I saw her arm was in a sling. She said she'd broken her arm in a fall, but that was a bad time for them. She wasn't able to work for a while. It was a sad situation. So, Father, do you think I should have told the detective all of this? Should I tell him now?"

Bella Sarver also wondered if she should pass on certain information to the Detective. She'd wavered back and forth for an entire day about that, until finally Art said, "Look, Bella, just call Detective Carlson and put the facts in his hands. He can decide for himself if it matters or not."

"I know, it's just that ...I mean, how likely is it that one of those artists whose work Shirley downloaded from the internet just happened to go into her store and see his or her own painting hanging there? And then, from that, to trace her back to her clubhouse, wait until she was in the shower, and then murder her?"

"Well, when you put it like that, it seems pretty improbable, doesn't it?" Art agreed. "And yet, this has to be more than just a coincidence, don't you think? It looks like at least two of the artists Shirley was ripping off are local people."

Bella crinkled up her face skeptically. "You can't be thinking Kasia Novik or Fabio Gompers killed her."

Art shrugged. "I admit it's far-fetched. But then, why *do* people kill other people? Is there ever a really good reason? Well, maybe in self-defense or something," he back-tracked. "But in cold blood?"

Bella nodded slowly. "You're right, Art. There's never a really good reason, is there? Except in the killer's mind. And then there's the scissors I saw."

"Scissors? What scissors?"

"Didn't I mention it?"

Art waited silently.

"Well, you remember that Kasia and I painted the co-op walls together? She wanted a little more blue tape so she could trim the ceiling. She pulled all kinds of stuff out of her duffel to while she was looking for it, and I was a little surprised to see that heavy shears among the other stuff. I mean, I thought that the police had confiscated all the scissors they could find from people who were in the clubhouse that day. And yet, Kasia still had hers."

"So you're telling me I need to be looking for a disgruntled artist?" Carlson said when Bella finally called him. "Do you have somebody particular in mind?"

"I don't know," Bella conceded to Carlson over the phone. "But as you know, Leo Schaeffer has been working on the books, comparing the inventory to the records he found and so forth. And when he asked me to take a look at the paintings, and I discovered they were just painted-over giclees, it seemed to us that you ought to at least know about it. That could be a motive for murder, couldn't it?"

Chapter Twenty-Seven

"So what do you think, Ron? One of the artists as Bella Sarver suggests? Do we have any sort of evidence?"

Ron Pepper shook his head. "We still haven't found the murder weapon. We rounded up all the scissors we could find, but none of them had any traces of blood on them, although some of the blades could have inflicted the wounds. So – nothing conclusive, or even suggestive.

"As far as the artists having been defrauded, though, we can place a couple of them more or less on the scene. Kasia Novik and Fabio Gompers were both in the building at the time."

"Enough for probable cause to do a search?"

Pepper shrugged. "We can ask. What about the son?"

"Jennings looked into him. Apparently, he's not doing so well at the moment. His fancy BMW is leased, as is that expensive apartment, and he's behind on payments for both of them. He needs money, all right, and his mother seems to have had plenty, according to Schaeffer. He resented his mother, blamed her for his father's suicide. He claimed to be out of touch with her, but we know they spoke on the phone, and he might have actually visited her store. There's enough motive, no problem, but do we have anything placing him on the scene?"

"No. He could have been there for all we know, but we haven't found anybody who says they saw him. That's a shame. Otherwise, he'd be perfect." Pepper brightened. "Maybe he was wearing some sort of a disguise? Or ...maybe he hired one of the artists to do the job for him?"

Carlson snorted. "You read too many detective stories, Ron. No, I'd really like him for the killer, but I don't see it. He says he didn't even know where his mother lived or that she had her own business. I don't believe that. He lied about being in touch; he's probably lying about that, too. And Rita Cutler thinks she might have met him at the store, as you mentioned. But the rest ....?"

"It's a shame. Sister Joseph said Shirley Rogers had a really hard time as a kid. Her father was a drunk who left the family and her mom had to struggle on her own. Still, that's no excuse for neglecting your own child. I can't even imagine leaving my kids by themselves to go gallivanting around. They deserve better than that."

"She loved him, though. In her own way. Or else why would she have kept those photos and the report cards? I think he had some feelings for her, too. When I showed him what she'd kept, he didn't say anything, but I could see he was moved."

"For what that's worth." Pepper wasn't impressed.

Kasia Novik answered the door wearing cut-offs and an old t-shirt, palette in hand and a brush in her teeth.

"Sorry to bother you, Ms. Novik," Carlson began, but he was caught short when he noticed that Kasia's whole body tensed when she recognized him on her doorstep. She looked at him warily, but said nothing.

Carlson cleared his throat. "I can see you're busy, but I just wanted to follow up on some information we received. If I could come in for a minute?"

"Why? What do you want?"

Carlson hadn't expected this sort of suspicious reaction when he decided to re-interview Kasia Novik. It was pretty routine, after all. *I wonder if I should have gotten a search warrant. Well, too late now.* He pushed on.

"I need to see your duffel bag, if you don't mind."

"My duffel bag?" Kasia asked. "I don't understand. What do you need my bag for?" She'd taken the brush out of her mouth and held it in a hand that shook slightly.

Don't tell me I'm actually on to something, here, Carlson thought. *She's scared, all right. What do you know? Maybe we've finally got a break.*

"It won't take long, Mrs. Novik," Carlson said, avoiding a direct answer. "I'd just like to take a look at it. You carry it everywhere, I understand."

"How do you understand that? Has someone been talking about me?"

"If I could just see the bag, Mrs. Novik."

Kasia frowned. She was too young to have many memories of Poland, but she remembered the tense atmosphere at home. Her parents would speak in whispers about a friend or a relative who'd suddenly disappeared. If her father, a university professor, sometimes made a disparaging comment about the Communist regime, he took care never to say such things outside the house, and not too loudly, even there. There was always the specter of a knock on the door in the middle of the night.

After the fall of the Soviet Union, when Poland was once again becoming a free and democratic state, they considered remaining in their homeland. The idea of leaving everything they'd ever known was scary, but ultimately, they opted for the dream of America. They built a good life for their family, but they never forgot where they came from, and they never allowed their daughter to forget, either. They taught her to be grateful for living in a country where the police couldn't just barge in to start searching your house and asking questions. They warned her how easy it can be to lose such freedom, if it was taken for granted.

"I'm busy right now," she said, her mind racing. Did she have to let the detective in? What if she didn't cooperate? Should she call a lawyer? If she made trouble, maybe the police could make trouble for her. If she let them in, would that be foolish? She studied the man in front of her. He looked all right. He'd shown her his ID. He was alone, but so was she. Her husband was at work and the kids were still at school. Well, she certainly wanted the detective gone before they came home. Feeling a little scared and not at all sure, she stepped back and let him in.

The duffel bag was on the floor in the entry hall, where she kept it ready. She *did* carry it almost everywhere. You never knew what you were going to need and she liked to be prepared.

She pointed to the bag on the floor, and he stooped down to unzip it and examine the contents. It was a not-very-large bag, with just the one central compartment, but it was capacious enough to hold a couple of t-shirts, a towel, a roll of blue tape, a pair of sandals, a smaller bag containing sample-size bottles of shampoo, conditioner, and hand cream. There was also a notebook, a couple of ball-point pens, and a comb. There was a plastic case containing a miniature stapler, a tiny tape measure, a small roll of scotch tape, and a few paper clips. There was also a thick, heavy pair of shears. Carlson removed an evidence bag from his pocket and deposited the scissors in it, handling it very gingerly despite the fact that he'd prepared for his search by donning a pair of latex gloves.

"Is this yours, Mrs. Novik?"

"No. It's not mine."

"Is that so? Then why is it in your bag?"

"I don't know. I didn't put it there."

Carlson frowned. Kasia Novik looked straight into his eyes, her expression giving nothing away. Her arms hung at her sides, but both hands were curled into fists. He could see that she was holding herself together, but despite her resolve, she was trembling.

Carlson had made plenty of arrests in his time as a cop. It never bothered him to cuff a perp and take him in. It was part of the job, after all. That's why he pulled down the big bucks. This time felt different. But he did what he had to do.

"Let's go, Mrs. Novik. We'll need to talk to you at the station."

Chapter Twenty-Eight

Bella Sarver had been in plenty of strange places in her life, but she'd never visited a jail before. She'd been in the middle of a painting and it was going really well. In between swirling bright colors energetically onto the canvas, she danced around her studio in time to the music, waving her brush and singing along with the Shirelles.

Mama said there'll be days like this ....

All of a sudden, the phone rang. She was on a roll and tried to ignore it, but after the third replay of *La Bomba* she glanced at the screen and saw who was calling.

"Hi, Kasia," she said. "I hope this is important, because I'm working."

At first she couldn't understand what Kasia was trying to tell her. The words were all jumbled on top of each other, interspersed with sobs. But when she finally grasped what was going on, she wasted no time. She still had her apron on and there were streaks of paint on her hands when she marched into the police station and demanded to know what was going on.

It wasn't until she'd made Kasia slow down and go over her movements on the day of the murder carefully, one by one, that she began to see the full picture of what must have happened.

"I don't understand why it took me so long," she told Len Carlson.

Bella hadn't left the interview room until she'd made sure a female police officer would sit with Kasia while she was went to talk to Carlson. She hugged Kasia hard, told her to stay strong, and stirred plenty of sugar into the coffee the officer had carried into the room before she left.

Carlson was working in his office when the door opened and Bella rushed in. He wasn't the least bit surprised to see her. Melanie Jennings had already informed him that Kasia Novik had asked to make her one phone call to Bella instead of to a lawyer. Carlson had expected nothing less than that Bella would step up where she was needed. He pushed the laptop aside, sat back in his chair, and stirred his own coffee.

"Have a seat, Ms. Sarver. What can I do for you?"

Bella told him.

Officer Melanie Jennings drove over to Martingale Manor with Detective Carlson in the passenger seat. It felt like déjà vu all over again.

"I didn't think we'd be back here, Detective," Jennings said.

Carlson grimaced. "Neither did I," he admitted. "But it's sort of beginning to feel like home."

Jennings grinned, but Carlson just stared out the window until they got there.

Ken Wilson answered the door when Carlson rang the bell. He clearly wasn't expecting visitors. He was still in his bathrobe and slippers, but he let the police officers in.

"I need to speak to your wife, Mr. Wilson," Carlson told him.

Chapter Twenty-Nine

A festive atmosphere prevailed over all of downtown Deer Creek. Main Street was aglow owing to all the colored lights hanging from the lampposts and draped across the store fronts. Tons of people were out Christmas shopping, and familiar carols streamed out from the loudspeakers placed on the building corners. If the crowds admiring the paintings and sculptures arrayed around the Deer Creek Co-op were any indication, the co-op was destined to do a land-office business.

"Can I have your attention?" Bella Sarver called out, trying to pitch her voice above the racket of multiple conversations going on at the same time. The champagne and hors d'oeuvres flowed freely, contributing to the hubbub.

Art grinned at Bella and pulled a chair over to the front of the gallery. Before Bella had a chance to react, he'd climbed up on it, wobbling a bit on the padded seat while Bella held her breath. He stuck a couple of fingers in his mouth and emitted a shrill whistle. The noise level lessened suddenly. "It's all yours, sweetheart."

Bella shook her head and grasped his hand to help him get down from the chair, but she was smiling, too. She addressed the crowd.

"I want to welcome all of you to the grand opening of the Deer Creek Co-Op Art Gallery. That's the last time you'll be hearing it called that, because the membership has voted, and the committee has ratified their decision. Leo and Art, if you please," Bella said, nodding at them.

The crowd followed the two men out the door into the street. Art and Leo each grabbed a corner of the large tarp that covered the window and tugged. The tarp drifted down to the sidewalk, revealing foot-high letters painted across the glass, black outlined in gold, proclaiming: "The Penny Pearson Co-op Art Gallery."

When the applause died down, Bella pronounced the words aloud, shivering a little in the November wind. "The Penny Pearson Co-op Art Gallery. Most of us knew and loved Penny. She was a founding member of the Art League. She was the moving force behind the Art League's annual art fair. She established our collaboration with the Park District in offering art classes to everyone from toddlers to seniors. And as her final act, she gave us a legacy that enabled us to open this gallery. For the first time, our local artists will have an outlet dedicated to selling their work to the public. As everyone knows, competition in the art world isn't for the faint of heart. It takes a lot more than talent. It takes thick skin, hard work, and perseverance, year after year. It also takes a lot of pure luck – being in the right place at the right time. And now, we have the right place. And the right time. So congratulations to all of us, and let's go back inside before we freeze to death."

The crowd didn't need to be asked twice. Laughing happily, they surged back into the gallery, heading for the buffet tables.

"Congratulations, Ben," Bella said.

Ben Goldberg had his mouth full of falafel. He held up a hand for patience while he chewed and swallowed, finally gulping some champagne to wash it down.

"Thanks, Bella," he said. "I feel a little funny about winning the contest, being on the Board and all."

"Well, you won it fair and square, didn't you? Your suggestion got the most votes. So just enjoy it. You can pay double membership next year, if you want."

Ben grinned. "I might do that. Let's see how this year goes, first."

There were strict rules to membership in the co-op. First, the work had to be juried in by the co-op committee. Only the most professional pieces were to be accepted. Once juried in, the artist had to work according to a fixed schedule, so that the gallery could be staffed at all times. Next, each artist had to pay a yearly membership fee, to help defray the expenses of rent, utilities, and such. Ben won a free membership for the first year, but he still had to comply with the rest of the rules. So it wasn't entirely a free ride.

"It's a shame about Fabio," Ben said. "How did you figure out what he'd been doing?"

Fabio Gompers had the distinction of being the first and only person in the history of the Deer Creek Art League to be expelled from membership. In the forty-seven years of its existence, the League had seen its share of bad art, but never before had one of its members disgraced the profession by perpetrating a fraud. It was bad enough that he and Shirley Rogers had conspired to cheat their customers, but to cheat their fellows was another degree of outrageousness altogether.

"It wasn't too hard once the pieces began to fall into place," Bella said. "You remember, we were all so pleased to have an artist of Fabio's status be one of our members?"

"Sure," Ben agreed. "I remember when he first joined, when was it? Maybe four or five years ago?"

"No, it wasn't that long," Mollie Schaeffer said, joining the conversation. "I remember, I was Membership Chair when he joined, and that was only about three years ago. I was working the desk when he just walked in one day. He spent some time looking around the gallery and then he asked me a few questions about who we are and what we do, and so forth. And then he took out his checkbook and became a member, right then and there. It was the easiest pitch I never made."

Ben laughed. "Right. And then he became active right away, and we were so impressed that he had his work in all these galleries across the country. He never showed his best work at our place, though. Just small pieces, more like detailed studies rather than major compositions."

"True," Bella said, "but we all just thought it was because he saved his major pieces for the 'important' galleries. I don't think it ever occurred to any of us that not only were the pieces he showed with us not important, but they weren't even his! What a let-down."

"I know," Mollie said, "and then it turned out he was trying to pass them off as originals, not only with us but with paying customers, too. You'd think he would have been smarter than to try to pass off cheap giclees as original oil paintings."

"Yes, but I think he didn't do that at first. He re-worked expensive prints, on good canvas backings. It wasn't until he took up with Shirley Rogers that he started doing the cheap stuff, and apparently, that was Shirley's idea, not his."

"But that's what finished him in the end, wasn't it, Bella?"

"Right, Ben. That day when Mollie and I saw the paint peeling from one of the paintings he had hanging in our show was the day it all began to fall apart for him."

"And Shirley, too," Mollie said.

"Yes, although she was already beyond caring by then. We never realized the scam she had going until we all went in there and started inventorying the stock. That's when Leo saw there were so many discrepancies in the books."

"So Fabio was trying to get out of the arrangement he had with Shirley, but she held it over him. It was blackmail, really," Ben said. "Fabio wasn't left with much choice. It was either get rid of Shirley or give up on making a living as an artist."

"You would have thought he could have worked around the arthritis, somehow."

"I think he was trying, Mollie. After all, he was religious about going to the water movement class at Martingale Manor. Maybe if he'd given it more of a shot, or tried working smaller instead of on those gigantic canvases .... I mean, if he could doctor the giclees, he should have been able to still paint his own compositions, don't you think?"

"Poor Shirley," Ben said.

"Poor Shirley?" Art said. "It was all her fault to begin with. If she hadn't been so greedy, it never would have happened. But apparently, this was just the same pattern she'd followed her entire life."

"What do you mean? I thought this scam only started a couple of years ago," Ben said. "You mean she pulled this before?"

"The scam?" Bella repeated.

"Yes, the scam. Isn't that why Fabio killed her?"

Bella looked at Ben curiously, and then her eyes widened in understanding. "Oh, I see. No, no, Ben. Fabio didn't kill Shirley."

Now Ben was really confused. "But I thought .... I mean, isn't that what you told the police?"

"No, no. Fabio hated Shirley and he wanted out of their business relationship, if you could call it that. But he didn't kill her. He just took advantage of the fact that someone else did to try to cover up what he'd been doing."

"So then ...? How was this Shirley's fault?"

"Well," Bella said, "It's as I explained to Detective Carlson, Shirley Rogers had been a shady character for practically her entire life. She was always looking for angles.

If there was an honest way to do something and a dishonest way, she always chose the wrong side. She had a nice little business going and she could have made it a success. She hired Rita Cutler to help out, which would have been a really good decision if she'd allowed Rita to do more than just wait on customers. Rita had all kinds of good ideas, but Shirley didn't want to hear about them. She was happier surfing the net and cheating artists who probably never even found out about it. She loved to feel like she was putting one over other people. She'd been doing that sort of thing since she was a kid. It was just her luck to have moved to a community where her past came back to haunt her."

"After so many years, she must have thought she was safe," Mollie said.

"Are you telling me that Kasia knew her years ago, too?"

"Kasia? She's years younger than Shirley. Decades, even. What does Kasia have to do with anything?"

Ben was really at sea. "Wasn't Shirley downloading Kasia's images to make note-cards from them? And didn't they find the murder weapon in her bag?"

"Oh, that," Bella waived Ben's comment away dismissively. "No, that was just a mistake. I felt so bad, because it was my fault that Carlson went to her house. I never realized that he'd actually think Kasia could have killed anybody. But when I was finally able to get her calmed down, she said the scissors weren't hers and she had no idea what they were doing in her duffel bag. That's when I remembered that Lily Turner couldn't find her shears that day she was doing the quilting demo in my class. I suggested to Detective Carlson that he ask Lily if the scissors were hers. Turns out, they were. So then it all began to make sense."

"Really?" Ben asked, still at sea.

"Sure. It was the past that caught up with Shirley. You see, she'd moved away from Bridgeport decades ago. She had a different name, and obviously, she looked different than she had as a girl. She probably never gave those days a thought anymore, like Mollie said. She certainly never worried about it."

Ben's head swiveled between the two women. He wasn't much further ahead, but they seemed to feel they'd exhausted the subject. Mollie squinted as she looked around the room. "Do you think the jewelry counter is in the right place, Bella? Maybe we should move it closer to the front, so people see it first thing."

"Whoa, hold on a minute," Ben exclaimed. "What does Bridgeport have to do with anything? And who killed Shirley?"

"Oh," Bella said. "I thought I explained. It wasn't Fabio. Detective Carlson thought it was, too, but that was wrong. Then he thought it was Kasia, for about a minute. Especially when the lab confirmed that the shears in her bag was actually the murder weapon. But then, as I said, they belonged to Lily Turner."

"So Lily Turner, whoever she might be, killed Shirley," Ben concluded, beginning to feel he was coming into the picture.

Bella shook her head. "No, no, of course not. How could Lily have killed anybody? She's so frail, a breeze could knock her over. No, the key to the whole thing was that they were all from Bridgeport originally. When Carlson understood that, he began to get it. You see, it turned out that her old boyfriend recognized her."

"Okay…" Ben said slowly.

"Not only him, but her old boyfriend's girlfriend, too. Who was now his wife."

"And...?"

Art Halperin had heard it all before, but he was enjoying Ben's bafflement. It made him feel he wasn't the only one who'd failed to see the connection. He stood aside and let the scene unfold, his grin getting broader by the minute.

"And - that's just the point I don't get," Mollie said. "She was his wife and Shirley wasn't. So why was she still jealous, after so many years? That's just silly, isn't it?"

Bella shrugged. "Sure, it's silly, and yet - who knows? Old wounds can run deep, can't they? Don't you still remember things that happened back in high school? Maybe even elementary school?"

"I guess I do," Mollie agreed, "but really, I don't let those kinds of memories rule my life. That's just stupid."

"I don't think Debbie Wilson let her memories rule her life, either. Not most of the time, anyway. It was just the coincidence of recognizing Shirley after so many years, and realizing that Ken still carried a sort of torch for her that set it all in motion. Still, I'm sure she never intended to kill anybody. But when she walked into the locker room and heard Shirley singing in the shower, she saw red. There was a scissors right there, sticking out of the quilting bag Lily had left on the bench. So Debbie grabbed the scissors, probably not even thinking, and marched over to the shower, ripped back the curtain, and shoved the scissors into Shirley's throat. It was all over in a second."

"It's amazing that she remained so calm after it," Art commented.

"Yes, it's like the act of killing turned on a switch in her or something. She was able to just go on as if nothing had happened."

"Except, not quite," Art said. "Right, Bella?"

"Right. It took me a while to put two and two together. As soon as Debbie came back to class that day, I could see something was different. It was as if she'd suddenly become a painter instead of a dabbler. She was confident, in control. It was pretty impressive to witness, and if I'd thought about it properly, I would have realized something pretty important had happened. I noticed her standing well back from the easel and let the length of the brush do its work, making nice, loose, long gestures on the canvas. Suddenly, the painting that was cramped and picky began to turn into a composition with energy and movement. The flowers no longer stood each in its own little place, but flowed into each other, and the colors flowed, too, into the background and across the canvas. It was a totally different painting. Silly me, I thought it was my teaching! I figured she must finally have started to pay attention to what I was telling her."

Art laughed. "I'm sure your teaching had a lot to do with it, hon. Your words seeped into Debbie's brain, little by little, without her even realizing it. And then it all clicked, and she was able to make it work."

"Maybe. It's a shame it took an act of violence to release her artistic abilities, though. Maybe they'll let her have some art supplies in jail."

"I still don't understand, Bella. What made you realize she'd done it?"

Detective Carlson had asked Bella the same thing when she told him about her conclusions. Thanks to her, he'd found the murder weapon and had the murderer in custody. Case closed.

Still, he had to admit that Bella's reasoning was sound. He couldn't ignore it.

"My wife? Why?" Ken Wilson said, facing the two police officers on his front step.

But Debbie Wilson had heard the commotion and come to the door. She was fully dressed. When she saw who was there, she knew it was finally over.

"Deborah Wilson," Carlson said, "I'm arresting you for the murder of Shirley Rogers."

"Murder? What are you talking about, Detective? My wife never hurt anyone in her life," Ken Wilson protested. "This is ridiculous. I'm calling our lawyer."

But Debbie Wilson put a hand on her husband's arm as pulled a phone out of his pocket. She was completely calm, almost relieved, in a way. "It's okay, Ken. I'm amazed it took them this long to figure it out, but it's okay. Really. I never meant to do it. But she was singing away like life was just peachy, and I got so angry, and the scissors was right there – so I did it. It only took a minute, and then …I don't know. It didn't seem real, somehow. Nobody else was there. Nobody saw what happened. So I just …I guess I sort of pretended that it had nothing to do with me. I'm sorry. It's just I got so mad."

"I was really slow to catch on, Art," Bella explained, while Ben Goldberg listened, light finally dawning. "Debbie brought up the subject of marriage when she was admiring my engagement ring. She loved the ring, but seemed kind of doubtful about the whole idea of marriage. In fact, I asked her, if she had the chance to do it again, would she have married Ken. And she said, and this is what's strange, given that we were talking about our own feelings, she said to me, 'You've got it backwards, Bella. It's not me you should be asking.'

"And then, somebody else asked a question about what color she should use, and I went to look at her painting, and the moment passed. But when I got to thinking about what Debbie had said, I think she meant that she thought Ken had never recovered from his feelings for Shirley all those years ago. I think Debbie always felt that Ken had picked her on the rebound, and he regretted it. And when she saw how he looked at Shirley, when she was singing at the karaoke event that night, she saw that he still had feelings for her, and it hurt."

Mollie nodded. "I can understand that. Debbie was still jealous. But it still didn't mean she killed Shirley."

"No," Bella agreed," but once I understood the connection, I began to put two and two together. The police figured Shirley had probably been killed with something like a scissors, and I remembered that Lily Turner couldn't find her scissors when she was showing my class about quilting. And then I remembered that Kasia had pulled a scissors out of her bag when she was helping me paint the co-op space, and didn't seem to know what they were doing there. So when I heard that the police still hadn't found the murder weapon, I suggested to Detective Carlson that he ask Kasia about her scissors."

"But wouldn't that prove that Kasia had done it?" Ben asked.

"Wait a minute," Art protested. "I thought Martingale Manor was for seniors. What was Kasia doing there?"

"Kasia's mother lives there," Bella said simply. "Kasia uses their pool all the time. She must have left her bag on one of the benches that day, just like Lily did. When Debbie went to return the scissors she'd just used to kill Shirley, she must have slipped them into Kasia's bag instead of Lily's."

"So Lily's scissors were the murder weapon?" Ben asked.

"Exactly," Bella said approvingly. "Once the police tested the scissors, the blood on them matched Shirley's."

"How is it that nobody noticed the scissors were still bloody?" Mollie asked sensibly.

"Good question, Mollie. The fact is, they weren't. Debbie rinsed them off under the shower, naturally. She's not a complete idiot. But there's always some residue left, unless you do a really thorough job of washing, and Debbie had no time for that. Once the police knew where to look, the evidence was conclusive."

"It seems to me that would have pointed to Lily, not Debbie," Ben argued.

"True, except that given what I deduced about Debbie's feelings, she's the only one with a motive. Lily went on to marry someone else, and they had a good marriage for fifty years or so, until he died. She'd been angry at Shirley in high school, but she had enough self-respect to turn that boy away and move on. She didn't think much of Shirley, but she'd gotten over her anger decades ago. No, it was Debbie who was still hurt and angry, not Lily."

"And not Kasia?" Art asked. "After all, Shirley had stolen the photos of her paintings off that website in order to print notecards from them."

"Yes, but Kasia knew nothing about that until I told her, and that was after Shirley was killed. Anyway, hardly a motive for such a brutal murder. I never thought it could be Kasia."

"Well, anyway, it's all over now. We can get back to our regular lives. And we have a wedding to plan, right, Bella? What kind of flowers should we have? What's your favorite? How about roses?"

"I don't know, Mollie. I've always liked daisies."

"Daisies? Really?"

"Yeah. What's wrong with daisies?"

"Oh, nothing. Daisies are fine. Kind of … simple, maybe."

"I like simple. The simpler, the better."

"Okay, so daisies, then. Let's see – I guess that means yellow and white for the colors. That'll be nice. Very Springy."

Mollie seemed about to continue, but Art put his arm around Bella and led her away. "The only thing we really need at our wedding," he said, laughing, "is us. Now if I can just stop Bella from finding bodies all the time …."

Chapter Thirty

"I'm glad this worked out, Peter. I hope the nuns at Our Lady of Cherubim weren't too upset."

"No, they were actually okay with it, Rita. And it was kind of nice to see Sister Joseph again, after all these years. I know Martha Ashton told me to let her handle it, but I felt like I really wanted to get over there and talk to them myself. It turned out nobody had told them my mother had left her estate to the school, but when I explained the situation to the principal, she understood my point of view. She said they'd never want to contest my contesting the will, not under the circumstances. So then I felt bad, but Martha helped us work out a settlement. Cherubim still gets a nice little legacy, but I get the bulk of the estate, including the contents of this store."

"It's a shame we had to throw out all those giclee paintings, and those nice notecards, but I agree with Leo that it's best to start fresh, and try to keep things honest. It'll be so much fun to get to run the store. I really think there's a lot we can do with it. I can't tell you how happy I am that you're giving me this chance."

"No, no – it works out for both of us, Rita. I get a nice business on the side and a built-in manager. It's a win-win."

"So you're not giving up your – what do you call it? Day trading?"

"In derivatives, yeah. Well, I sort of am. I'm moving into more standard investments. Not as exciting, but a little more secure. You know, in a way, my mother really did me a favor. It's a shame she had to get herself killed, but basically, she's given me a new start. I was able to clear my debts, and I'm not going to blow it this time. Safe and steady, that's me from now on."

"Well, anytime you want to take a turn in the store, just let me know."

Peter laughed. "Don't worry; you'll be seeing a lot of me. This Deer Creek is a nice town, isn't it? I think it could grow on me."

"People are funny, aren't they?" Art noted, as he and Bella walked along the River Walk a few days after the opening reception of the Penny Pearson Co-op Art Gallery. The air was crisp and cold and smelled of winter. The river was frozen around the edges, but they were bundled up warm and besides, they had each other.

"I know," Bella agreed. "In a lot of ways, I think we never really get out of junior high. We try to put a civilized front on things, but underneath, most of us are probably the same scared little girls and boys we were then. It doesn't take very much to trigger those old feelings."

"Is that why you're so skittish about getting married, honey? Because if it is, please remember – I'm not Martin Lewis. I absolutely promise, I will never take half the furniture and move out. I don't drink. Well, not much, anyway. I don't run around. I married Sherry when I was twenty-four years old and never looked at anybody else in all that time."

"Oh, I know, Art," Bella said, reaching to cradle his cheek with her hand. "You're a good man and I love you with all my heart. You're nothing like Marty. I know that. And I'm not skittish. I want to marry you. I want to live the rest of my life with you. It's just – I'm not twenty years old anymore. I know a lot of things now I didn't know then, like how things change when real life gets in the way, no matter how much you didn't mean for them to change. I don't think Marty started out to be a philandering drunk."

"No, there I have to disagree with you, honey. People are what they are. You can look at a kid at twelve, and either he basically has a good head on his shoulders and a good heart, or he doesn't. It's not that he isn't going to make mistakes sometimes. It's not that he doesn't have a lot to learn. But if he isn't solid by then, he never will be. And vice versa. If a kid is trustworthy and reliable by then, he always will be, no matter what."

Bella smiled. "I'm not sure it's as simple as that, but I suppose you're right, basically. I'm sorry if I seem – 'skittish', as you say. It isn't you, honey. It's me. It took a lot for me to start over again after Marty took off, and I'm a little afraid of losing what I achieved. But I'm willing to take a chance, if you are."

Art stopped walking and turned to face Bella. He put his hands on her shoulders and took a deep breath. "I've been thinking," he said.

Bella looked up at him.

"How about a nice Danube River cruise for our honeymoon?"

Bella felt something wet on her cheek. She raised her head.

The first flakes of winter were beginning to fall. She stuck out her tongue, caught one, and laughed. Then she wrapped her arms around Art's neck and pulled him close.

Made in the USA
Monee, IL
30 September 2019